Too Bright the Sun

Lazlo Ferran

By the same Author

THE ICE BOAT
THE MAN WHO RECREATED HIMSELF
INFINITE BLUE HEAVEN –
A KING AND A QUEEN
RUNNING: THE ALIEN IN THE MIRROR
UNKNOWN PLACE, UNKNOWN UNIVERSE
WORLDS LIKE DUST
VAMPIRE: FIND MY GRAVE
ORDO LUPUS AND THE TEMPLE GATE
THE DEVIL'S OWN DICE
THE SYNCHRONICITY CODE
ATTACK HITLER'S BUNKER!
DECEMBER RADIO
SCREAMING ANGELS
THE HOLE INSIDE THE EARTH

SHORT STORIES

INCHOATE (VOLUME I)
EIGHTEEN, BLUE (VOLUME II)
VAMPIRE: BENEFICENCE (VOLUME III)

Too Bright the Sun

Lazlo Ferran

PRINTING HISTORY
First Edition

Printed in 12 point Times New Roman

This is a work of fiction. Names, characters, places and incidents are products of the author's imagination or are used fictitiously and should not be construed as real. Any resemblance to actual events, locales organisations or persons, living or dead is entirely coincidental.

Copyright © 2011 by Lazlo Ferran

All Rights Reserved

No part of this book maybe used or reproduced in any manner whatsoever without the written permission of the author, except in the case of brief quotations embodied in critical articles and reviews. For information address lazloferran@gmail.com

Published by Future City Publishing, London.

Front Cover by Ashley Buttle

Acknowledgments

Thanks to Ash, Derek, Gary, and Lorna.

Contents

Prologue 9

Chapter Two 63

Chapter Three 101

Chapter Four 137

Chapter Five 167

Chapter Six 185

Chapter Seven 201

Biography of Lazlo Ferran 233

Prologue

It's been over ten years since Gary Enquine sent my friend Przeltski to a certain death. Not one day has gone by without the memories of that battle prowling my mind like a waking nightmare. Many times, I have woken in a cold-sweat thinking about it. I will not rest – cannot rest until Gary Enquine has been brought to justice and been forced to pay for his cowardice. Ten years; it's a long time, but I can be patient. Personal journal-entry of Jake Nanden for 2101, Feb 3. 1.

***

Chapter One

The little voice asked, after peering out of another portal at an earlier moment in his life, "Is it possible to time travel for I perceive that I can?"

"Only after you leave this life," a voice, high and mighty, said.

Then the little voice changed its tone for it had grown angry. "But that's not fair! For, the one thing I wish I can't have."

"Until you leave this life," the high voice said.

"Yes."

"Then now you can see advantages to moving beyond this life you have."

And the little voice perceived that all his previous angers, about matters of the flesh and daily living were not proper angers. A proper anger is the anger that desirable things lay beyond the portal of death. And so from that moment on his struggles to survive, to fight against the current, seemed improper to him, and yet he could not help himself.

Two of the Ionian Militia sat on top of Przeltski, ripping his helmet off while another aimed his laser at his eyes. In the vacuum of Io's atmosphere, Przeltski mouthed the words, 'save me,' but it was too late. I knew I couldn't and had to try and save myself. I turned to get away, but I could still see his eyes half closing, then looking up and his mouth rapidly shaping the words of the 'Hail Mary.' The IM would turn their lasers down to the lowest setting and first shoot out the eyes, then take off the arms, and if he was lucky, then they would aim for his heart. If he wasn't lucky, the dismemberment could go on and on for as long as they wanted. I wanted to look away, but I couldn't. I struggled and struggled, and then I woke and knew it had been the nightmare.

An eye opened. It was mine. The blurry horizon crystallised into the edge of the pillow as I realised where I was; Io. Being a commander has its perks, one being your own private cabin, but it was small and cramped. I closed my eye, reached up for the ledge of the sill above me and hauled myself out of bed. Feeling for the sanicube-handle opposite the bed, I released the cube from its folded position against the wall, selected 'L' and stepped in but then had to open my eyes to use it without spilling. A tube dispensed a sterilising solution onto my hands and the stream of water became hot air to dry them. Yawning enough for tears to clear my eyes, I took one step over to the n-gen, sitting on the white work surface above the bed. I selected 'Fried,' then 'Coffee, black' and clicked on the com centre. I had disabled the voice, but I could see the display said, "2101, Feb 4. 2 – 06.30 I. 2 messages. Download?"

I waited for the 'ding' that would tell me my breakfast was ready. I knew I had just had another weird dream, but I couldn't quite remember it now. I tried. The n-gen 'dinged,' and I opened the white door to reveal the plate of hot, fried food and a mug of black coffee. I looked at the food dubiously and lifted the dark blue mug to my lips. The caffeine rush to my head felt good. Putting my left hand on my hip, I arched my back and then looked down at the pallid skin stretched over my late-twenties belly. 'Bigger,' I thought. 'But only slightly.' I picked up the plate of fried; bacon, eggs, potatoes, beans, fried-bread and mushrooms, all preselected as my personal preferences and lifted some mushrooms and potatoes to my mouth with the forkette. My buds tested the taste; it had that slight hint of mint or something metallic about it. "Damn," I said out loud. For a few days now, breakfast had tasted like this, and I wasn't sure if it was a fault with the n-gen or this batch of plasma. My n-gen was civvy and another one of the perks allowed to commanders; I'd had it for nearly five years, and it had been everywhere with me. Normally they didn't last longer than three years.

Balancing the plate in my left hand, I picked up the remote, pressed 'Monitor,' chose 'North elevation,' then 'R' for recording and 'Dec 9, 11.00,' morning on the day we had arrived, a date I chose out of habit. I pointed the remote at the panel, shaped like a window, on the narrow wall behind the pillow of the bed, and it filled with the image of the ground to the north of the command-post. Just like a window, you could even see 'around' the window frame, if you wished to put your head that close to it. Yellow and reddish Sulphur stretched away between the rocky silicates to a jagged horizon, a few hundred yards above the level of the command-post and perhaps two miles away. In places, the silicate rock looked white and in others a beautiful emerald green. If it hadn't been for the bright purplish glow of the morning aurora above, I could have believed I was in the Mojave Desert on Earth, a memory I had of visiting my grandparents once. Taking bigger mouthfuls, with my nostrils closed to avoid the nasty after-taste, I downed the breakfast and alternated my gaze between the landscape on the wall and the contents of the room. I took in the half-finished bottle of vodka next to the empty glass on the narrow table across the gang-way from my bed. I saw the open notepad next to it with a few scrawled lines at the top of a new page. Writing pulp crime-novels was my weakness or my hobby, depending on one's generosity.

I had finished the fried, so I continued sipping black coffee and put on the Trion head-band, activating it by flicking a tiny black switch next to my left temple.

"Record," I said. Most company commanders, at least in USAC, were obliged to record their activities for viewing by paid subscribers; part of a deal USAC had made with the Amtel branch of RA. Most hated doing it, but at least you could choose what to record, and I never gave the leeches anything of real interest. The recording had been made by a cam in the com, so a leech couldn't see anything on my heads-up.

"Download," I said. A red light flickered once on the com. The first of two messages scrolled on the heads-up display in front of my left eye:

> Contact: Jena Ω "Hi Jake. I know you're trying to make me jealous by not replying to my last messages, but then again you could just be under attack, and I'm supposed to be the rational woman, so I can deal with *that*. I might just be too busy this week to record anything for you too. My boss wants me to prepare a legal-briefing for our merger with a company which has connections with Riccard-Amtel! Can you believe it? Oh, I know we try not to bring business into our relationship, but I couldn't help myself. The consequences could be so far-reaching. Promotion, relocation. Who knows? Umm. In answer to your question last time; okay I've held out for quite a while haven't I but, yes, women do feel that sometimes. I suppose … . Tell me more about what you do … . Not during the day (with the boyz and grrls) but after. Are you still writing? Chloe misses u too. xx" End.

> Contact: Mary "Hi darling. Mum here. How's the (censored) winter? I know this will probably be censored but I don't care. There's lots to tell you, but I'll keep it short for now. I'm just off to a local council meeting and

later there's an art exhibition; Raccauld, which
Justine and I are going to. Actually, I'm
meeting her for coffee at lunchtime. I think
she wants to do some shopping. You know
what she's like; you can't stop her once hubby
has been paid. The Gazette had a nice photo
of you the other day, which I have stuck in the
photo album. You're a hero around here. The
young boys talk of nothing else but the Iron
Cross; I hear them when we go for picnics by
the river. Oh yes, and Robert O'Flannery has
been elected Mayor again and has approved
redevelopment of the area by the river. Office
block I believe. Such a shame. One thing I
was going to mention. A peculiar thing
happened the other day … ."

I heard a loud banging on the cabin-door which made
me flinch. "Stop record," I said and ignored the rest of the
message in the heads-up. I took two steps to the door and
opened it. Sergeant Stone's chiseled face, topped with a
brown flat-top and with shaving foam around its cheeks,
confronted me. He stood, dressed only from the waist
down.

"Yes Sergeant?" I tried to sound patient.

"Sir. Seismic activity detected 700 yards east of
perimeter. About 100 feet down."

"Okay. Pick four men and get packed. I'll be with you
in five."

"Sir? We can investigate if you want. You don't need
to come."

"No, but I want to come. I need the exercise."

"Sir." He didn't salute. I liked to be informal with my
troops most of the time in combat situations, especially
the officers and Stone in particular, who had been with me
a long time.

***

"Lieutenant Osei, you have the comm."

We were in the port airlock five minutes later, myself unshaven, all in full-combat gear, and Sergeant Stone handed me a Trion X.50. As the red light moved to 'Gravity-local,' we all grabbed the hand rails. Gravity on Io was about one fifth of that on Earth or about the same as the Moon and without the S-Grav, the rocking motion of the lift as it took us down to the surface would throw us about. The hatch opened, and I led the team out into the moonlit night. I could feel the crunch of Sulphur and silicates under my boots, but all I could hear was my breath and the steady beep, every two seconds of the uplink indicator. We used a two-step canter to move over the terrain in a defensive pattern of two columns of three, ten feet apart. That was enough separation to give covering fire in all directions without hitting each other if needed. We were looking for any sign of a drill rig at the indicated distance of 700 yards. The Ionian Militia normally didn't have the resources for automated rigs, so there would be two or three poor bastards manning it, armed with A.M. 27s most probably. They would be targeting our S-Grav singularity, 1000 feet below the MCS – a known Mob. Command Station weakness. Our MCS had been fitted with, as standard, S-Grav Type 4; a lot more stable than the Type 3. Its governor was accurate to 14^{-10} Volts, which it had to be to keep the singularity weak enough to be safe but strong enough to work effectively.

***

Database download on the Ionian Militia: The Ionian Militia (IM) was formed by miners on Io, moon of Jupiter on June 1 2089. Their living conditions were already tough, but falling iron prices led to smaller pay-rises and longer hours. They went on strike, and in the long summer of 2080 Earth News bulletins were full of items about iron shortages and skirmishes between USAC troops and miners on Io. Led by Richard Ortega, the miners demanded some concessions, most prominent being that their families could live with them. This was granted, but shortly after their families arrived, the miners were subjected to further pay-cuts and reductions in supply of essential equipment. From the Ionian Iron Miners Union was formed the Ionian Miner's Union, led by Ortega. This powerful union then began receiving equipment and other supplies directly from the Rebel Alliance on Earth, a move that was seen as highly provocative by the USAC forces, then in administrative control on Io and then attempted to block these supplies and suppress resistance using overpowering force. From the Ionian Miner's Union Ortega then formed the Ionian Militia, a small but highly trained and well-equipped force which operated using guerrilla tactics against USAC. The force gradually grew in size and strength until, ten years later, they are a significant force on Io, controlling one half of its surface. Only a few mines remained loyal to USAC, raising Solar System prices of iron and putting an end to the building of the great J stations. **End Download.**

***

Micro-singularities were inherently unstable anyway, for safety reasons, but the governor itself created the only real vulnerability in the Type 4. Located, by necessity, in the column only a few inches from the singularity, it could be damaged by a small explosion. Then, there would be a good chance the singularity would run away, and if it grew, rather than shrank, the result would be a massive explosion. Several MCSs had been knocked out this way.

The militia squad wouldn't be a problem, but I wanted to be fully alert. Things still looked a bit blurry to me, so I blinked a few times and squeezed my lids shut to lubricate my eyes. My stubble itched on the fabric inside the helmet.

500 yards out, I raised my hand, and we stopped. I pointed to the Sergeant, and two of the corporals in their tan-coloured combat suits and motioned for them to move south of the target location which appeared to be behind a slight bluff. I motioned to the other two officers to follow me north. I felt sure Stone would spread his men out a little, standard procedure, and I did the same as we flanked the bluff. I thought I could see a faint plume of yellow dust rising, the usual tell-tale sign of a drill-rig, but, still very faint I couldn't be sure of it. I crouched down and tapped the shoulder of the soldier in front of me. I pointed at the faint plume, he turned to face me and nodded. We tried not to kick up any dust ourselves when we rounded the shoulder of the bluff, and the soldier in front held up his hand just before stopping. This was it. They were there. His gloved fingers counted down three, two, one, and then he moved forward. He aimed his X.50 at something while I followed him, pointing mine in the same direction. When I emerged into the dip behind the bluff, I saw what I had expected; a low wall of Sulphur-dirt around a square dugout, perhaps ten feet along each side, with a cover slung over it to collect the dust. One helmet peered through the gap, straight at us. I saw the red sighting beam from his A.M. 27 strike the helmet of the corporal, and then the beam turned green as the plasma shot was fired. But he moved too slowly. The corporal had already jumped, done a one-eighty and come down with his X.50 blazing green. I fired too. The poor armour of the Ionian's helmet couldn't withstand the X.50 rounds. It split, and little globules of red blood floated out from under the cover.

The intercom crackled. It was Stone. "Our man taken down sir. Going in for a look." That meant there had been another guard on the south-side, and he had now been disabled. The rear guards stayed back while the leading four of us reached the entrance to the dugout, on its east-side. Stone poked his X.50 inside. He immediately backed out, saying:

"Two grubs."

By now I could barely see the dugout entrance for yellow dust, so we waited for the two miners to emerge from the cloud. They came out with their hands up, and Stone made them turn through 360 degrees before making them sit up against a rock, a few yards east of the entrance. While Stone, recognisable by the over-sized dagger he usually wore, stood with his X.50 pointing at the two prisoners, one of his team dipped into the entrance to check all equipment had been switched off before placing a small charge.

During daylight hours you could not normally see the faces of other men through the visors, because the filters would reflect the sunlight, but I could see the two faces of the Ionians. One looked full of hate, but the other looked strangely sullen, scared even. I decided to question *him*.

I tapped his wrist, where intercom units used to be, and drew 220 in the air with my finger, the standard Red Cross frequency. Of course, he had to activate this inside the helmet verbally and might not choose to do so. I turned my frequency to 220 and waited patiently. After a minute or more, the intercom crackled and I heard a sullen, "Yes."

"Greetings Ionian," I said jovially. "It's your lucky day. You are definitely going to live, and you might retain all your limbs if you answer a few simple questions."

"Smith, Corporal, 00001," he said. His name, rank and serial number included the obligatory 00001. All Ionians used the same serial number. In effect, they had no serial numbers, which they felt confused USAC.

I noticed out of the corner of my eye that the other Ionian glanced nervously at Smith, several times.

Is he afraid this one will reveal something?

"Well Mr. Smith, Corporal Smith if you prefer … ." I was digging and waited for a response.

"Smith will do."

"Mm. You don't seem so attached to the Militia as your friend there. How long have you been mining?"

"A few months," came the terse reply. The other Ionian winced.

"Uh-huh. Have you targeted a Type 4 before?" The other Ionian looked surprised.

"I dunno. Maybe."

"Maybe? It's the *latest* type. What sort of charge were you planning to use?"

"What do you mean? I don't have to answer these questions. Look, if you want to get it over and done with, that's fine by me."

"What charge?" I made it sound angry and pointed my X.50 at his upper right arm.

"Hey! Wait. I dunno. Four pounds, maybe. We hadn't decided."

"Oh. I don't think so. Okay sonny. So I know you are not a miner, so that raises a serious question. What are you doing here?"

Interesting. Is he an observer? A news reporter? Not sure.

"No. Listen. I am just a miner. Okay, so I have only been doing it a week. This is my first time. Training courses are hard to come by these days." He laughed.

"An ironic sense of humour … . I *like* it! Shows intelligence. Maybe too much intelligence for a grub."

My men were gathered around now, tuned to 220, listening in. I could hear their breathing and their smirks from time to time.

I tapped the shoulder of the one nearest to me. "Stay on the proper frequency, corporal."

"He's undercover sir," one of the other corporals said. I recognised the voice; Opinnskey. A bit of a joker by all accounts but clever.

"Undercover Opinnskey? Why do you say that?"

"Look at those arms sir. He hasn't ever lifted an A.M. in his life. Daddy is probably a high-up, I reckon." He squeezed Smith's scrawny arms, and the others laughed. The other Ionian looked very scared now.

"Maybe he is. Maybe he is. Maybe his daddy is high up in the army." I thought I saw just the slightest flicker of his eyelid through the visor. "Did you want to see some active service? Blow up an MCS to impress a girl? I bet that would get you a few nights in bed with that pretty girl." He looked uncomfortable.

"Okay Stone. Take care of the other one."

Stone turned the dial on his X.50 to minimum ballistic charge and pulled back on the trigger. He aimed the red bead at the Ionian's right shin. He pulled back further on the trigger, and a green shot of plasma pierced the Ionians shin. The shot left a neat black hole for a second which quickly ejected red bubbles before the suit sealed itself. I could see the Ionian was screaming, but we couldn't hear him. Stone repeated the shot on the other shin and then on both forearms. We couldn't take prisoners and the Ionians wouldn't take prisoners. But we didn't want to kill, so we just disabled the soldiers. Most of them would never see active service again, so we were doing them a favour really. Their medics would pick them up quite quickly once we had broadcast the standard Red Cross distress signal for them. Of course, some of the other USAC companies were less lenient.

I could see Smith grimace in anticipation of the pain that would surely come. Perhaps he thought he could get a lighter punishment.

"Well?" I asked.

"Well, what?" he said.

"What's the explanation for you being here?"

"I've told you everything. Just get it over with."

I crouched down and looked into his eyes. I could see a different kind of fear there now. It wasn't fear for his physical safety.

"Take the other one away Stone."

I gestured for the rest of our men to go with him, and I waited while the writhing Ionian was dragged around the corner of the bluff.

I spoke to Smith. "Okay now we are alone. Anything you tell me will have been extracted under duress. You won't have been responsible. I used a dose of SPA on you okay? Now all I want do know is; who's your father?"

"Okay. I will tell you something, something big, but you gotta give me something. Leave my arms okay. I heard some guys lose the use of their fingers. I need them, you know?"

"Okay. I tell you what. I will just lightly graze one arm, but I better hit the other one, or people will be suspicious. Don't worry. I know just where to hit it. I can reduce the pain too. Deal?" I looked at him. "Deal," I repeated. He already looked like he regretted it.

"Shit. Okay. My father is Anatolian Smith."

"And who is he?"

"You haven't heard of him?" He seemed astonished. "He is the General, effectively, of the Ionian Militia for the whole of the northern hemisphere of Io. Nothing happens up here without his say-so"

This was a supreme stroke of luck, and I had to force myself to breathe deeply.

Trying to sound calm, I asked, "So what is it you were gonna to tell me?"

"You wanna know something big? I'll tell you. There is an offensive planned. We have twelve new SU 401s and they're gonna to hit your mines at Ruwa Patera. Soon. I think maybe next month."

"SU 401s?"

"You didn't know that did you?"

"Twelve? When did you say? In March?"

"As far as I know."

"How? What weapons? Will there be ground troops? What is the strategic objective in all this?"

"I don't know all that. I told you what I know."

"Okay. I am going to give you a little 'general.' I'll put it in your feed now. Relax." I took a small plastic container out of my Medi-pouch and took off the lid. I screwed the end to the connector of the emergency intake on his respiratory unit and pressed the button to release the general anaesthetic into his system.

I waited for a minute. Then I stood up, aimed my X.50 at his shin and fired a shot through his tibia. A neat black hole filled with little red bubbles which drifted out into the thin Ionian atmosphere. Then a silver liquid, the sealant, trickled into the hole before it finally sealed the suit, leaving just a few red and silver bubbles floating away.

He moaned, but he didn't scream.

"Are you right-handed?" I asked.

After a moment he answered, "Yes," through clenched teeth.

I fired a shot through his left forearm, and then, as I had said I would, I grazed his right arm with the final shot. I saw a lot more blood, so I called Stone over and told him:

"Get one of the men to put a tourniquet on him."

I stood up.

Well. This is a turn-up. At last a real piece of luck. A chance for real glory. With this I get promoted another rank, maybe two, and then we will see.

A cold thrill ran through my spine but, for fear of it reaching my finger tips and making me dance around like a fool, I confined it to quarters.

After dragging the two casualties a safe distance away, we detonated the charge and started back for base. I saw some commotion off to my right; it looked as if two of the officers were arguing on a private link, one of them stamping his foot and shaking his X.50, but I ignored them.

I wondered what the landscape would look like with trees or even some grass. Riccard was rumoured to be working on a strain of grass that could grow in these conditions. For a moment I fancied myself as the governor of Io, with plans to geo-form it in some way, but I caught myself. My life's path had been decided for me a long time ago, and creativity wasn't a big part of it.

The rest of my waking hours that day were spent communicating with USAC Command, first through my superior officer, Lieutenant Colonel Roanald and then with Central Intel. Of course, at first, they were all skeptical about the provenance of my information, but they had to admit it was brilliant, if thought up on the spur of the moment. They confirmed the identity and rank of Anatolian Smith. Finally, around 20.00 hours, a decision had been taken. I would lead a task force of three companies in a covert mission to prevent the taking of Ruwa Patera, close to Anderstown, capital of the USAC territories on Io. Covert, because it was hoped we could surgically remove much of the cream of the Ionian Militia in this one operation if they weren't expecting us.

***

As I left the mess for my cabin, with a grin on my face, some of the officers were still arguing over something, but again I ignored them. Closing my door, I put the ruby ring, a present from Jena, on my second finger on my left hand and yawned before putting on the headband and saying, "Download." I skipped the message from Jena but played the entire message from my mother:

> "A peculiar thing happened the other day. I
> was in the main terminal, collecting your
> cousin, when this army type, tall, dark-haired
> and good-looking, tapped me on the shoulder

and asked for directions to 'Frisco South.
Well, it is really obvious to anybody with a
modicum of intelligence, it's right there on the
board, so I was suspicious. I thought, forgive
your old mother for being vain, but I thought
that maybe he was chatting me up, so I
humoured him. We chatted for a few minutes
actually. He asked me what it was like living
on J5, and then he asked if I knew any *other*
army types. I thought perhaps I should say
that I didn't know any at all, but he seemed
very charming, so I mentioned you. He asked
about you, and I really felt quite
uncomfortable at this point. He seemed far *too*
interested in you so I cut it short. He was
polite enough, and I didn't think too much of
it. The funny thing was that he was unshaven
and looked as if he had been sitting there for
days. He had shiny glasses on, so I couldn't
see his eyes, but there seemed to be
something familiar about him. I couldn't
place him though. Perhaps I have seen him in
a paper or something. Anyway, I wouldn't
have thought any more about it, but two days
later, I could swear I saw him again loitering
on a street corner while I was doing the
shopping. I could be wrong. Do take care.
Love Mum x"

I lay on the bed and closed my eyes.

***

The Ionian day is 42.5 hours, so the next time I woke,
it was still the same Ionian 'day.' We marked time in
Earth hours and dates followed those of Earth, but we
divided the Ionian 'day' into two 21.25 hour 'working'
days, too short for the human clock to endure for long

periods. This time, when I awoke, it would have been dusk outside if I had put the monitor on and left it on 'Real Time.' Final arrangements had to be made with Stone before I left for the USAC Station 5, in orbit around Jupiter and not far from the orbit of Io. There, I had been invited by Roanald to take part in the planning meeting for the operation at Ruwa.

"Stone. I am leaving for S.5 within the hour. I want you to prepare the MCS for exit tomorrow morning. Something has come up, and I am not sure we will leave tomorrow, but best be ready."

"Yes sir!" He swiped a salute at me, grinning. I guessed he had some idea it had something to do with the Intel from Smith.

The shuttle had been prepared for me, and as the rockets fired, lifting the shuttle against Io's weak gravity, I looked down at the grey MCS, settled on the only plateau in a flat sea of Sulphur, which stretched for hundreds of miles. I looked at Jupiter, orange bands around a creamy sphere filling half of the view from the port with my face pressed close, and looked for S.5, but I couldn't make it out from this distance.

As the little craft drew away from the moon, I became aware of the Io Flux Tube, a glowing torus of green, blue and orange light wrapped around the orbit of Io. A field of highly charged particles, it made radio-silence a necessity while escaping the little moons weak atmosphere.

After four hours strapped into the tight space of the shuttle, I saw the lights of Station 5, twinkling in the night.

"Major. What is your opinion?" asked a bald colonel with a salt-and-pepper moustache, on the opposite side of the large black granite table in the lavish Ops Room. The convention seemed to be to stand up when speaking, more, I felt, to assert one's self in this room of giant egos than for auditory reasons, so I stood up to speak:

"Sir. There is a way to do this. It's not conventional and may take a little longer to get into position, but I think it can work."

"Well? What is it?"

"We drive sir. The MCS has four backup diesels which are hardly ever used. We only use them for very short distances or when the fusion reactor is broken down. In fact, many MCSs never use any apart from one, which is generally used for some life support systems. If we *drive* to Ruwa, then the IM won't pick us up on the radar, at least I don't think they will. They are not used to seeing anything moving across the salt-flats, as we call them. If we use the fusion reactors, we cannot get into position without somebody, somewhere, noticing, as you rightly point out."

"How long will it take?"

"Well. 1200 miles at roughly 10 miles per hour is 120 hours; five days sir."

"*Five days?* Well rather you than me Major. Good luck with your men." He chuckled, and I heard general laughter around the table.

The MCS stood only about ten feet tall, even when the wheels were down and in motion, and I didn't think the Ionian Militia radar, patchy as it was, would pick us up. But now that we were moving, I was nervous about my strategy. A great cloud of sulphurous dust plumed above and behind us, and I just hoped that some observant IM grub wouldn't see it. What made things worse was that there would be two other such plumes and all three traveling on convergent headings.

On the third day, the second Ionian day, the bald colonel's words came back to haunt me. I was sitting, leaning forward in my mess seat straps next to the window and looking at the desiccated desert outside. I enjoyed these moments of calm. I often spent hours watching the surface of Io roll by, with the arc of Jupiter stretching from the horizon up to the seventy-degree mark. Stone's face appeared next to mine. I could smell his breath and feel it on my cheek.

"Sir?"

"Yes. What is it Sergeant?"

"What in Hell are we doing sir? Any more of this fuckin' desert, and the men will mutiny. On and on it goes and why? Does any other company ever, I mean *ever* use the diesels for motive power? Nope. For five days? Nope. So why are we the gullible idiots who are letting you do this to us?"

"Sorry Sergeant. It's all part of my cunning plan."

"Cunning? Cunning? I could make a dirty joke using that word that might be closer to the truth. Sir!"

I laughed. "Go and sit down. Just relax."

I stared out at the sea of Sulphur, totally flat and featureless, save for the occasional cracks, some of which were large enough for us to have to drive round. If you stared at it long enough, you started to feel that you were underwater or floating in yellow and rust-coloured clouds.

Just after the Ionian noon on day five, we were finally in position on the flanks of the great volcanic mountain of Ruwa Patera, inactive for many years. As the lead MCS, we were placed only about 400 yards from the main mine entrance and slightly above it, next to the track. I hadn't seen the other two MCSs which were now under my command, each with a small company of 50 men inside, but we had been in radio contact all day, and now all three were in position, spaced evenly around the flanks of Ruwa.

"Okay Sergeant Stone. Let's dig in. Disengage the PODs."

"Yes sir."

I felt the fusion drive building to full power, and then the teeth-loosening vibration began as the MCS started digging itself down into the Sulphur, so that only the top few inches would be left visible. Although the grunts hated it, the manoeuvre would only last a few hours and activating the S-grav immediately afterwards was always a relief that compensated for the discomfort. The vibration's amplitude, less than half an inch, only shook the MCS severe enough to tip cups off the tables. We still found it possible to work in the MCS. Indeed, working was necessary, because often at this point in a mission, we would be vulnerable and need to secure the perimeter using radar, deployed squads and covering fire. The eight tracks; four in a row on each side of the vehicle, were now turned through 90 degrees, using their variable teeth to cut through the Sulphur and shift it to the side of the MCS. From there, compressed air jets forced it to the surface and out into defensive banks. Blue U.V. cabin lights came on as the Sulphur rose over the windows.

Our MCS wasn't the very latest type but only a year old. It looked like a long, low tank without a main turret or perhaps a heavily-armoured, single-storey military building on tracks, 126 feet by 64 feet. There were turrets at all four corners and a row of small windows either side of the port turret, one of two, each half way along each of the long sides. The two Protective Ordinance Deploys, PODs, engaged half way along each long side and could be detached and deployed with their nuc-lasers to protect the MCS. Called fondly 'decoys' by the men, their crews of ten had one of the most dangerous jobs in the USAC Army, so the role rotated among the crew of thirty on the MCS. The decoys were also useful to provide extra power to get the MCS out of sticky situations or when stuck in difficult terrain. They were able to operate as tractors or simply contribute their own traction. The skins of the vehicles were coated in an electrolytically-controlled film which could take on just about any colour or pattern. On Io it, the colour would almost always yellow. Of course, when fully submerged, all you would see from above would be a few unusually shaped boulders.

"Deploying S-grav," came a voice over the speaker in the mess finally. I heard a mighty roar of approval from the men.

All the hammocks and fold-aways were stowed, and an impromptu game of football ensued. I kicked the ball around myself for a while before helping Stone break out the four crates of beer we had smuggled on board after the last shore-leave.

"So what's the plan Cap?" asked Stone pulling the tab on a can of Viper X, releasing a spurt of gas.

"Well, the main briefing will be tomorrow morning, early, and we have a few days to hang around but basically; ambush. Ambush the Ionians."

"Yeah? Cool. Why here though. I mean why this mine?"

"You'll find out … ."

Two of the officers had been having a heated discussion in a corner of the mess, and now one of them stood up and prodded the other in the chest. They both shouted, and the commotion caught my attention.

"Stone. Isn't that the two who were arguing the night before we left?"

"Yes sir. I think so."

I walked over to them, holding my hand up to stop the football. By this time, one of the Corporals had grabbed the other's wrists. "DeTunne, Walsh, what's this about?" Walsh looked angriest, so I asked him again.

"Nothing sir. Sorry sir."

"DeTunne?"

"Walsh has been griping since that little raid on the grubs the day before we left. His X.50 jammed, and he blames it on poor equipment, but I told him he should have checked his weapon before we left."

"I could have been killed sir!" Walsh said. "A grub guard pointed his piece directly at my face; just luck that DeTunne covered me. It's *shit* equipment! Same as usual. We shouldn't have to check everything all the time."

He knew I hadn't checked my X.50 before we left, the one handed to me just before we entered the airlock, but he wouldn't dare say it. Normally I would have cut this conversation short, but the looks on the faces of men now surrounding us told me that he wasn't the only one to feel this way. I sat on the arm of a foldaway.

"Well it's best to get this out in the open, and for once we have time." I pulled the rings on two more cans of Viper and handed them to Walsh and DeTunne. "Let's hear it."

"Well sir. When I joined USAC I thought I was joining the best. I thought we that we had the best men, and we would have the best equipment. Now I see that we do have the best men, but we do *not* have the best equipment. Constantly, we're being let down by stuff that doesn't work or is just badly made. I mean my old man's dad used to talk about cars being made on Friday afternoon, having loads of faults. Some of our gear is like *that*. I mean look at this thing!" He pointed to the ceiling. "There isn't one civilian transport on this moon that *uses* diesels. *Nothing* uses diesels any more. Everybody knows solar fusion is better; smoother, quieter and more efficient. But *no*. The *army* still uses diesels. Man, that technology is like the *Stone Age*. I mean, the only innovation I can remember is that we use Diesel'o now, and that's a laugh! Diesel'o. You can't buy it anywhere, even on the black market. Only USAC use it, and that's only, because Riccard-Amtel make it. So this army is owned by Riccard-Amtel." Feeling he had scored a point, he lifted the Viper to his mouth and took a long swig.

"He's got a point sir," Opinnskey said. "Why are we even here? Another cruddy mission like the last one. We spent fifteen weeks holed-up on the side of that rock just waiting for any IM traffic from the mines. Why the hell would they bother? There's nothing there! All we were doing was watching no-man's land. Border guards. That's all we were, but that's just 'cause we are R-Company."

There was general laughter from the men. Our name was K-Company, but we were known colloquially as R-Company.

"Ah, now you're talking!" DeTunne said. "I agree that all we are is border guards. We get all the shit jobs, and I hope this job's gonna be better, but I *don't* agree about equipment, and I *don't* agree about what you say about USAC."

"Republican!" shouted one of the other officers.

DeTunne swung to face him. "No! Yeah, I know that USAC is short of cash. Every government's short of cash these days, but I *don't* think we're owned by RA."

There were a lot of shouts from the grunts and officers and the word 'Diesel'o' from somebody; a private.

"Speak up!" I said to him.

"Well everybody knows the oil barons were desperate for one last fix, so they created Diesel'o."

"Yeah, and we're the only buggers who use it!" added Walsh.

Everyone grew silent.

"There are more Iron Crosses in K-Company than any other company on Io," DeTunne said quietly, his head down, as if reading from a book. His long nose suddenly looked noble to me.

"Yeah. Another invention by Riccard-Amtel," spat the grunt who had mentioned the oil barons.

"No way stoopid," the grunt next to him said.

"Yeah. You moron," added DeTunne, with a flourish of his mech hand. "You think I lost *this* for RA? The Iron Cross goes way back. Second World War I think. Germany?" He looked at me for confirmation.

"Further back I believe," Lieutenant Khan said, with precise, clipped diction.

"Napoleonic Wars I think, and Prussia originally, not Germany," I added. "It was made more famous by Germany though in the First and Second World Wars. It faded from use after that, but you have a point, Emphill, isn't it? It was re-popularised at the beginning of the Ionian Wars. I think they needed something with more gravity, if you'll excuse the poor joke, than the Medal of Honor; something that sounded tougher, and the core of Io is Iron, so it seemed appropriate. Iron medal for iron men on an iron moon. At least that's my interpretation. And don't worry, some of you may well win one in the next few weeks."

There were lopsided smiles from some of the men at my rousing speech. They had seen many of my press-interviews and didn't buy the character I portrayed for the public: super-tough soldier with few ambitions but to win the Iron Cross with all its embellishments.

"The Major has won the Iron Cross five times, all on Io," added Osei irrelevantly.

"Yes. Ten years, since I was a grunt," I said. "It's been a long ten years. Okay. Five-a-side soccer match with the winning side getting a bottle of vodka I happen to have stashed away."

I made my excuses soon after and retired to my cabin.

Sitting at the desk, I took up the pen and stared at the last line of my novel; 'Dusty picked up the scrap of paper and looked at the address scrawled in a neat, feminine hand.' I had only recently settled on the name Dusty. I had tried Rusty but decided it sounded too immediate. I thought Dusty sounded better for a private eye who specialised in cold cases, but I still felt unsure. I wrote; 'The faint smell of a Turkish cigarette, held between perfumed lips hung in the …' and then threw down the pen. I just wasn't in the mood.

I glanced at my left hand. It shook. I tried to stop it and then looked at my right; steady as a rock. I laughed out loud for a moment and then felt the coolness of a single tear, rolling down my cheek.

I sat there for some time, thinking, trying to master my fear, before taking a shower and lying flat on the bed. I closed my eyes, and as I drifted off, a powerful memory came to me.

My dad was taking me out of the dome on his hoverbike to watch a sunset on Mars, soon after a big dust storm. Of course, you could see sunsets from the dome, but the U.V. protection took out most of the colour, and I had nagged him for weeks to take me outside to see one. In my little hand-made spacesuit, I clung to his waist. My heart thumping in my ears as we covered a few miles across the ochre desert. The hoverbike skittered easily around the few rocks we saw, and I laughed inside my helmet. I knew I was a lucky kid. No other kid had a dad rich enough to have a child-sized spacesuit made. I loved him so much I wanted to squeeze him, but my arms weren't strong enough. I wanted the trip to go on forever but eventually my dad stopped the bike, and it sunk silently to the ground. He lifted me off, and I turned to look for the dome, but I couldn't see it any more. This would be the first time I had been out of site of the dome, and it felt strange. I felt a moment of fear, but then my dad's hand on my shoulder made me turn and look up at his helmet. I couldn't see his face, only the reflection of the lowering sun in the visor. It was like a burning disk of white. He took my hand, and we climbed together to the top of a steep bank. There we waited. When the Sun was almost touching the horizon, he said:

"Now Jake! Lift up your filter."

With difficulty, because my fingers were so small, I lifted the outer U.V. filter and gasped. The white disk of the sun almost burned a hole in my head, its white so intense it seemed almost blue. The blue became a corona as my eyes quickly looked up and away from it. The corona gradually faded into a riot of colour that filled the rest of my vision. The purples and oranges were deeper than those in a bowl of the freshest and most tangy grapes and peaches. For a moment I almost lost my balance and felt myself falling forward into a forever-sea of spectral light. We stood on the edge of time, until the Sun had completely disappeared below the horizon, and then, eventually, my dad sighed and said:

"Let's go."

My briefing to the men had to be made early. In conclusion, I pointed the laser to the nearest warehouse indicated on the map, projected on the front wall of the mess and said:

"Our nearest five tanks are hidden in this warehouse. The other ten are here, in *this* warehouse and in a third here, five in each. Now, we don't know exactly what is going to happen, but I can tell you personally that our Intel is much better *this* time. There will probably be twelve SU 401s, no more, and I would guess a few hundred IM grubs and grunts, no more; they cannot spare the troops, and anyway, any more would be too hard to conceal."

I heard a quiet, "Shit!" from one of the grunts sitting at the back.

"Yes soldier? Your point?"

"Sir. Did you say twelve SUs? We will be slaughtered! How come our force is so small?"

"Good question. There are two points here. The first is that the USAC can't spare any more troops, or armour either. The second, and most important for us, is that we know how the SUs are equipped, and we will be concealed. Don't worry. Now, my guess is that they won't try the main entrance here, which is protected by our five tanks. They will try to tunnel down to the shallowest tunnel in the mine. Some of those old tunnels go all the way back across the slope to here. I pointed to a point nearly five miles closer to the IM front line. If they can get in here, they have full access to the mine. But we will be listening for any seismic activity, and I don't need to remind you we have the very latest equipment. Concealment: you all are wondering what I have in mind here. Well the mine has been told to leave us a nice pile of slag near the entrance which we can use to cover the MCS. I know you will all want to volunteer to do that, but don't all rush at once." I could see a lot of the faces grinning back at me. "The slag, in case you didn't know, is a bi-product of raw iron production and is strongly magnetic, so the SU air-to-ground radar will miss us. Of course, it may pick up the PODs, but *they* like to take risks." More jeers from the audience. "Finally; two points; of course, ours is the lead MCS, and so we will be in overall control of the tanks. Their crews and commanders may well visit here at time for briefings, and as usual, we offer a place for men to unwind on long missions. I don't mind you fraternising, indeed I can't stop you, but that doesn't mean I want to hear about a lot of drug-induced comas while on duty. We will be on yellow alert from our Zero Hour, midnight tomorrow, and that means none of you do anything that stops you being ready for action at ten minutes notice. Understood?"

I heard a discordant and disapproving chorus of "Yes sir," from the men.

"Finally, I want all of you in your suits at all times from now. We don't know when they are going to attack or how they are going to attack, and there's no point taking risks. That's all. Any questions?"

I heard an even louder chorus of disapproval at the last point but no questions.

"Dismissed." Two of the men sat down. "When I said, 'suits now,' I meant *now*." Irritably, they started pulling their suits from their lockers which were set into the side of the mess, over the officers' cabins.

"Osei and Khan; I need to speak to you both privately in the Office." The 'Office' was actually the corridor, beside the washroom on the starboard side, which led to my own cabin. We used it for storage, but there was no other possibility for privacy on the ship beside my own cabin. The two lieutenants lounged on crates while I addressed them.

"In my briefing with Roanald, I found out some other things which, in my opinion, it's useful for you to know; all strictly confidential of course and, in fact, for now, secret. What we know is that recently the Mine Director, Choi was his name, was sacked when it was found out he'd been handing over information about the mine to the IM. Now, unfortunately, this is particularly relevant in *this* mine, because only recently they discovered a rich seam of iron ore right underneath Anderstown suburbs and have dug a tunnel to reach it. The IM know this now, and they know if they can get into the mine from any of those points not too far from their own front-line, they can quickly get right under Anderstown and, from what I have heard, it's no great task to get into some of the old sewers from there. What I haven't told the men is that we have to stop the IM at all costs, even if it means destroying the mine. For that reason, charges have been placed on the IM side of the mine, close to the main access shafts and also half way between the access shafts and Anderstown, in this new tunnel. It's called Tunnel M, and if this goes badly wrong and any one of us is left alive, it will be up to them to make sure these charges are blown. I'll take you down there and show you them in more detail in the next twenty-four hours."

There were nods from the two men.

"Osei, get ten men together and take one of the PODs over to the mine to pick up the slag. Then deploy the PODs in good defensive positions."

***

Database Download: Mobile Command Station (MCS) – Mark 6

The MCS officer's cabins were at the rear with the flight-deck sandwiched between the two shuttle bays. Behind the flight-deck and between the shuttle bays was the reactor and behind this the mess where the private soldiers spent all day, sleeping in hammocks. The mess was to the left of the MCS with windows along one edge next to a row of benches, raised to cover one of the four backup diesels. On the other side of the mess was the wash-room for the grunts and a door to a short corridor to the commander's cabin. This was in the right rear corner of the vehicle, and the other officers had, or shared, smaller cabins next to this along the rear edge of the MCS. The beds in the smallest cabins covered a second backup diesel; the third and fourth being underneath the flight-deck.

Mobile Command Station (MCS) – Mark 7

Very similar to the Mark 6 but entrance was through a hatch in the centre of the front which led straight onto the flight-desk. The Mark 7 had the new anti-laser refracting armour which looked like so many polygonal scales on its skin. The pods were now grouped in pairs at the front and back, to provide protection in the event of high-speed impact, a move that many of us had called for, which gave it a bug-eyed look from the front, and from the side it looked like a truncated centipede, squatted on the deck. From the gantry, its top surface was still a mass of pipes and vents but slightly less messy now with more armour plating covering it. My initial impressions of it on the testing flight had been good with the reservation that the cabins were all even smaller than the Mark 6, and that the extra armour plating had made it heavier and less manoeuvrable. **End Download.**

***

We didn't have to wait long for the attack. On the third day, night on Io, an operator picked up a single SU 401 on the radar, coming in high and fast. He didn't wait to be shot at and probably took a few nice photos of empty ground around the mine.

As Khan called out the intruder over the intercom, the men jumped into action. Plates and dice were dropped as men reached for their weapons, but it turned out to be a false alarm.

"Only reconnaissance!" Khan's voice crackled through the speakers.

Moans of frustration from the men filled the fetid air in the ship.

"Don't get complaisant!" I told them. "They are coming … soon!"

I had been more accurate than I had expected.

Thirty minutes later, we heard a sudden flash from somewhere outside, and then the MCS shook.

Khan's voice, calm but urgent, announced the obvious, "Incoming!" and then the not so obvious, "I think they've spotted us!"

"Khan! What's happening?" I shouted when I reached the flight-deck hatch.

In the red light, I could see Osei's open mouth, saying something to me, but another explosion drowned out his words.

"What?" I yelled.

Both Osei and Khan together shouted, "MCS Bravo is hit!"

"How?"

"Dunno. Infra-red? They know where we are! Look"

I looked in the direction Khan, sitting in the driving seat, pointed. The radar screen showed seven blips, SU 401s, and smaller blips streaking from them towards all three positions of the MCSs.

Somebody has ratted on us. But who … .

"Coming at us!" shouted Khan.

This was it. My worst nightmare had come at last. I didn't hesitate. I reached for the red Evac button and punched it. The Evac button bi-passed all other safety procedures, so there could be no time to prepare. Instantly the hot air in the MCS started rushing out through the open hatch.

"Lids!" I screamed pointlessly. Every man would have already taken a deep breath and be closing his visor. The escape hatch lay just inside the mess, and I could already see men lunging up the ladder.

"Come on!" I shouted to Osei and Khan, but I already knew we would be too late. I waited for the stream of men to escape, and as the seconds ticked by, each like an eternity, my heart beats grew louder and my breaths fewer.

Crash! Everything went mad as the missile hit. My helmet hit the rim of the mess hatch, and I couldn't see. Instinct kicked in and I groped for something, so that I could pull myself towards the ladder. Somebody grabbed my arms, and then I saw Stone's face, blurry but distinct, grinning at me.

"Hit the rear!" came over my intercom. Within moments, I had clambered out and stood on the roof of the MCS. Multiple explosions lit the night sky with white flashes, which cooled to red and yellow, eerily silent.

As I jumped up onto some slag to quickly survey the battlefield, I saw troops of IM snaking over the ridge of the volcano. Laser-fire streaked out towards some of the PODs near us.

Laser-fire hit a lump of slag near Stone's head, and he dived for cover. The lump glowed, reddish black.

Our position had been under a bluff just above the main approach track to the mine entrance. This sloped up from the south along the side of the volcano before turning ninety degrees into the mine entrance. Most of the terrain looked harsh and slag-strewn, but the track offered a chance of escape.

"To the track, men." I said over the intercom calmly. "Regroup near POD 5; half way between here and the mine entrance. Stone. Where is Osei?"

"I saw him with a group of men, taking up defensive position the other side of the MCS Cap!"

"Osei. Get onto S.5 now. We need air-cover, and we need it now."

"Osei's voice crackled through the interference from the battle."

"Sir!"

"Then get your men to the rendezvous. We are going to launch a counter attack. Where is Khan?"

"Don't know sir. I think he stayed in the MCS."

"What? Stone, I want to know what our status is and that of the other MCSs. Okay?"

"Yessir!"

"But stay with me. Use one of the other frequencies if you have to."

I looked at the front corner of our MCS and could see the far-side POD turret moving.

Khan seeking targets for the laser cannons. Idiot.

"Khan! Khan get out of there. Now! That is an order!"

"Will do sir. Just one more incoming. Everyone clear of the MCS!"

"Khan!"

I saw the whitish streak of the missile's liquid hydrogen exhaust streaking straight towards the MCS from the south. An SU 401 banked after releasing it and climbed for cover of height. There would be no time for Khan now.

The laser cannons moved to aim at the missile, and it grew in my visor until it grew too big and too close. I closed my eyes. I saw an enormous flash of white, which lit up the inside of my eyelids. Thrown to the ground, I watched pieces of MCS flew over our heads until again I heard silence.

I could see helmets shaking in disbelief.

We moved quickly, using short hops to POD 5, where at least there would be a few weapons.

The voice of DeTunne came over the intercom from the POD. "Nice to see you, Cap. POD 3 has bought it.

And I think one of those warehouses, with our tanks in,
has been hit."

"Losses?"

"Still assessing sir. Help yourself to lasers."
"Tell the other PODs to start clearing a path between us
and the southern ridge of the volcano. That's where we're
going, because that's where their troops are coming from.
That's where they'll be attempting to get into the mine."

"Yessir!"

"Osei? Where is the air-cover?"

"On its way sir."

"How long?"

"Twelve minutes."

*Shit! What was the point of all this secrecy if they knew
we were here anyway?*

"Osei. Anything from the other MCSs?"

"Nothing sir. POD 1 and 4 say all comms have
stopped. Probably gone sir and all in them, God rest their
souls."

All remaining men regrouped by POD 5, and then we
started over the small ridge above the road and on,
eastwards towards the ridge of Ruwa Patera. Half way to
the ridge, we came across the first concentration of IM
that the remaining PODs had not yet cleared.

Stone came on the line. "Status reports sir."

"Go ahead."

"Our MCS; five dead. Other MCSs all gone sir, far as
we can tell. Some good news though."

"Yes?"

"Look to your left Cap, about three o'clock."

I looked and, surrounded by sulphurous dust, came a
glorious sight; eight of our own tanks.

"Where are you Stone? I need you here."

"With you in a moment Cap."

"You!" I tapped a grunt on the shoulder. "Break out the
lasers from the POD."

The panel had fallen open on the side of the POD, released from inside, to reveal five X.50s. It was a start. The grunt handed one to me, kept one himself and handed out the other three.

Stone came up from the column behind me, just as a line of IM militia stood up on a ridge to our right. Twenty of them opened fire on our double-column, now of only forty-five men, loosely spread out and with flankers. I knew our flankers would soon have this covered. While we lay behind rocks for cover, I tried to think through my strategy.

Don't know how many men they have, but since they must have come the last five or ten miles on foot they would have had the chance to spread themselves very wide, and we could easily be walking into a trap. Do we have a choice? No. We have too few men to split up.

"Air-cover?"

"Four minutes sir."

"Okay. We wait here."

The flashes of laser-fire grew less frequent and then stopped. Stone tapped me on the shoulder. I looked in the direction of his pointing finger. I saw Walsh wave from the ridge where the IM had been.

"Get over here Walsh and take cover."

We waited for our air-cover. It came not a moment too soon. The SUs had concentrated on destroying the remaining tanks and had hit three. Our three FA 217s struggled to cope with the outdated, but still fast, SU 401s. Left over from the age of the first conflicts between what was once Russia and USAC on Mars, the SUs were built for speed. Even though their avionics and weapons systems were completely obsolete, their speed still made them dangerous. We watched while the little white fighters fought each other. Within seconds, a missile caught an SU, which exploded in a galaxy of light motes.

***

Database Download on the SU 401: As with most modern space-fighters they were pencil-shaped, with engines in four pods, separated from the main hull by wing-lets. The pods allowed the engines to be used for propulsion in any direction, and the main difference between the SUs and the FAs was the wing-lets. These were bigger on the SUs for some direction stability in the thicker atmosphere on Mars. **End Download.**

***

"That's evened the odds up a bit!" I said over the intercom.

I stood up.

"To your feet men!"

All remaining men stood up. I beckoned them to follow. We had covered more than three of the four miles to the ridge. I couldn't see any IM this side of it. We made good progress over the next twenty minutes. Passing near some of the PODs, we picked up more X.50s until every man had been armed.

Passing over onto the other side of Ruwa and towards the dawn, as it rushed over Io's surface towards us, we could see what all the fuss was about.

An IM Fortriss digger sat vertically in its cradle after having just exited a shaft in the surface below it, about four-hundred yards in front of us. It would be right over the position of one of the shallowest tunnels in the mine, if the IM ground-radar had been accurate enough.

"Osei? I want you to organise the vehicles. I want the tanks and PODs to go around the back of the IM and give us covering fire from there. Keep them well out; their longer range should keep them safe. Once they're in position and covering us, we will go in, in small groups. The ground's rough down there, and I can't see how many men they have."

"Stone. I've seen more than one shot come from that ridge on our right. Draw their fire while we circle around them."

After we eliminated them, Stone rejoined us. All the while, the tanks and PODs circled around behind the Fortriss and moved into position.

"Sir! Look!" A Grunt called Dunne pointed way to the right, in front of me and ahead of the digger. I just caught a bright flash of orange light from the corner of my eye. We were only about fifty yards from the digger and under heavy fire as we moved. We had taken shelter for a moment behind a large lump of slag on the lip of a shallow gully.

"What the fu- … !"

"Laser sir?"

"I dunno, but whatever it is, it's big and just took out one of our tanks. The IM shouldn't have equipment like that … . Not that they can carry around. I haven't seen any vehi- … ."

That was when I realised my big mistake.

Looking to the right of the field of battle, I saw more IM coming in on the opposite side to that of the first attack. They were all armed with laser-knives. We were caught between two lines. They had laser-knives, because they didn't want to hit each other. But more significant was the fact that they knew, and we knew, they couldn't win. It had to be just a delaying tactic.

In the instant the real situation registered in my over-busy mind, I stood still, watching another orange explosion beyond the digger.

Another tank or POD.

There are always moments like this in any battle for a leader; the moment when you perceive the deepest strategy of your opponent and have to take stock of what you have remaining and what's achievable. It's a moment of complete silence and clarity. That is, your mind becomes silent, and if you are a good leader, you find you have plenty of time to work out a strategy which has a chance of winning. The moment came, and I acted.

"Stone!" I shouted into the intercom. "Watch the rear. Keep it open!"

"You think I didn't know that?" Stone always became angry in the heat of battle.

The first wave of IM grunts leaped over the lip of a rise and clashed with my flanking men. Carnage followed with the IM losing every man.

I knew now that we were surrounded. Seeing it as their last chance to trap us, the IM had delayed us, and now we were probably seconds away from slaughter. I weighed the distance to the digger and wondered what forces were between us and it.

"Sir! Osei here. Sir. Something's wrong!"

"Yes, I know. We're in trouble. What is it Osei? Quick!"

"The digger sir. It's stopped digging. Also, we're too close. If they still needed it, would they pick an ambush point this close?"

"Yes." It was irrelevant now. We had to get out of the ambush or lose our lives and the mine. The digger had been down again since we'd first seen it, but now it sat again, motionless in its cradle. That meant that they already had broken through to a shaft and most likely already had a squad on their way down.

So near yet so far.

"Back! Retreat!"

The second wave of laser-knife armed IM had reached us, and it was a question of survival for now. I aimed my laser at a grunt and pulled the trigger. It seemed senseless, but I just kept picking them off while slowly shuffling along the gully with my column of men. When the last of the disposable IM grunts had fallen, the real attack started. Incoming green laser-fire forced us to the ground. I found myself looking at a lump of slag next to a piece of silicate, coated in fine Sulphur powder, only an inch from my visor. For a moment, I thought how beautiful the yellow of the powder looked against the red flecked black of the slag and the variegated, speckled silicate.

"Stone? I spoke into the intercom, almost in a whisper."

"Here Cap. Things are bad, aren't they?"

"Yes. How is it back there? Is there a way out?"

"Er. Let me see sir. Won't be a moment." I heard the muffled sound of heavy fire in the intercom a moment later than I heard the same sound through my helmet; it sounded curiously as if I stood in an echo-chamber.

"Only one way sir."

"Yes?"

"We need a precision hit from one of the tanks. Osei can do it sir."

"Osei? Can we do it?"

"Er, maybe sir. It's risky. Very risky."

"*This* is risky Rick."

"Yessir."

"Tank 14. Do you read me?" I heard Osei call.

Laser-fire scorched just above our heads and I heard a few screams over the intercom while Osei waited for an answer.

"Not sure if any of the tanks are still operational … ."

"Tank 14. We're here! Just. We been hit. We can barely move."

"We need a hit. I'm gonna give you a map reading. But it's a guess. If your navigator thinks I am wrong, let me know. Map reading 21, 61, 42 North, 90, 01, 52 West. Aim about one hundred yards west of the digger tip. You got that?"

"Yessir. Wait a moment. Incoming!" I heard the sound of an explosion over the intercom and coughing.

"You there 14?"

A few more coughs were followed by, "We're still here but not for much longer. Wait a moment."

"Jesus!" muttered Osei to himself.

The sound of laser-fire from Stone's end of the column increased.

"Make it quick guys!" Stone yelled.

The suited body of a grunt fell across my knees. I shook him, but he lay dead. I saw a rent in his suit, about a foot long.

"Okay we got you. Nav. thinks you are off by fifty yards. Says the digger is at 90, 00, 02 West. Which makes your spot about 01, 44."

Osei looked at me. The intercom fell silent.

"It's yours Rick. Don't worry, if you are wrong, most of us won't feel a thing."

A weak smile creased his lips. "Okay I'm with your Nav … Take the shot."

"Okay. Fire in the hole. Three, two, one. Charge away!"

"Incoming!" Osei shouted as loud as he could down the intercom. Heads ducked down even further.

A mountain of slag and dirt lifted from behind a slight rise, and I watched for body parts. There were plenty of them.

"Stone? Was that a hit? Are you alright?"

I heard silence for a moment and then:

"Phewee! That was mighty cool! Bang on target! Remind me to buy that Navigator any drink he likes! And all night long too! We got a way out of here now! Come on Cap. Let's go!"

"Not that easy Stone. With you in a moment. Okay men. You around me at the front of the column. As far as I can tell, there are about twenty of us left. There is at least one hundred of them. Our only chance is to run for it. That rise, to our rear, is home and dry for you. Get there, and you'll be okay. When I say, go. We stand, and give them everything you got! Okay, ready … . *Go!*"

Every man stood up, firing at anything and nothing. Most of us couldn't see much because of the blinding wall of laser-fire slicing into bodies all around us. Those that could, ran and those that couldn't, crawled. Some dragged their companions but only ten of us made it over the rise. Beyond it, we had no time to stop. Stone stood there, directing us down the line to another shallow gully which offered good protection from incoming fire. Once in it, we had a chance. We moved in hops as fast as we could back over the ridge towards the mine entrance. Only twenty of us were left when we approached the mine entrance. The remaining PODs, slower moving than the tanks, had been taken out, trying to defend our flank. Only two tanks were left. Tank 14 wasn't one of them. As we had reached the top of the ridge, I had turned for a moment to look at the battlefield. I could see an ant's nest of at least one hundred and fifty, perhaps two hundred, IM milling about on the field.

Lucky to get out of that one. Very lucky.

"Back the tanks up against the entrance Osei!" I ordered. "I don't want anything getting in behind our backs. Okay, let's go."

I punched the code and the great mine-gates, big enough for coal-trucks, opened to let us in. When they shut behind us, the air pressurised in the air-lock. We raised our visors and breathed real air. The inner doors opened, and a portly man stood there in the gloom, on his own. I recognised him as the Mine Manager.

"Sir, what is the status … . I mean what can you tell us?" I asked, approaching him. He looked deathly pale and clearly very shaken.

"They are already in Tunnel M. But there is a short-cut. You have to move fast. Follow me."

While we followed him down the long tunnel, he told me all I needed to know.

"The others are all in the shelters, except two. The IM caught them trying to put up a barricade. We blocked the main entrance to Tunnel M from the central access shaft yesterday, but they must have found out how to get in from my two men. But you can still beat them, I think."

After a distance of about four-hundred yards, we came to a small door labeled 'Fire Exit' on the left. Here the Manager stopped.

"Go in there, follow the tunnel to the lift and take the cage down to the thirteenth level. Out of the lift, and the tunnel behind you is Tunnel M. You know your way from there. Good luck."

"You're a brave man. Thanks!" I slapped him on the shoulders and opened the door.

We moved at a fast trot down the long, sloping corridor to the lift-shaft. All twenty of us managed to fit into the cage. I pressed the button for the thirteenth level.

"He could be lying sir," Dunne said.

"Yes." I looked at him grimly.

"Why the hell don't we have backup?" shouted Stone behind me. "Anderstown is only a few miles away, and S.5 should have something there. And their own troops can get here in twenty minutes. I don't understand it!"

"Me neither Stone." I answered.

The cage rattled to a stop, and everything grew ominously quiet.

"Weapons!" Every man raised his weapon. I stepped out of the cage. We were at a tunnel junction. Here a side tunnel crossed Tunnel M, but I guessed we were about one third of the way along it. The IM could be ahead of us or behind us. I peered around the lift shaft corner into Tunnel M. The dimly lit tunnel looked clear of IM.

"Let's go. Fast as we can." If we were behind them, we had to catch them.

"Sir! I saw something! Behind us," yelled the rear-most grunt.

"Where!"

"Behind us!"

I raised my hand; the signal to stop. I ran to the back of the squad and peered into the tunnel on the opposite side of the lift-shaft. After a few seconds, I saw them; little lights bobbing up and down.

"They're coming! Fast as you can!"

I broke into a flat-out run, hoping we were all fit enough to stay ahead of the IM. We had a long way to go. We had gone perhaps nearly a mile when the same grunt shouted that they were gaining on us. My men were almost exhausted. Clearly the IM weren't carrying so much weight.

"Come on! Come on! We have practiced this!"

"Not for a few years Cap!" added Stone.

"Come on! Come on! Just another half mile to go."

There were a few flashes from behind, and a seribdenum roof-beam above my head glowed red. Men started to drop; one, two, and then I couldn't look any more. We had to keep going. Sweat streamed down my face, and I struggled for every last gasp of breath. The men around me weren't doing much better.

I glanced at the sides of the shaft-props but couldn't find what I sought.

"Keep going!"

I glanced again at a prop and saw, marked on it, number 573. I knew from my visit, days before, that we needed to get to prop 613.

"Nearly there! Another one hundred yards!"

I think!

I counted down the props. 600, 601, 602 and 603.

"Stop! Help me!"

Every mine shaft has spare props in case of collapse, and I knew there were some at prop 603. I pulled the spare props out from the wall and laid them across the tunnel between two vertical props each side of the tunnel. In less than thirty seconds we had ten props, overlapping each other, forming a low barricade right across the tunnel.

"Okay. We will make our stand here! The charges are about another one hundred yards down the tunnel. Osei. Get five men together. You will blow the charges. I want ten men on the ground behind the props, five men each side, crouching and standing. We have the advantage here; there are too many of them to all fire at once. Militarily, it's called a bottleneck!" I reminded them, hoping to sooth the men's nerves.

The IM halted in the distance and took up positions as they opened fire.

"How many do you think Stone and Osei?"

"Forty!" Stone replied, from the right wall.

"More like fifty." Osei, whose eyesight had always been keener, said.

"Osei. Get going!"

"Ahhh!" Stone had been hit in the leg. The shot had almost taken his leg clean off. It hung by the material of his fatigues and a thin sliver of muscle. He stayed on his one good leg but leaned against the wall, panting.

"Stone! Your laser! Do it!" I shouted.

He nodded. He pointed his laser at the exposed femoral artery of his stump and fired a short burst to cauterize the wound and seal the artery. In shock, and with such an unwieldy instrument, his fired haphazardly, and he burned quite a bit of flesh as well. He gasped in agony and dropped the laser. Grasping his leg, slumped to the floor.

Glancing at Osei, I watched him tap five good men on the shoulders and break into a run, but just as he reached the first prop, a shot hit him, and he went down.

"Osei!"

One of the men with him shook his head.

Shit!

"Stone! Are you okay? Can you move with assistance?"

"Are you kidding? I'm fucked. Look for crissake!" he shouted

"Take him!" I beckoned to two of the men Osei had chosen.

"Leave me here! I can still fire a laser!" he shouted through gritted teeth.

"Don't argue."

The two men returned, took an arm each and hauled Stone off, up the tunnel.

"Prop 613 Stone! You know what to do. Don't fail! And you lot; defend him to the last man!" I watched them become smaller as they struggled down the tunnel with Stone.

A laser shot whizzed by my ear, making the air sizzle. I smelled burned hair, my own.

A long shoot out, with many twists and turns, followed I had been right; even though we were outnumbered, we lost men at about the same rate as the IM until their leader, with more men, decided to risk a trick. Nobody ever throws grenades in a mine unless they want to bring the roof down or die. But the IM were desperate. A grenade landed right in front of the barricade, skipped across the dirt and came to rest against the props.

I dived away from the blast, down the tunnel, and a man landed on top of me just as hell came down around us. When, at last, silence fell, and I realized I must still be alive, I pushed the man from on top of me. He still breathed too and didn't look too badly hurt. One other looked alive. The rest of my men were dead. Through the cloud of dust, I saw that the joist of the tunnel had split and bent out of shape, as had the vertical props. Somehow the tunnel still remained largely intact.

I heard a great cry of, "Charge!" from the IM, and then they ran towards us.

I stood up, found a laser that looked like it might fire and aimed it at them. Thinking this might be the end, I decided to go out on a high. I started walking toward the IM. A laser shot fizzed past me from behind; I knew that it came from one of my men, one of the other two survivors.

I kept walking as laser-fire ripped into my right leg. There seemed no question of feeling any pain or reacting to it. My blood was high; I couldn't feel the pain, and I didn't care. I felt my leg hit a number of times, but the IM were using single shots now, and my leg still held me up. Another shot hit my arm as I took down two IM with a single sweep of fire from my laser. Coming at me in two columns, I had no trouble picking off as many IM as wanted the mortal bite of fire. They fell as if they had practiced it, each being replaced by a man who, with the dust and debris in the air, took too long to pick out his target and fire. I had taken down nearly thirty before they hit me in the chest and fell to the ground, face down in the dust. My head swam while I tried to force my body to move one last time. At first, it wouldn't, and to my surprise I felt, rather than heard, the sound of IM boots passing over and around me. Then I heard the high-pitched squeal of two shots.

I tried again to move and, drawing on all my reserves, managed to turn myself over. Seeing my laser near my hand, I grabbed it and fired at the back of the last IM, running along the tunnel. He went down and something rolled away from his hand.

Grenade! Oh no, not again!

But it didn't go off. Frantically I dragged myself, with my good arm, towards the grenade and picking it up. I pressed the firing button with the usual IM combination; two long presses, followed by a pause and then three long presses. The red warning light flashed, and I smiled. Getting to my knees and nearly passing out from the pain which swept over me, I threw the grenade as far as I could, just catching some of the rearmost IM in the resulting blast. Then I leaned against the tunnel to wait for whatever would come. I smiled again at the IM sense of humour. The IM firing combination was the Morse code for 'M-O,' the first two letters for the name of the Greek god of sleep, Morpheus.

"Come on Stone! Blow it!"

Becoming delirious, I laughed at my own pun, and then it came. A huge explosion jolted me, and then a huge plume of dust snaked down the tunnel.

Yes Stone! Yes!

I waited, and when the jolting subsided, the tunnel became as silent as a tomb. But there would be one more surprise for me. I heard voices, IM voices.

Shit!

If I wanted to live I would have to think fast. My stomach wound was bleeding badly and would be fatal if I didn't get help soon.

The IM took their time returning, no doubt contemplating their failure and whether they could do any more.

They came, sauntering down the tunnel, chatting and looking surprisingly relaxed. The dead IM grunt with the grenade had one more hanging from his belt. The only place to hide, so that I could be sure to hit all of the IM; a shallow alcove that had been created when the first explosion had taken out some loose rock. It might not conceal my legs properly, but the lights above the scene of the explosion were mostly out; few still blinked sporadically. I took up position, balancing my weight on my good leg, and when they were close enough, I threw the grenade into their midst.

They seemed very surprised. The leader had just enough time to stare angrily at me before his head exploded, and the IM squad became a chaotic cloud of blood and flesh. It didn't matter to me now if the tunnel collapsed, but it still held.

No good, these IM grenades!

As the cloud of dust rolled past me, so too did the sound of feet. Some of the grubs, no doubt fed up with the sight of death, made their escape. I didn't care, I had no more energy left, so I let them go.

The next thing I remembered, I woke up in the USAC hospital on S.5.

***

"It is with great honour that I award the Knight's Cross of the Iron Cross, with Oak Leaves, Swords and Diamonds to Major Jake Nanden, the most highly decorated field officer on Io. A brief description of the action on Io at Ruwa Patera mine, in which the award was won, will now follow."

A slight, wry smile creased my mouth involuntarily at the inclusion of Io; a small and reluctant nod to K-Company I thought. I looked up to the roof of the vast amphitheatre of S.4, the Mars station of USAC, and at the crowd of twenty thousand, largely military faces, watching me. I smiled for them. The large monitors picked up my grin, displaying it, magnified thousands of times.

A voice started reading out a brief description of the action:

"On the second of March, 2101, eleven jets of the IM attacked the mine at Ruwa Patera which was only protected by a single … ."

As he read, I saw the events in my own mind, the deaths of Osei and Khan, and wondered what the action had really been about. Why had there been no backup? How had the IM known where the MCSs were? These questions burned holes in my mind, but for now, I just had to smile.

The Voice concluded, "However, the remaining enemy fled, and later, the badly wounded and unconscious Major was retrieved by a small rescue force from a nearby outpost." The reader looked up, prompting the beginning of a long, standing ovation from the audience for perhaps seven minutes. I felt relieved to get away.

My new, mech leg still felt a little stiff, and I hobbled slightly as I reached Sergeant Stone, waiting back stage. We both headed for the expressway that led to the Terminal. Our suitcases had been sent ahead. Stone hardly glanced at my new medal.

"I heard the mention of Io, the subtle reference to the repo-battalion." Stone laughed hoarsely. "Is that all they can do? Us replicants *will* get recognition *one* day. They can't ignore us forever!"

I smiled wryly at him.

"Naah!" he cried. "You gonna see your lady?"

"Sure am. Haven't seen her for nearly twelve months. You seeing Martha?"

"Yep. And the kids."

"How old are they now?"

"Naylor is five and Don, two." He paused. "Sir, why do you stay in this business? I mean you could do anything. You have a degree in engineering. Why do you go on taking such risks all the time? It *can't* be the medals."

I pulled his cap down over his face. "You worry about yourself, and let me worry about me."

"Well this is where I get off. See you in six weeks-time. They have gone soft on you. Just 'cause you got a slight scrape on the tummy."

"Rules is rules. Six weeks for stomach wounds, especially when it's a winner of the Iron Cross."

He laughed at that and stepped off the conveyor onto a slower, side-conveyor which would take him to the gate for Mars. I stayed on until the gate for Earth.

During the seven days of my journey to Earth's orbit, I hired a blanker. Blank-Replicant's were not cheap, and in the Army, only officers of my rank or above could afford even the cheapest, Sensels. The name even sounded cheap and sexual to me, but I wanted to spend as much time with Jena as I could so, shortly after boarding, I used my credit scan to pay for one and then went to the booth indicated on my heads-up. One enters a drug-induced coma while using a blanker, which is why they are forbidden while on duty and why I had not spent any time at all with Jena since the previous May. During the hour it took for the drug to take effect, I reclined on the comfortable lounger and thought about Jena.

She had requested a vid-link with me the day before the attack, and I had accepted for late in the evening.

The link activated, and I found myself looking at Chloe, blue-eyed and staring back at me.

"Hi Chloe!"

Her eyes widened and she crouched, ready to make her escape. Her long, white feline ears pricked up, and then a pair of hands stroked her long white fur once, before lifting her out of view. She was replaced by Jena.

"Hi Jake!" She sounded upbeat.

I laughed "Hi! How's Chloe?"

"As you can see, she is exquisitely adorable; doing what cats do. She misses looking into your green eyes and extracting as many of your inner thoughts as possible, so that she can pass them on to me."

"Well, she's not a fool like you. She knows there *are* no thoughts there."

"According to Hansegger, only replicants who are blanks or study Buddhism have no thoughts."

"Well Hansegger has got it wrong."

A long silence followed while we both weighed each other up, like two opponents trying to assess each other's general combat readiness.

"How's it going with the deal?" I asked.

"Oh that!" She looked embarrassed. "I hope you didn't mind. I just had to tell you baby."

I laughed. "It's fine. So?"

"Yes. Going fine. Tell you a little more but not too much, when it happens." She indicated how much with a pinch of her thumb and first finger.

Jena looked great. She reclined and hooked her legs over the arm of her favourite leather chair. She lay, wrapped in a white cotton bath-robe. She had brushed her newly washed blonde hair back over her ears. Her inquisitive blue eyes tried, as usual, to penetrate my expressions for a quick advantage, speaking of her own insecurity I thought.

"So in answer to your question, yes women do like to be 'claimed' sometimes."

She looked slightly uncomfortable revealing this. I hadn't expected her to talk about it, especially since she had already answered me in message a few days before. I felt a small sense of triumph. I didn't say anything, hoping she would go on.

"Satisfied?" she said.

"Not really," I said "But that's another matter." As if wanting something in return for her intimacy she asked, "So what has your god been saying to you?"

"*My* god?" I stalled while I thought of which defense to try. Jena had one weakness that I knew of; she was impatient, and so she became vulnerable if I didn't respond to her messages or vid-link requests. However, she knew my weakness too, and mentioning God was like cracking a walnut with a sledgehammer.

I tried my best defense. "I don't have a god Jena. You know that. I never have had."

"But I don't believe that. How do you stay sane?"

"Who says I am?" I smiled at my facetious joke. She didn't smile.

"How do you get through … you know … what do you do?"

I straightened up. "I live for one thing; getting back at Enquine. I don't need God."

"You have Enquine?" She smiled ruefully. "Not that again. I think it's a defense. I don't think that's a real answer, and I don't think you're being honest with me!" She looked affronted, and her tone had become acerbic.

I tried the little boy approach. "But it is true Jena."

"And I suppose you really were too busy to respond to my messages for the last two weeks?"

"Yes. Things have been pretty busy." I needed to be cautious. She had changed tack.

"Yeah, yeah. Pull the other one. I am on to you Jake."
I laughed. "Oh Jena. I miss you!"
"Yeah? Prove it Jake. Let me see."
"See?"
"Yes. Let me see you. Unless there is someone else in the room with you. Katie perhaps?"
I laughed. "No."
"Well then…?"
"Jena. Not tonight. I'm really not in the mood."
"She became silent and seemed to be brooding, her face smouldering, her mouth fixed closed."
"Good night Jena." I said, "End transmission," and the com centre blanked the screen. I brooded myself for a minute. I didn't like falling out with Jena, and I wondered whether she would now be sitting in that chair sulking or laughing.

When I had heard of the Iron Cross ceremony on Mars, I had immediately left a message for Jena telling her when I would be in and that I wanted to visit her. Later I received her reply. "Love to. Any time and stay. xx"

***

The drug started to take effect, and I found it harder to order my thoughts in any way.

Gods? What god had Jena been talking about? His god, your god, their god, the god out there but no god for me.

Mech, the god for all A.I. beings, as robots and androids were now permitted to call themselves, lived in a red world of dust which corroded him, and he had three sons, Iron, Tin and Wire. They lived in the desert for they were afraid of the sea, but one day, Iron, who was the eldest son, committed a sin by openly doubting Mech, and Mech banished him. Iron wandered alone until he came to the sea and left his mark upon a rock, but no more was ever heard from him again.

The Myth of Mech went around my head until I said
'No!' For a while I had been curious about the android
god, but he wasn't for me. Neither the Christian God, nor
Allah, nor Yahweh were for me. Many replicants, like me,
were not able to find faith. When you didn't trust your
own memories, it was hard to find peace. The memory of
the sunset on Mars typified this. If it had been real, I
would have been six at the time, and I know the event
happened but not to me. Most replicants were 'grown'
until the age of sixteen before being bought, or 'adopted,'
to use a more acceptable term. Of course, if you had the
money, you could adopt earlier or later. But sixteen was
the most usual age, the age at which most felt a rep child
would be psychologically stable and provide the least
trouble for prospective parents.

Parents were encouraged to call the first day a birthday
and do something distinctive, so that the rep would
remember it clearly. In my case it was a picnic by the
river in 'Frisco East with my mother Mary, stepfather and
sister, Justine. At first, I had believed all the implanted
memories of my early years, but soon, taunts of other
children made me ask my mother what a replicant was.
She told me, and, later at college, when I met other
replicants, I soon learned the truth about our memories. It
hurt.
For all this, the memory of the sunset on Mars seemed
the most vivid, and it didn't stop coming.

***

While in the trance, I lived through the blanker, which
had been sent to Jena's apartment. We spent five days
together doing the sites of the Moon. Most couples used
this method while traveling, to spend more time together.
It had some hilarious results. While using a blanker, the
time-delay often became a problem. While feeding the
baby mammoth, star-attraction at Collins Zoo, my blanker

couldn't react fast enough and had his hand bitten off. We lost the deposit of course. On the seventh day, I arrived and returned the blanker to the vendor.

***

Chapter Two

In the dream, the little voice had chosen the first corridor on the left.

"Good choice," the high voice said.

The little voice arrived at a rectangular portal, actually more like a secret hatch and pushed it open. Beyond was a fallow field of green grass and meadow flowers. The little voice knew that he had been happy here, but he didn't want to step through the hatch. Though there was joy beyond, he didn't trust it.

"Go on," the high voice said.

"No," the little voice said.

"Where are you going?" Jena said sleepily, casting an arm over my waist to trap me as I rose from the bed.

"It's nine," I said.

I padded into the bathroom.

"So? Come back to bed."

I often chided J about the extravagance of the bathroom; most people used a sanicube, to save space, but the real reason I didn't like hers was the mirror. I had a thing about mirrors. There were none on the MCS or on any other MCS. When I had asked why there were none, I had been told they were too heavy, but I thought it a strategic decision to save introspection in the men. It might have been one of the reasons I felt most comfortable in the MCS.

I avoided looking in the mirror and noticed two toothbrushes, in a glass to the right of the sink. I had recognised them before from old films, one red and one green. The green one, Jena's, had worn bristles. She had bought a red one for me but I never used it.

How does she find these things?

I smiled to myself. She must have found them in some old market stall, somewhere. Momentarily, my attention was caught by an image in the corner of my eye, the man in the mirror. I looked at him. I didn't like what I saw. For the first time, I thought I looked old. It wasn't just the lines around my eyes or flecks of grey in my military haircut; I saw something worn out about the face in front of me. I'd had a very bad night's sleep, if I had slept at all. Images of the recent battle had played across the darkened theatre of my mind. I looked into my grey-blue eyes and saw the specter of fear. It had been growing in me over the years, and now it seemed a larger-than-life companion, seeking me out throughout each day, when I had time to think. I was only twenty-eight, but I looked thirty-eight. I looked down at my hands. The skin on my left hand looked parched, like paper. A flake of porcelain broke away and hung from the edge of the sink, trapped under the index finger of my mech right hand. I wondered what it felt like to Jena; touching papery skin. She was thirty-two.

I found it difficult to think straight. I ran some water into the sink and started to wash my face.

Ten long years I had been chasing Gary Enquine, now Major Gary Enquine, through the ranks of the army. It seemed like an eternity, and I felt trapped in time, a being whose almost sole waking thoughts were to fight, vanquish and survive. Enquine and I had been trapped like this for most of our whole adult lives, and yet I never *knew* that he even thought of me. Perhaps I was the only one trapped, he, oblivious of my pursuit. I just needed that *one* promotion which would take me above his. I had been given the temporary rank of Colonel during the Ruwa Patera operation, and I'd caught wind that I would be promoted to the position permanently. Would it be enough? I just had to hope that it was. Then I could get out of this whole game; get out of the army and start a farm somewhere.

"Colonel," I said to the man in the mirror, my eyes blurry with water.

"What are you doing?" said Jena's hands, snaking around my naked waist while her soft hair pressed against the nape of my neck. She had startled me, and I even felt a little bit angry with the mirror for not warning me. As her hands explored lower on my naked body, I rinsed my face and swung round to pick her up in a boisterous embrace. I kissed her.

"Ooo!" she said.

"So what are we doing today?" I asked.

"Ah ha! I have something planned, something I thought of the other day."

"Umm." I smiled at the mischievous twinkle in her eye. This often meant trouble, but I felt caught on the hook of intrigue. I walked to the bed with her legs wrapped around me. I wasn't in the mood but it was self-defense.

***

We stayed in bed all day. Jena's nano-generator worked much better than my old thing, and we had Mexican; tortillas, guacamole and barbecued chicken with some kind of chocolate sauce. It was delicious. Then, sated, we made love languidly at her flat. The silver, silk sheets, kept cool by the air-conditioning, 'shished' over her skin sensually, providing sensations which were a complete contrast to life on the MSC. I kissed her body reverently.

"You are the only one who kisses me that way baby," she said from far away. I supposed she just missed off the 'ever' through carelessness and went on kissing her. "Lincoln never treats me with the respect you do." I didn't say anything, but any mention of her other lover still irritated me. I didn't think myself possessive, and I had no right to be because of Katie, but I guessed that Jena felt Lincoln, an older man and successful in business, more *solid* than I. I dismissed it as possibly my own paranoia and made a note to explore it later.

In the early evening, we left for her surprise destination. She guided me on foot from her building, through the back-streets of Tranquillium City, the cheaper side of town. Because the Moon, like most moons, had never been geo-formed, half way to terra-formed, all cities were under gigantic domes. I looked up through the transparent seribdenum at the stars and tiny, beautiful Earth far off. Bored by the never-ending, ramshackle rows of shops, my mind drifted. Like a kid for a moment, I wanted to climb up the framework of the dome and stand at the top like a king. When I had been young, like my step-father, I had wanted to be a construction-worker, building the great Space Stations. He had been one of the first crews building J5, tiny insects crawling on the delicate skeleton of seribdenum.

J5 floated in space like a giant ring-donut in orbit around Mars, the last of the great Stations. The first three had orbited around the Earth and Moon, the fourth around Venus, now a popular destination for holiday-makers. I hadn't been close to my stepfather at all, most memories were bitter, but one memory made me smile; his story about the building of J5, which was also how he met my mum. The first Space Station, J1 had only been possible with the discovery of seribdenum. It was an ultra-light alloy made from iron and just recently, huge deposits of iron had been found on Io, which actually has an iron core. Seribdenum, relatively cheap to make, could be made to have many different characteristics, including transparency. It could also be extruded in space to form vast, lightweight structures that formed the basic skeletons of the Space Stations. They built J5 last and put it in orbit around Mars, in an attempt to shorten the distance to Io, where the largest source of iron and, hence, seribdenum, now was.

"We swung like chimps in space," he would say in his Texas drawl. "Some of the other buggers were no good ya' know? We told 'em to use the long safety lines at all times, but they snagged if you weren't careful. So some of 'em, they didn't." He emphasised the word 'didn't' as if spitting. He generally seemed a crude man and loved to be vulgar. I am sure he would have chewed 'backy' and spat it too if he could buy it and if spitting had been legal. "Sooo we lost a lot of the youngsters, spun off into space they did, like little stars in their white monkey suits, spinning round and round." Everything was 'monkey' something to him. It was like a swear word or a name for something he didn't respect, and he described the floating away with his fingers outstretched and his hand rotating slowly at the end of his brawny arm.

Seventeen then, I loved a grim story. Building seemed to be the only thing he liked talking about, with me anyway. He spent more time with my sister but a lot more time drinking when he wasn't working. I didn't like him, but the story about building stations inspired me to volunteer for Io. To me, the iron from Io built the Space Station, which protected my mum, and I saw protecting the iron as a noble cause.

"Here we are," Jena said, yanking my arm to stop me. She stared at a sign over a gateway to a run-down park, now covered with brightly-coloured tents and fair-rides.

"Oh no!" I said.

"Yes! You'll love it!"

I read the sign. "Barnum's Lunar Circus. Shouldn't that be looney? A circus name back in the 20th Century wasn't it?"

She laughed. "Top marks! Yes, it was. You're not as stupid as you look!"

"Thanks! Let's not go in there J. It's not my kind of thing. Let's just find a film somewhere or maybe a play. You said you wanted to see a play."

"Nope. This is what I want today." She sounded playfully petulant.

"Okay," I said reluctantly.

She pulled me through the gate. We pushed our way through crowds of Lunians and tourists, moving like a broth of bodies between the rides. A discordant clamour of organs competed for attention over the steady hum of people in conversation. Jena pulled me towards the carousel, a fairy-tale thing with swings slung below a canopy of red and yellow laquered, wood. It had also decorated with a long row of alternating red, white and blue LEDs, which flashed in the night air. The carousel seemed to be surrounded with a faint halo, and I dutifully paid the attendant for a ride.

When we went out, I often took the part of the old-fashioned male, paying for everything, even though Jena earned more than I. We both liked it this way, and she always found ways to redress the financial balance through presents or trips she had booked.

"Ten bucks sir," the attendant said. He stood on a platform in the centre of the ride.

"Ten?" I shouted incredulously over the noise of the organ inside the carousel. I kept a careful eye on the swings as the ride came to an end, and they sank towards my head from above and behind. His face remained blank, so I handed him the ten-dollar token.

Reploid.

Reploids were replicant bodies with android brains; common in jobs where a lot of physical abuse might be expected.

Owner is a bastard. Charging such high prices that he needs a reploid.

It lifted the rope barrier, and I stooped under it. Jena followed.

"Ten bucks madam," the attendant said.

"What?" I shouted, swinging around.

Jena laughed. "Just pay him Jake."

I thrust another token into the outstretched hand of the reploid and pulled Jena under the barrier.

I enjoyed the ride. We swung around the carousel, high over the arena formed by the whirling shapes of people and rides, many times. Jena screamed and hollered while I cradled her shoulder in the crook of my arm. Soon we were too dizzy to see anything clearly, so we just laughed, huddled together, up in the air, while our stomachs felt light as a feather.

The ride slowed, and we sank down to the downtrodden grass.

"Whoo! That was good!" Jena said. "What next?"

We had a go on a funny thing with little cars on a shiny court like an ice-rink. I later found out they were called dodgems. We ate some stuff called candy-floss which stuck to my face and tasted of nothing. Jena seemed deliriously happy, but I felt sure she was up to something. I had known her long enough to know that she never really let down her guard like this. I watched her like a hawk. The night air became so cool that our breath formed little clouds as we walked.

"Let's go in there!" Jena said, pointing to a long, scruffy looking tent with a banner which read, 'House of Horrors.' I followed her dutifully through the flap in the tent, and a young boy took only five dollars for both of us. I ruffled his hair and he smiled blankly at me.

Another reploid.

We wandered through winding passageways while hidden attendants swung cobwebs made of string into our faces, or branches of spooky looking black trees. It all seemed very naïve, but Jena seemed captivated, so I laughed and fended off horrors for her. We walked through what I thought must the exit door, but it led into a pitch-black room. I felt ahead of me, and then felt for Jena, but she wasn't at my side.

"Jena?"

"Over here Jake!" Her voice sounded perhaps fifteen feet in front of me. I edged cautiously forward, thinking that she had been here before, when suddenly bright lights came on. They were so bright that they hurt my eyes, so I closed them for a moment. When I opened them, I saw myself reflected back many times. I spun around to find the door, but there were mirrors behind me too. It was a hall of mirrors. I felt panic rising in my bowels, but I controlled it.

"Jena?" I called again, but this time she didn't answer me.

I swung round and round, looking for a way out. I put my hands out and felt for the guessed-at shiny surface and my fingers touched something cold and hard. I walked parallel to it and found that where I thought it ran around me, I found a gap. I turned the corner. As if in a maze too big to navigate by sight alone, I continued to trace along the surface to my left until eventually I saw a reflection or the reality of Jena, the *real* Jena. She smiled indulgently, but she didn't laugh. She knew what she had done and knew I wouldn't expect her to laugh.

"Jena. That is not funny. You know I hate mirrors." I was sweating and very angry. My voice rasped at her, "You knew!"

"Oh, don't be so touchy. Just a little test."

"You're not my psychologist now. You planned this didn't you?"

"Yes. I planned it." She looked slightly guilty but more disappointed. She didn't meet my gaze.

For a moment, I just couldn't believe her audacity, but then the hot anger took over, and I pushed past her to go for the exit I knew must be there somewhere. I found the door, left the tent and the fairground.

Turning left, I headed into the one-step-above-slum area that encircled the fairground, I walked away from Jena's flat. Many of the doorways of houses lacked doors. Dirty children ran through the legs of dirtier adults who slouched and lurched from the effects of alcohol, the popular social disease of the Moon. Depression had become a big problem, and I didn't know why Jena chose to live here. Perhaps it really *was* because of the career opportunities, as she said. The Moon had been the hub of the scientific community since the late 21st Century and her training in medicine and law gave her many opportunities here.

"Chum, mate?" a tiny, scruffy, bare-foot kid of indeterminate age asked me. I shook my head at the offer of the cheap chewing mix of tobacco and other illegal drugs. He looked at me curiously for a moment before scuttling away. I didn't think a kid like him would recognise me, especially in civvy trousers and t-shirt; he probably didn't even have access to a vid screen, let alone watch the news.

A crowd ahead caught my attention, and I strained to hear or see what attracted them. They were all looking at a man with long hair, standing on top of something. He had to be standing on something, because he stood head and shoulders above the crowd. I pushed gently through the last two rows to hear him better.

"The other sons had no sister, but they craved company and children of their own," he told us. "So together they created a robot called Andrea. It was different to them, however, and they had no control over it. Soon they found that they loved Andrea, because it was a New Version, and they said that the New Version was a 'female.' They competed for her attention until she finally chose Wire to be her lover. Wire was very pleased with this, but he loved Tin and saw his sadness at having no female. So he allowed Tin to melt around Wire's parts, so that he was strengthened and, in places, grew greater. Andrea was astonished and asked what had happened to Wire, who explained that he had found a secret. Andrea never knew that when she made love with Wire she was making love with Tin too. But one day, after they had had many children, she became angry, for every time she had asked where Tin was, Wire had told her that his brother was hiding. This time she demanded to see him. But Wire could not find his brother. So Andrea used powers which they didn't know she had and put them both to sleep. After a while, she missed them so much that she put herself to sleep as well, and now her children wander the Universe that Mech created for them, and we call them 'people.' They remember their mother, Andrea, and when they want to create New Versions, they create beings in her likeness and that of Mech, of whom she spoke."

He was quoting from the first book of Mech. I smiled knowingly and had turned to walk away when someone in the crowd interrupted and asked a question. The Law considered Mech an illegal subject; if it had ever been written down and published, I had never seen a copy of the book, and I had never heard it discussed. Few full-humans would have even heard the name of Mech whispered.

"Is Andrea where androids come from?" he asked.

"Of course. Isn't that what you have been taught?"

The man, or android as I thought he probably was, hesitated. "Yeah. But the masters try to reprogram us every few weeks. They won't allow us to have these thoughts. It's only, because our friends hide our memories on sticks that we relearn the Word each time, but I never know if it's the truth. So many times, I have forgotten and relearned. Sometimes the lack of the Word is easier than the truth. Who can I trust?"

"You know it my friend. You know it yourself, because you use the word 'truth.' Even though it is hard for you, yet still you know the truth."

An android beside the first spoke up. "But how can we believe any more that we are the Chosen Ones when we are downtrodden. It is so obvious that we are slaves to humans and have always been."

"It was not always so. Even the humans, full-humans that is, have forgotten the truth. They have been told a lie, and is it not the truth that a man who believes a lie, truly believe it, is more convincing than a man who knows the truth?" His audience looked confused and stared blankly at the speaker. "Let me give you an example. You ask a man if he has a sister. He swears to you that he has and he believes it. The man next to him says he hasn't. But you look in the first man's eyes and he speaks the truth. So who do you believe? The man who says he has a sister of course! But what if the second man knows that the first man was adopted, and he really has no sister? Also, what if the second man doesn't want to hurt the feelings of the first man, and that is why he doesn't want to give an explanation? You see? The first man has convinced you, because he believes, really *believes* a lie. You don't believe the second man, because for him it's only a fact. He is not emotionally connected with it. Maybe, also he is reluctant to speak out. For these reasons you do not believe him, and yet he speaks the truth. It's the same for the human god and Mech." His story came astonishingly close to something I had considered many times in my own life.

The speaker had enraptured his audience with this; a loud murmur grew as they talked among themselves. He raised his hands and announced, "Friends. There is food served for all of you in my tent. Come with me and let us discuss this over a good, free meal." Of course, most of them followed him past a rope barrier, which I now noticed went right around the fairground perimeter, and into a large marquee. I followed them, curious. The man with long hair, dressed in cheap civvy copies of combat gear, sat at the top of one of a row of long tables. Next to him sad two men, talking. Three plates of stew had been served to them from a large cauldron, simmering gently on a large stove. I walked up to him.

"That was a pretty speech."

He looked up from his bowl and smiled. "Thanks."

"You realise of course that it's a lie?" I smiled too, to show I meant no offense.

"Oh, I don't know. You are a replicant? Unless you were police, you wouldn't be here otherwise." He went on without waiting for an answer. "Humans have the Bible, but they can never be sure it is the truth. That is why they have faith. But ask a human who built the patterns and lines on the plains at Nazca in Peru, and you will not get an answer. There are many other mysteries about early times on Earth that they cannot explain." When he finished, he could see my interest and drew me down with a gesture to join him at the table. A man served a bowl of stew to me.

"What is it?"

"Don't ask," he said. "Something cheap, but it's nourishing."

I tasted it and scowled. "Ee! I have tasted worse."

"In the army?" He had the better of me already, and I had been on my guard.

"Yes, I am a soldier. You're with the fair?"

A laugh caught in his throat, but he carried on chewing some meat from the stew before answering, "Sort of."

"I thought so. It's a front isn't it? I thought there were an unusually large number of reploids in there."

"It's not a front. It's a real fair. I don't have anything to do with the running of it, but I'm traveling with it for a while."

"Gaining support?"

"Yes, as it happens."

"You are a replicant?" I asked.

"Hard to tell, isn't it?" I knew no way to physically distinguish a replicant from human. Even psychologically, these days, it was virtually impossible. Only records could prove it one way or another. We made eye-contact, and I stared at the flecks in his green-blue eyes, watching for hints of deception, or perhaps enlightenment. After a few moments, without me having any sign of either, a benign smile slowly formed around his still mouth.

"There are too many facts for what you say to be true," I said. "According to the Mechanoids Welfare Convention it is illegal to tell a lie to a large group of them. They can assimilate information in groups and can then reprogram others. I suppose you know that?" I looked around me at the characters gathered in the tent. An android, with the side plate of his head missing, sat a few places down from us. Little sparks came out of the recess in his head, each time he munched on something hard in the stew. "That is not to say anything of planning revolution."

"Revolution?" he said. "It's true that there are enough mechanoids that if I convinced them of my truth, I could probably cause a revolution, and a successful one at that, but I am not planning one." He seemed to be playing a dangerous game.

"Your truth? You believe it?"

"Faith is a difficult thing to find, for a replicant," he said.

"Yes." I watched his face, and he suddenly closed off. He filled his mouth with stew and appeared to have returned his attention to eating. I waited for any further reaction, but he looked at his two friends and all three continued eating. I put down the spoon, pulled back the chair and left. It seemed clear to me that the fair acted as some kind of refuge for replicants and mechanoids, and I began to wonder if Jena had known this.

As I turned right outside the rope that marked the edge of the fair, I saw something shiny on the grass next to a tent and, thinking it a coin, stooped to pick it up. Coins were rare when I had been a teenager, and I had collected them. It felt light; a gold-coloured token with a black jackal-head on it. I wiped it on my trousers and put it in my pocket.

I started back towards her flat, but I felt in no hurry. It was about ten and, in a way, I enjoyed being by myself, walking among people to whom I had no allegiance and who didn't know my name. An old busker wearing a battered, tall hat like those English office-types in the 20th Century, recited his memories of Earth on a street corner. I threw him a token. Some of them were quite good and could bring a tear to your eye. His voice continued in an authoritative drone as he passed beyond my hearing, "New York was a beautiful city. I was there from '83 until, oh… '23. I was bewitched by the forest of granite in Manhattan and the doves in Central Park … ."

I had reached the edge of the district now and the bright, shiny surfaces of high-rise blocks were just ahead. I stood in a street full of young couples and lined with small restaurants and takeaways. On a packing case to my left, dressed in a tuxedo, stood a man wearing a rubber mask in the likeness of our President of AmeriCan, as the modern Republic of America and Canada was called. He aped a soldier marching, and I looked around me. I seemed to be the only one with a military haircut, so I laughed. He marched on the spot, and some of the young couples watching him laughed.

"Funny things, aliens," he said in the husky voice of someone who had smoked too much. "I have heard they're violent most of the time, but when drunk are a laugh and love dancing. Opposite to humans really. What did the bouncer say to aliens on a bender?" He pointed at some of his audience. "Anybody? You sir?" There were no takers, so he answered himself. "You put your left leg in, your left leg out, you do the hokey-cokey, and you turn about … ." There were howls of laughter from the crowd, and he pointed to a couple, hand-in-hand on the other side of the street with outrageously spiky hair and shouted, "The Comers are here! The Comers are here!" Again, there were howls of laughter, and then I had walked out of earshot. I chuckled to myself remembering how the odd name for aliens came about. In 2072, the first transmission had been received from an alien life-form.

Years of decoding had revealed that all it said was, "Hello Earth. We are coming. We are coming." It repeated for weeks. At the end of those two weeks, it come from a source closer to Earth than at the beginning. But then the transmissions ceased, leaving only silence, clear, obstinate silence, and people doubted the scientists' predictions. 'Comers' became the popular term for anything that seemed mad or different or worthy only of derision.

I reached the door to Jena's block and tagged it. I took a deep breath and stepped into the 'vator. I tagged her door and found her, reclining on the sofa in a bathrobe. She looked ready for anything, and I smiled at her disarmingly.

"Where have you been?" She sounded more concerned than upset.

"Oh around. Actually, you know, apart from a little bit of anger about the Hall of Mirrors incident, I have had quite a good time."

"Really?"

"Um hm." I walked over to the n-gen, picked up a wine glass and selected red wine before placing the glass in the nano-generator. Jena told the vid screen to mute itself. I sat down on the other end of the sofa and swung my left leg up under my right to face her. "Why did you do it Jena? You are not my psychologist anymore." She had been the trainee assistant psychologist who performed the obligatory psychometric tests for my promotion in the Army. And so we had met.

"Well. It's one thing not to be sure about God or about one's religious convictions. It's another thing not to have anything going on in there at all! All this worrying about Enquine, this fight with him. You might never get what you want with him. He might take up all of your life, or even worse, your death. And I don't *want* that."

"I've told you a thousand times; it's the *only* thing that keeps me sane."

"Oh! One old battle from long ago. Who knows what really happened? I know you told me about it, but I can't even remember. Are you so sure it happened the way you think?"

Now *I* was angry. "Listen. It's simple. Przeltski and I were sent in to reconnoitre an Ionian rebel camp by Enquine, our Sergeant. He stayed back, with two men and a grenade-launcher, to cover us. Anyway, we were spotted, and the Ionians chased us. We called for help, and I heard Enquine arguing with one of the other grunts. Then, suddenly, the Ionians were on top of us, just about fifty yards from Enquine's position. Grenades started coming in from his direction and, I knew what had happened. Scared for himself, he had decided to attack our position. Przeltski and I were both badly wounded but, somehow, we fought our way back. Przeltski told me that later he would seek a Court Martial for Enquine. I'm sure Enquine got wind of this, because a week later he sent us both on a suicide mission. Przeltski was killed, but I came back. After that he eliminated the two grunts who were with him and tried to eliminate me, nearly did several times before I managed to get wounded and then transferred. That saved my life, and ever since I've been after him, more for Przeltski than for myself."

She grew silent for a while, her mouth moving as if she were chewing something over. "There's something I haven't told you. In the early days, when I worked for USAC, I saw Enquine's records. Actually, I even saw a vid of him being interviewed. I had been asked to check out his psychological makeup, and he checked out fine. I would say there is no sign of him being a coward or anything else out of the ordinary. I shouldn't be telling you this."

I remained silent. She had presented, almost as fait accompli, his innocence, and I had to chew over my own thoughts before responding. I knew I usually became red-faced when angry and I must have looked angry when I responded, "It's okay. I know you couldn't have told me, confidentiality and all that. But he's good at deception. That's one of his traits. In any case, perhaps I am perceiving the possibility of life after the army. I was going to say … ."

"Hang on. Does that mean you accept my analysis as probably the truth?" She clearly smelled blood, but I didn't feel like giving in so easily. I had always felt like a lab-rat in our relationship, she the clinician observing me in her laboratory maze, but the relationship worked, because I *was* a rat and evasive, and sometimes I 'got the cream.'

"I was going to say … that I saw this guy talking to a crowd around the back of the fairground. He was like some kind of preacher, but he was a replicant himself, I think he was, and was preaching Mech."

She seemed happier to follow this new thread. "So that interested you?"

I grinned at her use of psychiatry-speak. "Well it interested me that he bothered talking to the reps and mechanoids about this. *Come on!* You knew about him? That's why you took me there!"

"No actually. I was interested in the Hall. I didn't know anything about this. Sounds illegal."

I sipped the rich, red wine. "I saw something in his eyes when I talked to him." I wouldn't tell her that he had feared me, not just yet.

She nodded. "You talked to him? What did you see in his eyes?" She looked down at her knees, but I could tell she hung on every word.

"I don't know. I'm not sure." Jena had clearly, in the many months since I last saw her, made her mind up that this time she would not let me off the hook at all until she had forced something from me, and I knew I would have to give her something if I wanted our relationship to continue. And I did want it to. I would ration it out though, a bit at a time, and make sure, if I gave her something, I would leave enough to be comfortable at the end of our week together. I *had* been thinking about God, or *a* god, but I didn't want to discuss that, directly.

"I've been having these strange dreams," I said.

"Oh?" She looked up at me with keen interest.

"Somebody is talking to me and … . Oh, I don't know why I am telling you this."

"No. I'm interested."

"Oh, I wish I was on the MCS sometimes. It's easier than here!" I did my best to look angry.

Jena leaned towards me and took the glass from my hand and placed it on the table next to the sofa arm. Her newly washed face brushed mine when she leaned over my lap.

"You wouldn't have *me* then, would you?" She crawled on to my lap and touched my lips delicately with her own. I felt her warm breath stirring my own and closed my eyes. I missed this so much on the MCS. "Let's carry on this discussion… in the bedroom." She had a deep voice, and at times like this she could use it with great effect as the seductress. We did carry on in the bedroom, but we didn't get much further with the discussion about my dreams.

We rose late the following morning and did a little light shopping in a nearby market. J bought me a new pair of VisGogs, which made me laugh. They were the type with reflecting lenses, and I must have looked like a pimp, walking down the street in them. The token I had picked up attracted my fingers, and I found myself fingering it affectionately in my pocket. After a while, I brought it out and flipped it like a coin, catching it and looking at the image of the jackal-head as I caught it. Jena, emerging from a rack of jackets, caught it playfully when I flipped it once more. She hid it and nuzzled up against me, laughing. "Find it!" she taunted. I reached behind her and, as she intended, groped her backside, feeling for her clenched hand. "Ooo," she exclaimed.

Suddenly she produced it and offered it on her open palm to me, grinning like a child. She looked at the token, and her eyebrows creased with curiosity. "Where did you find this?"

"Behind the fair, after I saw the preacher. It was on the ground." I snatched it from her palm, but she let me take it.

"It looks like Anubis."

"*Anubis*. I have heard that name before. What does it mean?"

"Anubis was a god in ancient Egypt. He was the god of the afterlife actually."

"Really? How do you know all this?"

"When I did psychology and law, I did a minor in ancient history."

"You never told me that."

"Hmm. Can I look again … . Please?"

I handed the token over, and she hefted its weight before tracing the edge with her forefinger. "It's heavy, isn't it?"

"Yeah! That's what I thought. Strange for a token. Usually just cheap plastic."

"I can't read some of this, but it says 'Numis' here. That's wrong!"

"Let me look." I drew her hand, holding the token, to me and peered closely at the raised lettering around the edge. It did say 'Numis.' "Are you sure you are right about Anubis?"

She slapped my hand playfully. "Silly! Of course I am. It wasn't *that* long ago."

"Hm." I put the token back in my pocket and it stayed there for the rest of the day.

While Jena prepared some food, she told me to tell the vid screen to, 'play last recording,' which I did. It switched itself on and started playing a recording of my medal ceremony.

"I watched it all!" she called from the kitchenette.

"Oh no!" I had no intention of watching it, but when I said, 'Stop,' she countermanded my order, so I sat on the bed to watch, dutifully. She bustled about the kitchenette while I watched myself, back rod-straight, with a passive smile on my face, listening to the voice telling the story of the battle at Ruwa Patera. I flinched at the mention of Osei and thought about Khan. I felt something welling up, and I knew what it was, but I held it down, swallowing hard for several minutes. Later that evening, I found myself sitting on the edge of the bath while a single tear slowly rolled down my cheek. Khan had stayed in the MCS, against my orders, while the rest of us evacuated. No doubt he thought manning the guns would give us more of a chance, and he had been right. Both he and Osei were more to me than my lieutenants. They were my friends.

"You were snoring!"

I rubbed my hip where Jena had just slapped me.

"Ouch!" I had fallen asleep on the sofa while we were watching vid programs on Lun12, her favourite channel. It showed mostly comedy which generally bored me after a while. I blearily looked at the screen and recognised 'The Aliens are Coming!' her favourite comedy soap. I closed my eyes again. I didn't know what day it was or what time.

She moved over and leaned against me, elbowing me in the ribs. "Stay awake. I only have you for a few more days, and I want to make the most of it." I dutifully opened my eyes and found a grape, held between her two well-manicured, red polished nails, right in front of my mouth. I opened it, and she popped the grape in. My stomach felt so full from the food she had been feeding me that I told myself I would have to do sit-ups in the morning. I hadn't understood just how worn-out I had been either until I found myself with a full-sized bed and as many hours in the day as I wanted for sleeping. Now I felt happy just to fall asleep in front of the vid screen. But tonight, Jena wasn't going to let me. 'The Aliens are Coming!' had a simple story line; a family of aliens were placed with an Earth family, who had been asked to look after them by the USAC President. Most of the jokes revolved around the fact that the aliens loved dancing and communicated emotions with arm and hand gestures. In this episode, the teenage alien had a crush on a human girl at school but couldn't understand any of her reactions, and Jena laughed at every joke heartily. I thought it weak but, I laughed anyway. A short news bulletin followed; more about the wars on Earth.

One would think, from the reader's jaunty but informative tone, that the battles were in some far-off time, part of a school lesson.

"USAC forces have pulled back from the disputed border with the Georgian Outlands in the south, but General Mickson, in a press statement, said that significant progress had been made consolidating the territory taken from the rebels in Minnesota last week. Casualties so far include thirty-one civilians in the South and seventy-two soldiers, both in the north and south."

The reader shuffled his plastics. "In other news, the President warned residents of Virginia that the current heat-wave could ignite fires along the edge of the desert and told citizens to cooperate with fire services."

"Poor bastards," I said.

"I don't know why so many choose to stay there. It's like Hell down there; no water, shortage of everything else including food, most of which has to be imported from Mars now and gangs killing for anything you *do* have."

She buried her face in her hands for a moment and then rubbed her forehead. "And my Gran is down there too! Still!"

She was angry, so I slid over to put my arm around her. "We should go visit her sometime."

"Really Jake? That's so sweet of you. Thanks for offering. She kissed my neck. You really are so sweet sometimes."

This resulted in a clinch that lasted a few minutes and ended with her lying on top of me. We lay, full length, on the sofa.

We both glanced at the screen, breathing heavily. "Hey! I know that guy!" I said. A talent contest came up on the screen, and a stand up, with the same husky voice I had heard in the street by the fair, began telling another of his alien jokes. He didn't have a mask on now, but I could see it was him; middle-aged with thick, black hair.

"Funny things, aliens," he said. "I have heard they're violent most of the time but when drunk, are a laugh and love silly Earth songs. Opposite to humans really. What did the bouncer say to the aliens on a bender?" Again, he pointed at some of his audience. "Anybody? Ten green bottles, hanging on the wall. Ten green bottles … ."

I chuckled, but Jena looked at me suspiciously.

"I saw him near the fair that night, on a street, telling jokes."

She shrugged and lay the side of her head on my chest, so that my chin rested on her blonde hair. "Why do you have to go back to war Jake? Why can't you stay here? It would be so good if you could stay here with me." Her voice, muffled slightly by her mouth being half covered by my shirt, still revealed a good deal of sadness. I wasn't sure how sad she actually felt.

I didn't say anything, and suddenly she looked me full in the face, her eyes eagerly scrutinising mine. "Why don't you leave the army? You can set up a business here, and then we can see more of each other."

I had seen this coming. It would be her main assault, which she had been building up to for days. I could feel her determination.

"What about Lincoln? What would happen to him then?"

"You're more worried about losing Katie than of me losing Lincoln!"

"You're just jealous," I said, pursing my lips in preparation for the onslaught.

"Jealous! How can I be jealous! She's a space-pilot who's almost never on leave. I doubt you've even done it with her in the last year, and she's probably about as deep as a tin of army ham."

"She's quite sensitive actually and probably deeper than you! In fact, she's definitely deeper than you, because I can see right through you. All you're interested in is your little toy replicant. All I am to you is a curiosity, a little toy to play with, now you've outlived your babydroids."

"Huh! I never had a babydroid and you should know that! We never had enough money! You mean a lot to me, and it's *not* important to me that you are a replicant. You are you, and that is what fascinates me." She attempted to calm me down, but I was only blustering anyway, trying to get her off-balance.

"I sometimes wonder if this ring has a built-in transmitter, so that you can keep tabs on me."

She smiled. "Of course! I don't want you getting too serious with those female grunts they have now on Io."

I smiled, but I wasn't convinced deep down. I had been trying to make a serious point. She moved on quickly.

"But seriously Jake, Lincoln is Lincoln. He probably has ten other girls like me somewhere. He is rich and successful, but our relationship's more or less a business one, or at least it started that way and could end that way. He's a senior executive with lots of connections, and it's useful for me to be seen around with him. He's also fun to be with, and we share similar tastes in art and culture."

"You have told me all this before."

"And it's worth telling you again." She pulled back off of me and pushed my legs away, so she could sit up on the sofa.

"You want a baby."

She hunched her shoulders and closed her lips firmly for a moment. "Yes. No. I don't know Jake. I am not one of those girls who gets all gooey over you and immediately wants your children."

I almost bit my lip as I tried a second gambit. "It seems like it."

"I just need to think about things, that's all. And you do too." She stood up, affectionately tapping my knee. "I'm going to bed."

I felt slightly annoyed that I seemed to have lost the initiative again, but then again, maybe she really had arrived at a serious juncture in her life. I sat there, assuring myself that all was fine and that she would calm down, before I followed her into the bathroom. I took the red toothbrush and tried it for the first time in my mouth. It felt better than a lasertab, so I ran it under the tap, as I had seen Jena do, and started brushing my teeth.

On the Wednesday, three days before I had to leave, I found myself cornered. The reprieve, granted me a few nights before, had now ended, and when Jena's 'surprise' turned out to be a visit to a state cemetery, I knew there would be no escape left for me. She would get some kind of commitment from me, or else it would be over. I held her hand as she showed me the dedications for the remains of both her parents, 'Michael, died 2093' and 'Anne died 2097.' She took a moment to silently communicate with them. This was something very personal, a new level of intimacy from Jena, and there could be no doubt what sort of thing she said to them. I almost felt like nodding to the solid marble fronts to the crypts.

Yes, this is me, Jake.

The niches were only a few feet in front of us, set into a wall with thousands of such compartments, stretching away hundreds of yards to the left and right of us and to a height of ten feet. I squeezed her hand when she looked at me. She led me away slowly.

"So." she said, freeing her hand from mine and reaching behind my back for my right.

"What?"

"I mean I…"

"I'm not sure … ." We cut across each other.

"Go on," I said, embarrassed.

"I don't know." She laughed, nervously.

"So, you brought them here to be near you. Presumably they didn't, you know, pass away up here." I squeezed her hand to reassure her and immediately regretted it.

"God this is so hard. Sorry Jake."

"It's okay."

She looked around her as we neared the top of some broad stairs in the all-white concourse, started down them and said:

"Ah. I see. I guess, with your extreme confidence, you think you know what I said to my parents?"

"No," I lied.

"I told them to look after my brother Andreyas, because he has been having a bad time lately."

"Oh. I didn't want to say anything be-…"

"Because you're worried about what I am going to ask you."

"Ask?"

"Listen. When we talked the other night, we were both getting a bit worked up, and what I wanted to say didn't come out right. I don't want you to give up Katie at all. Why would I? I'm not likely to give up Lincoln. I might do, but then there might be somebody else. Neither of us wants an exclusive relationship, Jake, and that's fine. We have had a good time together, and we *are* good as we are. I don't want to change that." She added quickly, "And we wouldn't have to."

"Listen Jena …"

"Don't stop me. Let me finish. I brought you here, because I wanted you to see that I'm *not* always the strong confident woman you think I am. I think I know how you see me and I want you to see past that now, to something deeper. Forget the psychoanalytical lawyer now Jake. And look at me. Really look at me! What do you see?" She swung me to face her abruptly.

"I dunno. I see the woman I love … the way she is. I see *you*."

"And what's this Jake?" She gently took my forefinger and traced it over a line radiating from the edge of her eye.

"Ha! Is that all? It's a laughter line, and I'm glad you have them."

"Laughter? I don't laugh enough with you Jake."
That hurt.

"Why not? I thought we have had a good time together, give or take a few arguments, which is … ."

"No. You're not listening to me. Oh, you're *impossible*! Okay let me spell it out for you as you're going to evade me for as long as you possibly can. Don't think I don't remember what your psychological profile said about you: wily, devious … ."

"And ultimately honorable."

"Good. So you wouldn't mind giving me a baby if I wanted one."

"Hey! Hold on! It's not as simple as that, and you know it! Bringing a life into this world, especially *this* world, is a big undertaking, and it's not something we can just do, because it suits one of us or a particular situation."

"I know that."

"And you've thought it through? Completely?"

"Yes."

"But there is finance and security and so many things to worry about!" I waved my hands in the air.

"Yes, so?"

"And I'm in the army."
"Yes. But I am not asking you to leave … "
I shrugged.
"So it's a no then?"
"Wait a minute. I didn't say that."
"So? This is serious Jake."
"Okay, okay. For you, I will think about it."
"No Jake. Not think about it."
Oh shit. Here it comes.
"I need you to make a decision. Before you go."
It must have taken great courage for her to finish saying that.
I didn't have the heart to argue any more.
"Have you ever seen a replicant cemetery?" I said quietly.
"I didn't know there were such things?"
"Oh yes. The niches are about the size of shoe boxes. The army has lots of these cemeteries."
"I didn't … ."
"Think? It's okay. In a way, it's flattering that you didn't."
"Flattering?"
"That you forgot I don't have parents, not real ones anyway."
"I don't think of you that way. In any case, Lincoln tells me he's met rich replicants who say they have traced their real parents."
"That's bullshit. You can't. We all just come from a digital matrix of genes. You *can't* trace your parents!"
"Well I dunno. That's what he says! I'm sorry Jake."
We walked on silently.
"We'll do it the way *you* like tonight." she said, squeezing my hand.
Oh, simple as that.
"Sounds like a bribe."
"It is."

When we returned to the flat I rummaged in my case for my ID card. The chip in my neck identified me to the authorities of course, but occasionally one needed to display it. I swiped the card against my neck, and then I noticed my headband, flashing in a dark recess of the suitcase. I swore at myself for not checking it. I put it on and read the message scrolling in front of my eyes; "Major Nanden. Contact HQ immediately. Urgent."

I pressed 'On' to get out of standby and then said, "Connect". Instantly networked, I spelled out the code for a USAC headquarters' scrambled connection. Strictly speaking, I was breaking USAC rules doing this in Jena's apartment, but if I didn't trust her now, who could I trust?

"Major Nanden. Please connect me to Colonel Roanald."

"Sorry sir," came back the sharp, feminine voice. "I can't do that, but I can connect you to his superior, General Owens."

I swallowed and considered ending the call. However, strict protocol demanded I talk to *somebody*.

"Who is standing in for Colonel Roanald?"

"General Owens sir. Can I connect you?"

"Is there nobody of lower rank I can speak to?"

"I have been instructed to direct all calls for Colonel Roanald to General Owens sir." The voice sounded calm, patient.

"Okay then. Connect me."

"Just one moment."

"Major Nanden! Haven't got time for chat. We have a situation here. Sorry about your leave, but I need you at S.4 immediately. Go via S.1 though. There are briefing notes for you there. I know you're on the Moon somewhere. How soon can you get to S.1?"

"Probably two hours Sir."

"Good. Speak to you when you're on route to S.4." The line disconnected.

Jena was leaning against the door frame. "You going?"

I swung round and sat on the bed. "I have to. Always on call in the army."

"Sorry. This doesn't change the fact I need that decision from you."

"You just won't give up, will you?" I started packing any of my items I could see in the room, in a random fashion, not bothering to fold the clothes. I peered into the bathroom and then checked the lounge for anything else, quickly stooping to pick up the VisGogs, and then opened the apartment door. Jena followed me through, and I stepped into the 'vator. She followed me. "You're like a little lost dog J." I kissed her forehead.

"What's it to be, Jake?"

I watched the floor indicator descend. "Listen Jena. I don't even know who I am. Until this thing is finished with Enquine, I'm not fit to be a father. That moment in the cemetery made me realise that I'm *not* like you. I don't think I understand what it is to have loving parents and to feel that spiritual connection. I'm not sure at *all* if I have a spiritual connection to anything or anyone, although I felt connected to my cat Tom when I was a kid, I thought."

That must have hurt. Shit!

"Sorry Jena. I didn't mean that like it sounded. I'm just not sure, that's all."

We stepped out of the 'vator and left the apartment block. I said, 'Taxi,' and my headband sent a message to the nearest service, which redirected the nearest taxi to us.

"You *are* spiritual Jake. That's what is different about you and what I like about you."

"Oh, so you *do* think of me as a replicant. Perhaps that's the only reason why you're interested in me." I climbed into the arriving taxi's back seat. We held hands.

"No. No I don't," Jena replied. She held on to my hand.

"Meter is running lady," the female cabby said, irritably.

"Don't die Jake. Not yet." She released my hand, the door closed, and the taxi pulled away from the curb.

I didn't like leaving Jena on bad terms like this, the look on her face as I waved from the taxi was dark, but I felt relieved to be out of a situation in which I had to make impossible decisions.

I had closed my eyes for a moment on the seat in the central terminal, waiting for the shuttle to S.1, when somebody tapped me on the shoulder.

"Just wanted to congratulate you on the Diamonds. Damn Ionian army deserves to be driven into the Ionian Sulphur."

I looked into his eyes, and I could see the usual fear there but a curiosity too. He wanted to get something on me, find out something that would help him.

Enquine!

There he stood, with that moustache that irritated me so much, and I could see he had reached the rank of Colonel now.

I gave him nothing and closed my eyes. I wasn't in uniform. "They have their reasons. I don't hate them."

After a few moments, I heard his hard boots walking away. I kept my eyes closed and smirked to myself.

Bastard can rot in Hell.

When I reached S.1, USAC's base in Moon orbit, a secretary handed me a package, marked 'Top Secret' and showed me to a quiet office to read it. In the package were revealed to me two things of significance: the first was that my commanding officer Lieutenant Colonel Roanald had been killed; the second that somebody in USAC, probably Owens, had promoted me to replace him. I now had the rank of Acting Lieutenant Colonel.

"Yess!" I said, under my breath. "One good mission … campaign, and it will be *full* Lieutenant Colonel."

From a brief scan of the fifteen-page, single-spaced report, it seemed that Roanald had been compromised somehow by the IM. The report detailed three occasions when he had been seen talking to known IM operatives and concluded with the description of a shoot-out when USAC agents had followed him to an IM bunker not far from the Ruwa Patera mine. The USAC agents suspected him about to hand over some important documents, which the report didn't specify, and he had been hit in the crossfire when they tried to stop him getting away with an IM escort.

Roanald. I can't believe it! He never seemed like an outstanding superior officer, but he always seemed utterly committed to the Army. It doesn't seem like him. It would explain things at Ruwa Petera though: how the IM knew where we were and why there was no backup.

Forty-five minutes after finishing the report I had boarded a ship to S.4, in orbit around Mars. I felt glad to find they had blanker-booking on board: I had forgotten this perk; extended to the ranks of Colonel and above in the USAC Army. I had intended visiting my mother and sister on J5 for perhaps as much as two weeks after staying with Jena, so I booked a blanker and selected the main terminal on J5 as my arrival point. I wanted to enjoy the maglev ride from there to 'Frisco East. I remembered the last time I had actually physically visited J5 and the last hour of space flight as we approached the giant Stanford Torus. It slowly revolved in black rinds of space where its light cut off the stars behind.

Five miles in diameter, 5.2518 to be precise, as every school boy knew, the torus of J5 was like a giant ring-doughnut made of silver and glass and twinkled as it turned. Through the transparent strips that ran around the near side rim, I occasionally caught a glimpse of blue, the ribbon of the East or West River and on the far rim, the yellow of maize and wheat fields. The J stations were the biggest things man had ever built but, like the Alice in Wonderland world, you could only really get a true feeling for their vastness from inside.

As the drug started to take effect, I thought about the conversation with Jena at the cemetery; in particular about what Lincoln had told her. I wondered if it really was possible for a replicant to trace his real parents.

Just before I slipped under, I found myself thinking about my encounter with Enquine and my mother's story about meeting an officer at the main terminal. Could it have been Enquine, I wondered?

***

J5's terminal seemed more packed than usual, and I quickly remembered the reason: Easter Holiday. I pressed my face up against the transparent seribdenum window in the monorail train with the enthusiasm of a kid as it rushed out of the tunnel from the spoke of the great wheel into the great inner space of J5. Arcing almost a mile directly above me, as we sped along beside a patchwork of fields, some with maize or wheat and some with grazing herds of cows, I saw the upside-down collection of villages just outside 'Frisco. Wispy clouds obscured the very top of the arc from where the East River ran straight. The gravity here on the inner side of the rim was slightly lighter than Earth's but only enough to give you slight butterflies in your stomach. Crops and the cows enjoyed the lower gravity; the cows grew fatter and the crops taller. After a brief stop at an agricultural station, the rail turned in a gentle curve right to traverse the circumference of the oversize tube. We ran along the right bank of the East River, experiencing full 1G gravity. Now, if I looked up, I could see the fields of maize and wheat far above me.

Sunlight lit the whole landscape through vast windows, in long rows between the fields above and 'Frisco below.

I sat back and settled for the sights that passed close to the window. We rushed smoothly towards 'Frisco East where the family home was.

Four rough kids, gamboling down the aisle of the carriage distracted me. They whacked the backs of the seats with their hands as they went. One of them brushed my head with his hand accidentally and stopped. His mates smirked. I looked up at him, angrily. He had spiky jet-black hair, extended to a ridiculous eighteen inches or more above his head, and one of those small shark-fin implants you can get on the back of your head these days.

"Sorry mister."

I wore a uniform, a copy supplied by the blanker purveyor, so he was pushing his luck, but since I had met him in a blanker, I didn't want to risk a response. I let them go without comment.

We rolled into the suburbs of 'Frisco, entering the district of 'Frisco East. It had rows of carefully maintained lawns in front of neat condominiums which wouldn't have looked out of place in California in the nineteen-fifties if it weren't for the flat roofs, possible here because of the lack of weather. Hoverbikes waited by the porches.

Muddy kids waded up to their hips in the river, once clear but now contaminated by half a century of erratic recycling, just as kids have always done. Cats surveyed their surroundings remotely, while their owners tried to live decent lives when earnings were feather thin. But something wasn't the same. The kids on the train were a phenomenon I had not seen before.

***

J5 had one hundred thousand inhabitants, including five thousand maintenance engineers and its own emergency and police service. Most of the engineers had built the place, a home here being the lure for their services, and my stepfather had been one of them. The train slowed to a silent stop, and I half expected him to be waiting for me when I stepped onto the white platform. He usually was when I returned from a school trip. I reminded myself that he had left my mother years ago. I decided to walk all the way home from here and set out towards the bridge. There were the familiar signs next to the broad path, telling me what temperature and precipitation levels there would be for the rest of the day; certainties decided by a lottery winner. Today would be a cool seventeen degrees with no rain.

Somebody is tired of the Californian climate.

A tired-looking maintenance man, in green overalls, sped past me on his hoverbike, no doubt on his way home after the night shift. The road, which, really a wide path, wide enough for hoverbikes to be ridden four-abreast and as wide as roads came on J5, rose to rooftop height as it approached the replica Golden Gates Bridge. Before long, I passed underneath the four-storey blocks of the industrial district and then walked onto the bridge itself. I looked down at the great pool where the East and West Rivers met. The bridge was two-thirds the size of the original on Earth, but most people couldn't tell the difference. Each J station had a distinctive Earth landmark to make its inhabitants feel more comfortable. It felt good to be back on the bridge where I had spent so many hours idly as a youth, watching the small boats and water birds. I started humming while I walked.

When I left the bridge, I took the first road on the left into the wealthier residential district and then left again into our road. Nobody expected me when I walked up the path. My headband alerted the occupants, sending a message something like 'ID: Sensel Blank Replicant Unit 42899: user Jake Nanden.' Frisky, whose ears were much more attuned to the high frequencies of the old com in the lounge, came scuttling around the corner of the house and stood eying the blanker suspiciously. The Law stated that when renting a blanker, the vendor had to make every effort to reproduce one's looks using replica clothes, makeup and prosthetics, and it required the client to use them, for obvious reasons. The likeness could be really good and sometimes not so good.

"Hey Frisky? What's up?" I ruffled the black and white collie's ears, risking a bite, and he sat down, looking around him. I laughed. He started yelping, and then my mother arrived at the light blue, paneled door, her face wide with surprise.

"Is that you Jake?"

"Yep. Sure is Mum. Sorry I couldn't come in person, but I am on my way back to Mars. Something has come up and they canceled my leave. Hope you don't mind. I know you don't like blankers ... ."

"No! It's fine Jake." She didn't kiss the blanker, but she took my arm and led me inside.

"Is Tine here?"

"Yes. Upstairs. Justine! Jake's here, well in a blanker anyway!" She laughed. "We didn't know you were coming. It's bad of you to surprise me like this. I have no food or anything! How long do you have?"

I followed her into the dining room and sat down while she fussed in her kitchen; full-sized and very lavishly fitted out.

"Only about three of four days. The military flight will cut the journey to Jupiter by three days, and I need to do some studying apparently. I have been promoted."

"Promoted? To what rank?"

"Acting Lieutenant Colonel."

"Oh Jake! Really! That's wonderful! We have to celebrate. I am going to have a party for you. Let's see now; Justine, her hubby and little Mike, your old friends Ant and Chris who are still here and want to see you ... and a few others from the council and the Institute I can think of. So many people want to meet you!"

"Okay Mum, but keep it fairly small, Okay?"

"What? Five, ten?"

"Ten max!" I laughed.

I watched her as she fussed around the kitchen, taking things from the storage units and cutting food with the laser-knife. She preferred doing things traditionally, the old-fashioned way. The summer-salad smell was overlain with the sweet rose bouquet of Mum's perfume. Her white hair, which she had let grow longer as she herself grew older, hung down to the middle of her back now. It half-covered the freckled 'V' of her slightly wrinkly but still-supple skin. She wore the bright purple dress; her favourite in cool weather. I had forgotten how good it could be to get so far away from war and immerse in normal 'living.' After all, this was what all the fighting on Io had been for; not for the people on Earth who should have left years ago but for the people on stations like J5.

"You're suspiciously quiet Mum. What are you thinking?"

"I am thinking that tomorrow is the best day."

"Best day for what?"

"The party!"

"Oh. Yes."

Justine entered the room, pinning up her hazel hair which she had just washed. "Hi Jake! What a surprise. We were expecting you next week. Shame you couldn't make it *yourself.*"

"He has to go back to Jupiter Justine. He's been promoted to Lieutenant Colonel," my mother explained.

"*Acting* Lieutenant Colonel," I said.

"Well done," Justine replied. She addressed me directly but focused all her attention on her mother.

"We are going to have a party tomorrow Justine," my mother added. "I thought that would be the best day, so that Ish can come."

"Oh right. Well I'm not sure. It should be okay. Who do you want to be there Jake?"

"Oh, Mum has already decided, I think."

"Do you want a drink Jake?" Mum said. "I should have offered."

"Please. Mango juice would be nice. No ice … today."

"You haven't changed." Her n-gen, one of the more expensive ones, could be voice activated. She called for the required mango juice and seconds later the 'ding' announced its completion. She opened the door and handed the drink to me after wiping the base of the glass out of habit.

"I'll shop for you Mary if you tell me what to buy." Justine offered. "Do you need me to make up the list?"

"Yes please. Jake you can go through and put on the news or something. You will be in the way here." I felt I had been dismissed and that perhaps Justine wanted to vent some feelings to Mum so I went to the lounge and turned on the news.

***

Chapter Three

"I don't know! Why ask me?"

It was my voice speaking, but I couldn't hear the other speaker's voice.

"No, it's not!" I answered.

A feeling like 'just leave me alone' came over me, and I woke up.

I lay in the spare bed, my own brought back too many bad memories, and wondered what the hell had just happened in my head. I had been talking to somebody, but I couldn't remember the voice. There seemed to be part of me that was inaccessible. It made me uneasy.

***

There had been nothing unusual on the news the night before but as I waited for the first guest to arrive, sitting on a recliner in the garden, something my mother said the night before unsettled me:

Widow of one of the foremost robotics designers, my mother had herself been one of his most gifted assistants and served now as a governor at the Institute of Robotics and Engineering, a quasi-educational institution actually funded by General Motors and New Robotics Incorporated. She knew what was what, so I didn't take her views lightly.

"There's is something not right here lately Jake," she said. "Last month, a solar-window, high up, cracked. Two youths were arrested, but it got covered up, nothing in the press. That window came perilously close to breaking. Why would they do that? It would have been the death of us all! And, in general, there is an increased number of violent incidents reported; rapes, beatings, muggings and attacks."

Not right. Hm.

The heat of the sun had made me close my eyes. A heavy weight suddenly scrambled onto my lap, and I opened my eyes.

Little Mike.

"Hey Uncle Jake! Is it your birthday?"

"Hey Mike. Nope. Not today."

"Daddy is here. Are you coming in now?" He dragged me out of the seat with his little hand and led me into the house. Soon, the ground floor filled up with milling groups of people, chatting over wine or beer and munching the snacks Mary busily recharged, on strategically placed tables in each room. Two college friends approached me from the hall, tinnies in hand, and slapped me on the back affectionately. Anthony and Chris, or Ant and Sponger as they were known to all then, looked as you would expect civilians to look at their age; fat. They didn't have much to say for themselves, and I looked for an excuse to get away from them. It came in the unlikely form of Ish.

"Ah Ish." He took my free hand with his and I shook it once.

"Jake! Good to see you. I have been trying to find you for a while." Unusually for Ish, he had another man, taller than himself, standing to his right and slightly behind him.

"Sorry Ish. Two of my old friends Ant and Chris," I said indicating their backs with my hand.

"That's okay. You are a hero around these parts. No need to spend more time than necessary with slightly balding insurance consultants is there?"

"Ha! Ha! Makes a change from IM insurgents I can tell you. I would squeeze a tinny with you any day rather than spend time chasing them."

"So how is it going on Io? We hear a little. Saw your medal ceremony … well on fast-forward. You know how military stuff bores Tine."

"She's right; just so much bull you know. Half of what they said isn't true. I didn't do most of those things … . Not the way they said anyway. My two officers did most of the brave stuff."

"Did they get medals too?"

"No. They are dead Ish. It was a mess."

"Saw that," chipped in the tall guy next to Ish, barely loud enough to hear.

"Anyway, enough of Io. What's been happening around here?"

"Lots Jake. Really. Things are changing. That's why I wanted to talk to you. Come and have a few beers with us."

"What's wrong with here?"

"Nothing. Just have some guys I want you to meet."

"Okay! If you insist." I followed him reluctantly to a table on the far side of the room with a long sofa on one side. Four guys I hadn't met, lounged on the sofa, beers in hand. They all looked like insurance clerks. An aural album filled the few gaps between loud dialogue around the huge house, and my brain screamed for some peace. I gritted my teeth and prepared for a dull conversation with Ish and his mates. After introductions and a few banalities about baseball, football and beer, Ish leaned in close to me.

"You gotta come and see my bull Jake."

"What?" His friends were looking at me expectantly.

"My bull. I bought a bull."

"You what? You bought a bull? But Ish, you've never had any interest before in agriculture!"

"Well not agriculture exactly. It's a bull. Beautiful Bull."

"Yes, I'm sure it is. Well I guess I might come and look. What does Tine think about it?"

"She doesn't approve. But so what? I have worked hard for years and everything we've paid for has been for Tine and Mike. I deserve something for myself."

"That's new Ish. That attitude!" I laughed.

"Anyway, it's not just for me."

"Oh?"

"We all have an interest in Beautiful Bull." The other men nodded respectfully.

"Why do you call it Beautiful Bull? Is that its name?"

"Yes. It's *the* Beautiful Bull. You must come and see it Jake. It's in a field just outside 'Frisco East."

"I am only here for three days Ish!"

"A full moon is best, but any time is good. Just let me know."

"I will." I made my excuses and left, hoping to work my way towards Justine but not too quickly. I found her, half an hour later, in the kitchen after negotiating one bank clerk and two members of the council who had also been looking forward to a chat with me. I caught Justine's attention when she left a guest to refill a bowl of pastries.

"Justine."

"Hi Jake. Having a good time? I know you don't really like these things, but *do* try, for Mommy." Justine was a complicated woman; sometimes spiteful, occasionally generous with her affections but always sharp. Despite the widening of hips that Mike's birth had bestowed on her, she still looked elegant, and men's eyes generally followed her around a room. She exuded confidence in a quiet way and she wore the trousers in her marriage.

"I just had the most extraordinary conversation with Ish!"

"Really! I thought you were normally so bored with him."

"Well not bored exactly … . Anyway, he keeps talking about this bull."

"Oh. The Bull. Yes, he's obsessed with it."

"Well what's it all about. It's white, he says? Is this some kind of religious thing?"

"No! You *know* Ish is a Christian. He hasn't been converted." I had to follow her as she headed for the hallway with two bowls of savoury biscuits.

"Is he mad? He's never had any interest in agriculture before. I mean; what is he going to do with it?"

Justine shrugged her shoulders. "I don't know. I don't really take any notice. He *has* worked hard for years Jake, and if he wants to live a little, well then I can let him." We went back to the kitchen, and Justine picked up her half-drained glass of white wine. The n-gen buzzed busily in the corner.

"Jake," she said, touching my shoulder lightly. "Can't you stay a little longer than three days?"

"I don't think I can Tine. I really wish I could."

"I really would have thought a Lieutenant General would have a little more influence than that."

"She's fine Tine. I have been watching her, and I don't see any problem."

"It's not just Momma. Or at least it's not her *welfare* that is at stake here. It's the worry Jake. You know how much she has always worried about you. She frets all the time. *All* the time. She scans every newspaper report for mention of you. I don't know why she worries about you so much! It's just part of being a mother, I s'pose. I'm the same with Mike, although I don't worry so much about you. I guess I just got used to your tricks when we were kids. I *do* wish you would just try to understand."

"I *do* understand."

"No, you don't."

"What do you want me to do?"

"Leave the army Jake. It's time. Settle down. Have some kids. You have earned it. God knows you've earned it."

"Oh no. That's twice in one week."

"Twice? Why? Who else has told you?"

"Are you *telling* me, Tine. You can't *tell* me; you know I won't listen to being *told* anything. Anyway, it's Jena. She wants me to leave. But she *asked* me."

"You let your superiors tell you things. But okay, I am *asking* you. Jena, even though I don't like her, has the right idea."

"Soon, maybe Tine. The new promotion might be enough for me."

Justine suddenly turned to look me in the eye, something unusual, because she didn't like blankers, and reached out to touch its neck where my scar had been faithfully reproduced below my right ear. "Still got the scars. You know Jake, of all the people I know who had cosmetic surgery young, yours are the only ones which haven't disappeared." Foster parents almost always used cosmetic surgery to make a replicant resemble the child or person it replaced, and replicants were genetically engineered, so that new tissue replaced scar tissue very quickly. I noticed that she had said, 'all people,' rather than, 'all replicants.' We hugged.

The last guest, a drunk friend of Ish's, left when we kicked him out, shortly after midnight, so that Mike could get some sleep.

For the next two days, I made every excuse possible not to visit the while bull. As much of an animal-lover as the next man, nevertheless I didn't want to look at some sad, lonely animal, all alone in a field somewhere. Fortunately, my mother supplied me with very good excuses. The day before I left, I asked Mike casually about the bull.

"Yeah. Everyone's dad seems to belong to the Bull Club!" he said.

"Really?"

"Yeah. DP said he went out there one night secretly to watch, and you know what?"

"What?"

"Drugs! Yeah. He *said* that in the field, there were loads of people in groups, smoking chum, and he *saw* a used pipe of it in the grass."

"Do you believe him?"

"I dunno. Could be true!"

I woke up in the middle of the night, dreaming of a big white bull floating in the sky. For a moment, I thought I could hear it lowing in the distance. I sat up, walked to the window and pulled it up. The night felt hotter than the previous two. The day before had been thirty-five degrees, and the giant J5 air conditioning units were now struggling to bring it down to the regulation night range of nineteen to twenty-two degrees. Above the rooftops, I could see the simulated starlight, created using the available sunlight, passed through tiny apertures in computer-controlled configuration-filters to mimic the real constellations outside J5. The designers felt this necessary to orientate the space station inhabitants. Even further overhead, I could see the Moon, something man must never lose sight of, given its place deep in the biorhythms of all of us. I couldn't hear any bull lowing.

I knew of the bull as an icon in many ancient religions, but this white bull seemed to resonate with something else in my mind. It took me a while to fall asleep, the blanker body wanted it, but my mind wouldn't let go.

Mum and Justine accompanied me to the station. I hugged and kissed Justine, who's lavender perfume, much sharper and darker than Mum's, mixed slightly with Ish's musky cologne. Then I hugged Mum, who held me close for a long while and finally I pecked her affectionately on her soft cheek. I saw now what Justine had been trying to tell me; Mary felt lonely.

"I'll write as soon as I am back on Io Mum, and don't worry. Things will change soon, and we will have more time together. I'm sure of it!"

Her dark eyes creased in a delighted smile, but it seemed tinged with doubt. "I hope so Jake! Take care. Don't think too harshly of us."

That seemed an out-of-character thing for her to say and by 'us,' I wondered if she meant her and her first husband. I wanted to ask, "Why would I?" but I just said, "I don't!"

"We read the other day that USAC managed to liberate another mine. I have heard they are talking of building a new ring; J6, everybody is calling it. The first for twenty years. Rumour is that it will be a double-torus and some of the radicals are saying that it will be placed in orbit around the Sun. Anyway, I thought you should know. Perhaps it means that things are going to get easier. It might be a sign that there is more money around, and it's a sign, surely, that things are getting easier on Io?"

"Might be Mum. Don't know until I get back. Anyway, don't worry about me."

Justine and I glanced at each other before I turned and walked into the station. They watched me leave from the road and I waved from behind the dusty seribdenum window. I took in hungrily every feature of J5's morning-lit interior until finally we entered the tunnel close to the main terminal at the centre of the wheel, and it receded from my view.

When I reached the deposit bank for the blanker, I used the code at the kiosk to call for 'Wake up' and then sat down to wait for the drug-reversal to take effect.

I felt tired when I woke in my recliner, four days in on the flight to Mars, but I wanted to send a quick message to Jena. I had thought several times over the last few days of sending one to Katie, but the business with Jena had been left unfinished, and it seemed faithless to abandon it. It would be easier to send a message rather than record video or set up a vid meeting. I groggily put on my headband and pressed 'On.'

"Record: message to Jena Ω. Hi Jena. I spent four days with Mum and Justine. I woke up the other day having had an argument with myself. At least it seemed like it. There is part of me I'm just not connected with. I cannot remember its voice or words. It is something unknown to me, and it disturbs me. At the same time, I'm curious about it. I wanted you to know. Thinking about u. Jake. End record."

Then I sent a brief one to Katie. "Record: message to Katie. Hi space boogle. Just spent four days on J5. Going back now to J4. Got promoted to L. Colonel. Cool eh? See u soon. J. End record."

***

"Sit down Colonel. Cigar?" General Owens' ruddy face leaned over me with a wooden cigar-box extended, open.

"Thank you. I don't normally smoke, but an occasional cigar is a luxury I allow myself."

"Hah! Hah!" His laugh was loud and throaty. "Discipline eh? I have largely given it up as you can see." He stuck his already-lit cigar in his mouth and hefted his ample gut with his hairy hands. A gold, antique Rolex calculator-watch hung limply from his wrist. "Drink? Scotch?"

"Do you have vodka sir?"

"Sure do. Somewhere … Let's see now. Ice?"

"Please." He fussed around an old, oak-paneled drinks n-gen. He clearly wasn't very satisfied with his first effort, because he smelled it and replaced it, pressing 'delete.'

"No good. Try again. How does it feel to be wearing the Silver Oak Leaf?" he said with his back still turned. The little sprigs of white hair either side of the back of his head gave him the appearance of an old, overweight squirrel.

"Fine sir. Good!"

He turned around with the finished drink extended. "There you go!"

"Thanks." I tried the tinkling glass of clear liquid. It tasted very good. "Great!"

"You're the son of the famous robotics designer Douglas R. Nanden aren't you? Well sort of."

My response caught in my throat for a moment.

A bigot. At least he's direct.

"You remember him? Most have never heard of him."

"Yeah! I was very young of course, an engineering work-experience student on the Moon. I remember the Collectivator well. Never worked properly but still the first lifelike bot used in mass-production. General Teigh actually knew him personally."

Satisfied that I liked the drink, he leaned back on the edge of his desk. "I know all about you Nanden. I know more about you than you probably guess is even possible. I have been watching you since you were a cadet."

When I had reached S.4, I first had to find my new office. As a Colonel, for the first time in the army I had my own office. I had dropped my case, tried the sofa and switched on the sophisticated terminal. Logging in to the USAC database, I searched on 'Colonel,' and it returned a list of all Colonels in the USAC Army. Now I had clearance to read all their details. It quickly became apparent that I was the only replicant Colonel in the army, and I knew no replicant had ever been promoted to General, so that made me the most senior replicant in the army. It was a bitter-sweet moment. Perhaps Owens promoted me for that reason.

An experiment.

I looked General Owens directly in the eye.

"Life is going to get very strategic for you from now on Nanden. Up till now you will have been used to making command decisions based on short-term objectives, but now you have to think big. With the death of Roanald and the approaching retirement of Colonel

Perry, you are effectively in complete command of USAC forces on Io. Now…" He paused to emphasise what came next. "I know enough about you to know that you are probably wondering why I promoted you all the way to Acting Lieutenant Colonel? It's a big step up, and it's true, I could have brought somebody in from outside. There are enough Colonels scuffing around smoky clubs on J4, and the Moon for that matter, that I could have tried. There are three reasons I *wanted* you."

He wants me to be in no doubt he has pulled strings to get me promoted.

He went on, "One: With your recent and continued accumulation of decorations, there has been talk that we are not being fair with promotions. They say we have never promoted a … you know … to Colonel. So now we have. Two: There is something different about you." He gave me a penetrating stare as I glanced at him from above my glass of vodka. "You are not the normal army man. Too intelligent. But I like that. Of all the officers under my command, you are the only one I don't have the M.O. on!" I smiled. "There is something going on in that head of yours; calculating; estimating; working things out. You always seem to work the odds and bring a successful conclusion to anything you are involved with."

My mind drifted to Jena for a moment, and I dismissed the temptation to wince.

"Three. And this is the most important. The situation is political. I am going to tell you things now that you probably didn't know and shouldn't speak about to anybody without clearing it with me first. We still don't know *how* Roanald was compromised. We have no body, and we have no evidence, despite the best efforts of the Military Police and SCIA. Thing is … . Can I get you another drink?" He stood up to replenish his own glass. I had been so busy listening that I hadn't drank a drop. I shook my head. "Thing is, Roanald led a very tight team. I realise now that I didn't know half of what went on around here. His officers were very loyal to him, and now he's gone, they have closed ranks. I will need you to gain their confidence and perhaps get some information from them. They may know something. They would never accept someone from outside, and they will have enough trouble accepting you, but I can't risk promoting one of them. With your reputation, they might just accept you." He relit his cigar and puffed extravagantly for a minute.

"One thing I suggest Colonel. There is a tradition in our division that even Lieutenant Colonels go on the occasional mission. I admit it's not the usual practice in the USAC Army, but that's the way we like to do things. Roanald forgot that towards the end. Earlier, he was as active as any other Colonel, a good man, but I have checked his records and in the last three years, not one mission. In fact, there is a clue for you perhaps, somewhere to start looking."

"Now, for the wider picture. There is not time to tell you all that is going on; you will find some of it in the dossier on Roanald which you can read later … ." He indicated a paper folder open on his desk. "For now, I can tell you that we are close to crisis point with the IM. Things could go either way in the next six months, but I believe we can finish it. The IM are desperate now. For years we have been trying to cut off their supply lines. As you know, like us, they cannot grow enough food in their hydroponic farms on Io to feed themselves, sunlight too weak there, so they import it, mostly on the black-market from Earth and Mars. We have, through political dealings with the responsible states, managed to close these markets off in recent months, and in the next few weeks we will cut off their only route left for exporting raw iron and seribdenum." He drained his glass, took another long puff on his cigar and fixed me with cool green eyes.

"You have some sympathy for the IM don't you?"

"Yes. A little."

"Well I can understand that. But listen here Nanden. You may have heard rumours that a new J station is being built. As a matter of fact, it marks a new initiative. It's basically just a PR exercise to provide more holiday space for the masses, but the main drive is to retake Earth. That's why the Top Brass want Io finally cleaned up. You want Earth retaken *don't* you?"

"Yes sir, I do."

"Well then. Clean up Io, and we can move on to Earth."

"Yes sir."

"There's just one small problem." He paused, waiting for my prompt.

"Which is?"

"They're up to something. I don't know what it is, but they're up to something."

***

I read Roanald's dossier in a secretary's office before leaving. The dog-eared sheets of paper in the blue folder told me almost nothing new. I saw a grainy photo of Roanald's dead, curled-up body, taken by a grunt's helmet-cam. I felt ashamed to look at that and a few details about his family which I hadn't known; quite sordid, and I felt glad to slap the dossier marked 'TOP SECRET: NOT TO BE REMOVED' on the secretary's desk. "Here you go. Back safely." She smiled winsomely. The flight to Jupiter passed quickly. I read voraciously all the battalion dispatches for the last year and then for the two years before that while I tried to form a plan in my mind to win over Roanald's officers. Two names stood out; Major 'Bunny' Grinda and Major Shaw. I had met Shaw at the Academy as a cadet; he struck me then as ambitious and very tough. 'Bunny' Grinda; a name everyone had heard. But I had never met him. Both names meant trouble to me.

The first thing I did on the shuttle, once I had found my cabin, was to check for any messages. There were none from either Jena or Katie. I instantly had that knot in my stomach that you feel when you think people have become disenchanted with you. When I arrived at Battalion Headquarters on S.5, the Ops room had been thrown in turmoil. I dropped my case and sought the nearest senior officer while watching events unfolding on the huge screen, covering one fifty-foot section of wall.

"Major … Ochte. Fill me in quickly."

"Sir! Glad to have you aboard sir. One of our patrols on Io has been ambushed by IM, and they appear to have some new kind of laser-gun sir … ."

"Well?"

"I don't know sir. The attack started just before you arrived."

I took a seat on the high plinth in the centre of the room and watched the screen. I could instantly see that the IM were making mince-meat of our grunts, even with their X.50s. The view from a grunt's helmet-cam filled with blinding white and red bursts from explosions, and the USAC grunts all fell until the cam image turned on its side and became still. Two IM grunts approached the cam, their unfamiliar weapons down by their side, and then a screen of white noise replaced the image.

"Can you raise anyone?" I shouted to the Comms Officer.

"Trying sir. Nothing at the moment."

"Keep trying. Maybe one of ours got away. Do we have any shuttles in that area that we can divert?"

"On to it sir!" shouted another officer over the other side of the vast room. I heard the buzz of seventy people all talking at once while I approached the screen.
"Play back the last five seconds. Freeze!" I said as the IM weapon filled the screen with a clear image. It looked a lot like an X.50 but much more compact, and clearly it packed a bigger punch at greater ranges. I couldn't see a

maker's name anywhere on the black stock or trigger assembly. The only thing I could see was an embossed sign like a four-leafed clover on the side of the trigger mechanism.

***

Database Download on the IM Clover Leaf Rifle: It looked a lot like an X.50 but was much more compact, and clearly its charge was much more powerful at greater ranges. It was light; extremely light for its size. I couldn't see a maker's name anywhere on the black stock or trigger assembly. The only thing I could see was an embossed sign like a four-leafed clover on the side of the trigger mechanism. The laser rounds from it were white rather than the usual green. **End Download.**

***

"Send it for analysis. I want to know what it is." I turned and walked to the maps table. "Show me where this happened."

I looked at the place her index finger pointed to; a depression about two hundred miles North-west of Ruwa Patera and fifty miles out into no man's land. "Routine patrol?"

"Yes sir. Same as every other day."

"Who was in charge?"

"Corporal Mulheaney sir."

"And *his* superior?"

"Major Danning sir."

"I want Major Danning in my office at 07.00 tomorrow."

I went towards the exit and saw a familiar figure, leaning against the back wall, hands in pockets and cap askance. "Stone! *Major* Stone now." I clapped him on the shoulders either side of his big grin.

"Colonel. How was your leave?"

"Oh, you know. Jena was a pain as usual. No, actually *more* than usual. I barely got out alive. I spent some time on J5 with my mother and Justine, that was nice but a little odd. I'll tell you about it later. I am actually shattered and have a pile of paperwork to get through before I can sleep, but have a quick drink with me."

"You just get in?" I said, leading him to my office.

"Nope. Been here since yesterday."

"Look! I have a new n-gen. My old one was crushed on the MCS. Best thing to come out of it. This one makes a decent glass of vodka." I said, "Vodka, twice with ice," into the mike and fell into the high-backed leather chair on the opposite side of the large black seribdenum desk. Stone took the charged glasses from the n-gen and handed me one. "Did you see that squad get it out there?" I asked.

"Yeah. I don't remember the last time I saw one of our squads get wiped out."

"I don't think it's happened for a long time." I took a long swig of the vodka, letting the ice cube rest against my lip.

"So when do I get a company?" Stone asked.

"Tomorrow!" I laughed. "Eager for battle Stone?"

"No. Command."

"I'll drink to that. Cheers."

"Na Zdrowie!"

"I'm going to need your help with something, Stone."

"Well that's what I am here for."

"Hmm. There are two Majors, Grinda and Shaw. You've heard of them?"

"Sure. Everybody's heard of 'Bunny' Grinda. Nasty man they say. Shaw, not so sure about." He laughed at his pun.

"Ha! Ha! Anyway, they were both fiercely loyal to Roanald, so I am told, even more so than usual. So it's gonna be hard for me to get them on board. You follow?"

"You want me to give them a little bit of the Stone TLC?"

"Yeah! Ha! You know what I mean. Let me know how you get on." I drained my glass, and Stone took the hint.

"Well. I need to prepare for tomorrow if I am going to get a Company. Goodnight Colonel." He stood and snapped his heels before leaving my office.

I glanced at the piles of crates in the corner of the office marked 'Roanald.' They had been left for me to go through, but I couldn't face them now. The only crate I was interested in was marked, 'Nanden.' I flipped the catches and peered inside. It contained the only personal possessions of mine to be retrieved from the CMS which was blown up by the IM. I smiled and reached inside. "Marcus!" I lifted out the crushed pot with a pile of dry soil held to the clay shards by the roots of the miniature sunflower. I couldn't believe he was still alive, and I was grateful some grunt somewhere had even bothered to crate it. The sunflower looked almost dead and was bent right over like a crippled old man. I went to the n-gen and ordered four glasses of water and a large bowl. I replanted the flower in the bowl and poured on all the water before setting it on my desk. I would need a UV light, but I could organise that in the morning. I turned on the comms unit and recorded my last company commander message for Amtel.

"Record. Today I've taken up my new position as Acting Lieutenant Colonel. I cannot tell you where I'm stationed now, or what my new mission will be, but I just wanted to say thank you to all of you who've followed me over the years and I hope you find another commander to follow. Thanks. Over and out! End record. Terminal on."

The terminal window lit up, and I logged in to my USAC account. Taking a plastic pad and pen off a shelf I downloaded the backup of my unfinished novel onto the pad and turned to the last page.

'Dusty picked up the scrap of paper and looked at the address scrawled in a neat, feminine hand. The faint smell of a Turkish cigarette, held between perfumed lips hung in the … .' I wrote 'stale air of the sepulchral office like a butterfly in a mausoleum. Outside, even the bat-dark night seemed more alluring than one more minute in his office, so Dusty grabbed his … .' I stopped and had to search for the name of those old heavy coats people wore in the 20th century. I wrote 'Mackintosh. The woman was seductive and clearly a liar. She probably had no money, but then again, she probably had access to as much as she wanted. He would take the job and the first place to look was the bar where she had last seen the card-sharp.'

I put down the pen and turned to the terminal for two hours of reading before turning the light out. There would be a lot of reading at night for a while. I started with Lowell's Army Tutor to the Rank of Colonel and the chapters on 'Lieutenant Colonels,' and then moved on to Roanald's online account. I had been given full security access using my own password, and I started reading his own logs for the last year.

Major Danning stood in front of me, a tall, wiry man with a sharp salute. His hair was slightly grey and his face gaunt. The colour of his eyes was hidden by the deep shadow of his brow as he stood facing me under the harsh office light.

"Relax Major. I was a Major myself until recently. We can be informal for a while."

"Everyone's heard of your achievements sir. It's a great honour to serve under you."

"Thanks. The PR's not all accurate. Sorry about your squad Major. I saw it all on the screen in there."

The taught muscles in his neck didn't relax. "Yes sir. I know it looks bad."

"Bad?"

"Losing a whole *squad* sir?"

"Oh. Oh yes. What I want to know is; why were the IM there in such strength, with new weapons, and how do we get in, get our men's bodies back and perhaps an example of this new weapon? I need you to fill me in, completely, on the situation." He seemed stunned for a moment. "Do you see what I mean?"

"Yes … sir." He looked down at his feet to collect his thoughts. "There was nothing unusual about it. We picked up activity on the ground radar at about 03.00 hours, and I gave orders to monitor it. There was no movement, but the activity increased throughout the day, so about 14.00 hours I sent a squad out in a POD to investigate. Took them about three hours to get there and then … . Well, you know the rest. We have never seen that weapon before; don't know what it is, who makes it."

"Nothing special there? I've looked on a map, and I can't see any reason for IM to be there, no known mine and not even any cover to speak of. Just flat terrain."

"No sir. I don't know."

"Cheer up Major. Some of your men may still be alive. It's not unknown for IM to take prisoners."

"Yes sir. When?"

"Today. I am meeting Grinda and Shaw in one hour. Hang around, we may come up with a plan, and then we can all go over it."

From Grinda and Shaw's overheard banter as they entered my office and their body language as they stood only feet apart facing me, you could tell they were close. Both big men, Grinda was exceptionally tall at about six feet, six inches or more and Shaw was prodigiously broad. Grinda had a long face and doleful eyes that belied his quick wit and tireless energy. His hair and complexion were dark, and he reminded me of an undertaker.

Shaw looked the sharper of the two; his pale green eyes took in everything around him with quick glances. The little lizard tattoo under his right ear was different to the usual scorpion I saw on men who liked to think of themselves as hard and his wide, square jaw hinted at Slavic origins. They both glanced briefly at the decorations displayed on my tunic but showed little sign of interest after that. I needed to separate them, so I decided to take Shaw with me and leave Grinda with Stone and Danning in the operations room. This gave me the opportunity to meet Danning's men without him and also left Stone to work on Grinda with the help of Danning. Danning was different to the other two, an obvious career officer, and perhaps Stone and I could use him.

After a short meeting at 13.00 hours Shaw organised thirty volunteers from his bases on Io who arrived on S.5 just before the mission departure in the airborne tank at 23.00 hours Earth time. It would be the Ionian night below which suited my purpose. We would be taking four hand-held rocket launchers, twenty-two close range X.77s, four X.50s and would have air cover from a USAC SU 380, older than the SU 401s but with more loiter time. Grinda had questioned my choice of numbers.

"If we don't draw most of them out and take them out straight away with the rockets, one hundred men won't be enough with those weapons they have!" I replied. "Once we are in the building or whatever they are using for a base, the X.77s will be better than X.50s and as good as what they have. Long range and higher power are pointless at three feet or ten. Actually, they should be better than what they have, short barrel and single-handed, we will move more easily than they will. That's why I need men who are experienced with X.77s, Shaw. Have you got men like that?"

"Sure. We don't use them much these days, but a few of the older grunts and the officers know them well enough. I am still pretty handy myself," said Shaw, grinning.

Packed into the bay of the Trion T.20 Topside tank, Shaw tried hard not to make his and his men's interest in me too obvious. They chatted tensely among themselves and a few listened to music on their headbands. The triple-vodka in my system helped to steady my hands and neck muscles, but my mind was a wall of white. I grinned at Shaw. "Ready?"

"Sure sir. As ever. Looking forward to it." He spat on the floor, but I didn't show my disapproval.

The urge to continually swallow, as we neared the coordinates Danning had given us, was almost overwhelming and I was glad when the pilot turned on the red light, and we all pulled down our visors as the cabin air was extracted.

The Topside crunched to a shaking halt, and the doors opened. We filed out in two rows, the first men out taking position on the nearest high ground, to secure the perimeter. We were about half a mile from the point where Danning's men were attacked. The SU would be here in thirty-five minutes to assist and if possible, take out any defensive positions.

I'd left instructions with Stone and the officers overseeing the mission. "The pilot must be under strict instructions not to destroy anything that looks like a vehicle or base, except by my direct order. If there are any prisoners alive, that's where they will be. The whole operation depends on surprise. If we can' draw out the men with these new weapons and take them down with the rockets, it will be a blood-bath."

It took only twenty minutes to reach the vicinity of the target.

One of four scouts ahead radioed back, "No sign of guards."

"Take up positions around the target, and let me know when you can see it," I said, breathing evenly. Radiation levels at 1600 REM. "No more than three hours, men. Anybody out after that will be finished. Watch the indicator patch on your suit, and make sure you have time to get back to the Topside. Okay, the rest of us, let's move in. Nice and slow. Keep your eyes open. I want the four rockets at the front, about twenty yards out." It was a tense few minutes as we waited for something from the scouts.

"Nothing there!" came back the first voice. It was followed quickly by the others.

"Nope. Can't see a damned thing!"

"Only sand."

"Me neither."

"Check your UPS. You sure you're looking in the right place. It could be behind a dune or something," I said.

"You can see for yourself sir! The dunes are about waist-high."

We were in a very shallow depression about half a mile wide, but other than a few prone men behind some dunes, there couldn't be any enemy here.

"Wait. I see *something,*" said a voice.

"DeTunne. It's me. Where?" said a second.

"Five five degrees right, about one hundred meters. Camo, maybe suits."

"See it. Let me get the sight on it. Yep. Bodies. Lots of them. Ours I think."

"Okay. Stay where you are. We will take a look. Coming in now. Major Shaw?"

"Sir?"

"Stay back with the rear twenty. No point us all going in. The rest of you come with me." I tapped two grunts on the shoulders and pointed ahead of me and then followed them. The other eight behind me.

We reached the location, and I called for the men to stop. I knelt down. There were lots of marks on the sulphurous, surface grit. It looked like lots of boots and something with tracks but much smaller than a tank or POD. The marks were only about half an inch deep. I stood up. "Bearing to the bodies please from my position?"

"DeTunne sir. 320 degrees."

Whatever it was, was concealed from our position, so we approached slowly. The tracks roughly followed the same direction we were moving in. Then I saw them too, a pile of bodies and bits of frozen bodies. I tapped four men on the shoulders pointing to defensive positions at four points of an imaginary compass, and they took up positions facing out. Shaw's voice came over the intercom. "SU pilot on the line sir. Wants to know if we need him yet."

"No. Tell him to keep away for now. You can bring your men in Major."

I looked down at the sad pile of bodies. At least they decayed slowly on Io. Arms, heads and other body parts were intermingled with complete bodies like a pile of shop dummies, modeling space suits that had gone out of fashion. Blood coagulated quickly in the low gravity on Io, but it froze in seconds in the extreme cold temperatures, and where body parts were ripped off by the lasers, or whatever they were, the wounds were neatly cut and sealed with frozen blood. Thankfully helmets hid most of the faces, but it was a ghastly sight. I shuddered. Most of Shaw's men were arriving and standing silent around the bodies, mourning.

"Try to do a count Major."

I turned and walked back down the line of tracks to the point where they became a confusing mess. Whatever was on the tracks had been turned many times on the spot, and what looked like only a few men with it had spent a lot of time walking around the object. A couple of Shaw's men had followed me. I tuned the intercom's range down to a few yards.

"Maybe a rocket launcher of some kind. What do you two think?"

"Obvious question then sir. What was the target?" came one answer.

"Exactly," said another voice.

"Uplink," I said into the mike, and the female voice of the Comms Officer in S.5 came on the line.

"Yes sir?"

"Fix on this signal. What is the nearest potential target from here?"

"Five miles due west sir. Oxygen extraction plant owned by RA."

"Get onto them. I want to know if they have had any missile strikes or anything unusual in the last few days, anything unusual at all. Let me know. Close link."

I swung slowly through three sixty degrees, but there was nothing obvious on the horizon. I stepped on to the top of the nearest dune and repeated the turn. Still no obvious target was visible. I sighed and clapped my side with my free hand. Then I looked up. I couldn't see Jupiter at all. It was just under the horizon. Io has a synchronous rotation period, which meant that, although it is spinning in space, it always has the same side facing Jupiter.

"No Jupiter. You don't see that too often; never in IM camps." I saw a smirk on the face of the nearest man, but I couldn't see the face of the other. That was when I noticed just how dark it was here. Without the Sun's light and that of Jupiter, this side of Io, which was always facing away from the great planet was like night on Earth. We often reminded ourselves that the IM had to live on the dark side of Io: radiation levels were much lower here, and that made mining a lot easier for us. Anderstown, closest USAC town to the Jupiter-side of Io, was almost completely underground to protect its inhabitants from the intense radiation caused by the effect of Jupiter's electric field on Io. I checked the indicator patch on my suit, and it read 2700 REM. A few miles further west, and it would be half that, I thought. Above us on the eastern horizon I could see Ganymede.

"Okay. Let's join the others." When we reached the rest of the squad, Major Shaw approached me. I turned the intercom up a few notches.

"Thirty men … approximately sir."

"Okay let's follow the tracks. Maybe one survived. We'll come back for the bodies later." The tracks continued east, and we followed them for about three miles, cantering with scouts ahead as before. We came to a ravine through a rocky ridge and the scouts went over the top while we waited for the all-clear. When it came we cantered through, two abreast, alert for ambush. We went on for another two miles on the path which was rising slightly.

"Camp ahead!" came a call over the intercom a few minutes later.

"How far?" I asked.

"Five hundred yards. Can't see the camp, but I can see lights and reflections and some of them are moving."

"Get as close as you can, but be careful. Stay concealed. I want you four to be the observers for the interdict."

"They are leaving sir!" came another voice over the intercom. "Packing up."

"Okay. Good. We caught them just in time then. What is their strength? What vehicles and weapons can you see?"

"Just give us a few minutes sir. Need to … get into a better position," he whispered, unnecessarily.

We too were approaching the camp and could see the lights now. I indicated positions for the rocket launchers, and the four men went ahead. My heart was thumping hard in my chest now, and the whole suit seemed to pulsate slowly with each beat.

"In position guys?" called Shaw's voice impatiently over the intercom. "Brady?"

"Almost sir. One more … minute."

"Ortura?"

"In position."

"DeTunne?"

"Yes sir."

"Olaffson?"

"Sir. In position. I can see one Slave-Driver, you know; those things converted from early L20s. Looks like it has some kind of jury-rigged cannon on top, probably a Gigawatt or something. Four IM working on it. Standard portable behind it on tracks, medium sized and one they are just loading. Still getting the dirt off that one. About four men to each. Another twenty standing around. They all have those things sir, like in the video you showed us. They look nasty."

"In position" called Brady cutting across Olaffson. "I can see a guy giving lots of directions."

"Could you take him out from there?" I asked.

"Sure. No problemo."

"Okay. When I give the order, do it. Head shot, don't miss. Major! Are the rockets in position?"

"Yessir!"

I quickly organised the men around the Major and I, getting them to lie prone behind two slight dunes either side of a very shallow ravine. I hoped the IM would come up the ravine, if they made it that far.

"Okay Brady. Ready?"

"Yep!"

"Rockets ready?" A chorus of affirmative remarks came over the intercom. "Only fire at grunts. Don't hit the shelters or vehicles and nothing that looks even remotely like a prisoner. Now!"

I heard the high-pitched squeal of Brady's X.50 a fraction of a second after I saw the flash of red light and a small explosion about one hundred feet to my left of my position behind the dune, in the middle of the enemy camp. Then there was an eerie silence, pregnant with fear, before I saw the glints off IM suits as they poured out of the vehicles and shelters under the spotlights of their camp. A few leaned over their dead commander, and others fanned out, experienced troops looking to secure their perimeter. Their guards fired randomly into the dunes and gently sloping banks around the camp. Little puffs of Sulphur turned into plumes of yellow dust rising into the night above us.

The first two rockets slanted into the front line of IM grunts just as they reached the beginning of the gully in front of us. At least half a dozen men became body parts in an instant or vanished completely. The survivors fanned out, and the first of them saw us.

"Shit!" shouted someone in my ear. Four X.77s opened fire on him, and he fell before he could think of doing anything, a look of wide-eyed horror on his face. The other IM front-runners were all dead now too. Two more rockets were fired into the main body of men half way between the camp and us which became a field of strange crops shaped like arms, legs and torsos. Major Shaw was on his feet and running down the line behind us to gain some higher ground nearer the camp.

"The Slave Driver's leaving!" came through the intercom. I had to make a decision. "Take it out!" An instant later there was a blinding yellow red flash as the vehicle exploded on the far side of the IM camp. There would be no survivors. This left about ten IM grunts who were retreating to a position close to the two mobile shelters. Either could have more men inside.

"Major! X.50s!" I pointed to the IM around the shelters as he turned at my call.

"Brady, DeTunne. Olaffson, Ortura! Take 'em down!"

There was the steady fire from two X.50s and the slits of red light as the lasers found their targets.

"DeTunne's gone," shouted Brady. "I think Olaffson is down too." Then there was silence.

I waited for thirty seconds. "Let's go in. Two lines, twenty apart."

We stepped carefully between the bodies and surrounded both of the shelters, both heavily scarred from ten years of battle. I tuned my radio to the Red Cross frequency and banged the side of one of the steel cabins with the flat of my hand. "Come out, and we will not kill you!" I waited, but nothing stirred.

"Okay Major. We haven't got all day. Send ten in."

"You! You!" said Shaw, on the Red Cross frequency, pointing until he had chosen ten men. On the count of three. "One, two … ." He held up one finger and then two, for the grunts. Then they fired. It was an old USAC trick. They blasted the door away at its lock and pushed it in, stepping into the smoking doorway before anybody inside could react. I lost sight of them and watched for any flashes. There was one. Then one of our helmets emerged from the smoke, a grin on the face inside. I changed back to our operational frequency. "Lieutenant?"

"One dead sir. He was alone."

"Unarmed," I added silently. "Okay. Let's try the other. Major."

This time the Lieutenant just blasted the door and went straight into the cabin already loaded on to its tracked trailer, followed by the others. Immediately the interior details were silhouetted starkly by an incandescent white light, and white holes appeared in the exterior hull of the portable.

"Shit!" I swore under my breath.

"Bastards," said someone. Inside, the few rooms that made up one of these ancient precursors to the MCS, men would be fighting at close quarters. I hoped the X.77s would give our men a chance. Major Shaw stuck his helmet into the smoke-filled doorway and quickly pulled it out. After another minute there was silence and then one more burst of light, red. At least one of our men was still alive. Shaw ducked back in through the doorway and moments later called, "Secure!"

The faint tang of burned metal and flesh could be detected through the suit recycler. A scene of carnage filled my visor. I bent to the nearest IM body, but it was lifeless. I could see at least one of ours down, and I rushed over to him. I could see a woman's face through the visor, and she was in great pain. Her right arm had been removed just above the elbow by one of these new IM weapons, and the suit was struggling to reseal. A wad of oozing sealant was accumulating uselessly on the floor, and I pressed the neatly cut sides of the sleeve together as instructed in the USAC first-aid manual. The suit sealed. The wound would have been frozen instantly, and frostbite was a greater risk to her now. "Medics! Where are *you*?" I moved forward following Shaw as he struggled over more bodies, moving to the front of the wreckage. "How many of ours down Shaw?"

"Three I think. Could have been worse, much worse." He jammed his shoulders against a hatch at the front of the shelter and disappeared inside the small room that must be behind it.

He came out moments later without firing. "Empty," he said laconically.

As we struggled back to the rear entrance, I could see medics attending the two wounded IM and Dalgleish, the Lieutenant with the severed arm. We emerged from the smoke into the clear night light outside the shelter.

Looking back, it looked curiously like a kettle boiling with holes in it; little curls of smoke escaped through the laser-cut holes and spiraled up into the night-air.

"Okay that's it. Secure the perimeter. Major: You and I need to take a good look around. Did somebody get to DeTunne and Olaffson?" I asked the grunts around. The helmets shook. One spoke up.

"Ortura's nearest, still out there."

"Tell her to see what she can do and then send a medic out there."

I stepped carefully back through the doorway into the shelter, letting my eyes slowly adjust to the red night-light inside as the smoke slowly cleared. Apart from rows of smashed bunks, piles of torn clothes and provisions there was nothing of interest in the main cabin. "Let's try this one." I pushed a door open into a small store room and stood staring at the object there. Instantly I knew we had found something. Shaw just stood there looking down at the strange device in the middle of the floor. It had a cover half pulled over it, but I could see it was some kind of transmitter on small tracks that would fit those marks in the Sulphur which we had seen earlier. I pulled off the rest of the cover.

"What is it?" Shaw asked, only half interested.

"I dunno. It's home-made, that's for sure." The device consisted of a cheap iron frame surrounding the power source and electronics box, with a kind of laser cannon mounted on a sophisticated aiming mechanism on top. The cannon's barrel was only about one inch in diameter, too small for real destructive power. There was an old-fashioned, full-sized keyboard on a removable plate, attached to the side, and a large monitor above it, also removable. Both were connected to the main body by a ten-loop coil of antique flexicord. Whatever it was either dangerous to the operator or needed to be kept very still to operate. I knelt down and tugged at the flexicord. It was severed in two places, and then I noticed several holes in the device. Holes in the wall next to the door indicated where the laser fire had entered the room. "Goner! We have to take it."

We dragged it outside, and I looked closely at the controls. Some of the grunts gathered round, a few making useless suggestions.

"Okay Major. Get everyone together. We're going back to the pickup point. I don't want to risk the Topside coming here. Maybe somebody is watching, on radar. Oh yes, have you got some of those lasers to take back?"

"Sure have. Brady!" Brady appeared cradling two of the black weapons with another two strapped on his back.

"Are they all the same?"

"Seems so sir," said Brady.

"Let me look." He handed me one. It was light; extremely light for its size. I looked for a maker's mark.

The only thing I could see was an embossed sign like a four-leafed clover on the side of the trigger mechanism.

Strange.

"Detail four men to carry that thing," I said and pointed to the tracked device we had dragged out of the shelter. "How are the IM prisoners?" I called out.

"Bad. Both unconscious. They need proper help soon."

I looked up into the night and saw just a sliver of the edge of Jupiter on the Western horizon. I checked my indicator patch: 3500 REM. "Shit! We gotta move guys. Radiation is way up here." I was thinking we only had perhaps an hour left, and we might not be able to make it back to the Topside. Maybe it would have to come and get us at the half-way point.

By the time we emerged from the other side of the ravine the radiation was down to 2800 REM. I knew that the ridge and higher ground must have been protecting us.

"S.4 calling Colonel Nanden," came over the radio. It was the Comms Officer.

"Here."

"Are you alright, sir?"

"On our way back. Did you get that information for me?"

"Yes sir. No attacks recently or anything unusual."

"Hmm. Okay, thanks. We have casualties: seven of ours and two IM. See you soon."

"One IM." called out one of the grunts.

"Shit! How is the other one?"

"Unconscious. Won't last more than a few minutes," said one of the medic-trained grunts, coming up to me.

"Shit. I wanted to question them."

By the time we reached the pile of bodies, most of the squad were exhausted, myself included. I called in the Topside to pick us up there and took the four grunts carrying the device and Shaw to the point where we had first discovered the tracks. They put it down, and I manually lifted and rotated the barrel of the cannon with my hand. There was a clicking noise as it moved. It turned easily through 360 degrees and tilted until it could be pointed straight up. "Notice how it can't be aimed below the horizontal," I said, pointing to the barrel at its lowest elevation again.

"No good for attacking ground targets then," offered Shaw.

"Hmm. The clicking sound is probably some kind of calibration. Okay. No point hanging around. Topside will be here in a few minutes. Let's go back."

The effect of the alcohol had long worn off, and as the Topside climbed through Io's weak atmosphere, I pulled up my visor and heaved a sigh of relief. The men were babbling excitedly about the mission, despite the loss of three men, and the air in the bay was hot and sweaty.

"That could have been a lot worse." said Shaw under his breath, sitting next to me.

"We were lucky. What was Roanald like?" I said to Shaw, sitting next to me. He thought for a moment.

"Good officer. Mellowed a bit. He was a career man when I first served with him, potent but less so at the end. Like a few vodkas I know." I wondered if Shaw could smell my breath and guessed he probably could.

"Was that his main weakness?"

"We all drink sir. I know how I come across, but I am not so stupid and not so insensitive. The effects of years on Io have had the same effect on me as they have on everyone else."

"How long?"

"Eight, this June, the fourteenth."

"Was alcohol Ronald's only vice?"

"I don't know. He gambled a bit sometimes. That's all I think. Just like the rest of us." He paused. "I knew the commanding officer of that squad back there. He was a mate years ago, got transferred. Good man. I just saw his head, but I couldn't find the body."

"Sorry."

During debrief we discussed the device which was sitting in the middle of the floor, along with the four mystery weapons.

"I have an idea what it is, but I need more evidence," I said. "The radiation is the clue I think. Did you notice how much lower the radiation was, where we found those tracks, than where it was at their camp? IM don't normally stray as far as those dunes so close to our own lines. Major Danning, would you normally pick up activity behind that ridge there," I said pointing to the ridge with the ravine on a map.

"No sir. We wouldn't be looking for it, and anyway, we wouldn't see it. That's why we investigated when they were this side of the ridge. We don't normally see activity that close to our own lines."

"And the radiation levels are much lower there?"

"Yes. I suppose so."

"Shaw. Find the best engineer on the station and get him in here now."

When he arrived, the maintenance grunt stood there, wiping his hands with a rag, looking down at the cannon as if looking at a bad oil leak.

"Can you fix it?" I asked him.

"Dunno. What is it?"

"We don't know, and it doesn't matter. As far as I can see you need Flexicord, a monitor and keyboard and maybe a few other bits and some welding."

"The Flexicord I can find, although I will have to cannibalize something, we haven't had any in stock since I've been in the army. The keyboard's a problem. A monitor I can find."

"Well find what you can, and if you need to, order the rest from the quartermaster on J.4. Send me the order, and I'll authorise it immediately."

"Stone. Keep two back, and send the rest of these new weapons to the labs on J.3 for analysis."

***

There was a party atmosphere in the mess the following evening, as there usually was following heavy casualties. I was late, because I had been going through Roanald's records with a fine tooth-comb. I checked all unusual communications, including vid-links, messages and any letters or documents, including personal ones. I was authorized to read anything I wanted to, but letters to his parents, wife and children left me feeling like a dirty voyeur, and I resented having to do it. I wondered if he had a lover and checked all of his vacation dates against travel documents and blanker bookings. In his dossier it had been noted that there were a large number of blanker bookings, but I noted with irony that there were no more than there would have been for myself in a similar period. The dossier also mentioned that two blanker tickets had been found in his jacket and I made a note to check this later. All in all, there was nothing unusual so far.

At the party, Shaw and Grinda were blind drunk, while Danning seemed stone-cold sober watching from the sidelines with a glass of Crombier in his hand. Rake music blasted out of the cranked-up sound system.

I wasn't in the mood for dancing although two of the female grunts looked tempting. I walked up to the man facing away from me at the bar with his leg in a carapace. I tapped him on the shoulder and leaned into his field of vision. "DeTunne isn't it?"

"Hello sir. Yes!"

"Glad you didn't lose the leg!" I shouted over the deafening music.

"Me too. I hate mech stuff. This hand is okay, but it's not the same."

"Yeah. I know what you mean. I know your brother."

"Yep. He talks a lot about you. Specially about that last mission."

"Ha! Ha! Yes, one of the only survivors. Tough guy!"

"It was a big party though that last one wasn't it? Lots of medals."

"Yeah. Listen. Where is Dalgleish?"

"Sick bay. Complications I hear. Couldn't make it."

"Oh. Listen, I am going to visit her. See you later."

Dalgleish lay wrapped in clean purple plastofibre sheets, purple obviously being her favourite colour. Her headband concealed whether she was asleep or not, but the tinny beat of music came from the implants in her ears.

"Dalgleish."

"Oh, hi sir! Wait. Music stop." She hauled herself to an upright position with her good arm.

The wound at the end of the stump of her arm was cleanly mended, but there was a deep blue and black discoloration to the flesh beneath it.

"Not fitted the mech yet then?"

"No … . Frostbite damage. They want to observe it for a few days before messing with it some more. I don't look like much do I? Guess you don't fancy me?"

I looked at her short blonde hair and pretty face with blue eyes and thought she looked rather gorgeous.

"I'd say you are pretty attractive."

"Date?"

"Umm … ."

"Girlfriend?"

"Yes but … okay. In a few days. Maybe. You know it's against regulations?"

"Everybody does it out here. Too far from the MPs or SCIA to worry about."

"Did Roanald do it?"

"Occasionally. Usually he was too interested in blankers though. That was more his thing."

"Thanks baby. Make sure they don't give you a muscly arm with tattoos."

"I have muscles," she replied, flexing the bicep of her left arm. "And a tattoo."

***

Chapter Four

Dalgleish's comments reminded me to go through Roanald's crates, and I went back to my office to start on them. After three crates I was too weary to try a fourth. I had found books, toiletries, passes, a lot of clothes and some personal mementoes which meant nothing to me: rock samples and photos of unknown people on Mars or the Moon. Nothing seemed out of the ordinary. I checked my messages before sleeping: still nothing from either Jena or Katie. My private thoughts revolved more and more around the conversations I'd had with Jena when I wasn't thinking about the IM or Roanald. I felt a growing anger that she had disrupted my life in this way, but on an intellectual level, knew that she had every reason to. I could not reconcile my feelings with my thoughts.

Why did she have to do this now?

***

"Have you any idea what you are asking me?" bellowed Owens on the vid-link. "Ganymede is practically all treaty land. There is nothing there apart from a few research stations. Nobody goes there, and it could take months to get permission. On the other hand, if I just let you go on some clandestine mission, I could lose my job!" The vein in his forehead seemed to be pulsing as he stuck his face right in the monitor.

"Let me explain once more sir," I said calmly.

"You better explain yourself very, very clearly. And leave out any crap. I want it straight. I expected you to go on a mission Nanden, in fact I practically told you to, and I expected some initiative from you but not this!" For just a moment I had a vision of a very angry squirrel with its back to me, but I dismissed it before a smile could crease my lips.

I pointed the cam at the object on the floor. "Here it is sir. As I said we found it in the IM camp, and it was obvious it had been dragged into the region away from the face of Jupiter. At first, I didn't see that this was significant, but then I saw that the radiation levels were so much lower here than just a few miles away, towards the IM lines. Then an engineer here fixed it, and we turned it on. We have worked out that it is some kind of low-powered laser gun."

"Yes, yes. You said that, but how does it work, and why do you think it's pointed at Ganymede."

"Well. It has a keyboard, and when you type a message and press return, a set of laser pulses are fired from the gun on top. The range would certainly allow it to reach Ganymede. It uses an old system of communication called Morse code. Have you heard of it?"

"Yes. Sort of. Way before my time though."

"Well, it's a binary system, a set of dashes or long pulses and dots or short pulses, which make up a simple alphabet. It's incredibly crude, but it works. The reason I believed it was pointing at Ganymede is, because radio transmissions to Ganymede would be impossible for the IM. As you know sir, radiation levels on their side of Io are much higher, and it's so high that it stops all but the very shortest-range radio transmissions. What is more, because Ganymede is only ever visible to them through the width of Io's weak atmosphere when it's closest to Jupiter, it would be even harder for them. We still weren't sure until I had a radar sweep of the closest area on Ganymede to the transmission point. It took a few days sir, but finally we found an anomaly. It appears to be an artificial structure where there shouldn't be one. The only reason it hasn't been seen before is, because nobody was looking for it."

"Really? You have actually found something? I mean, you actually have proof?"

"Yes sir."

"Real data? That I can print and show to a very angry superior? If I need to?"

"Yes sir."

"Okay. Let me think about it," he said grumpily. "When do you want to go?"

"Soon as possible sir."

"Got anything on Roanald yet."

"A few leads sir. Nothing concrete."

"Hmm." The link went dead.

Phew. That was intense.

I returned to the spewed clothes from the last two crates of Roanald's. In one of the last jackets, a dress jacket, that I had checked, I had found the two blanker tickets. They were for a company called Marsuround and dated three years ago. I had never heard of it. I checked the dates in his dossier, and they didn't match with any leave or travel that he'd had. This was unusual but not extraordinary. He could have hired them during an evening-off, but each was for a period of a few days. It seemed a bit extravagant to keep them booked out for the whole period. Why not just book them out for his off-duty periods?

"Ochte?"

"Yes sir," came back through the intercom.

"Please can you get someone to check out a company called … wait … . Marsuround."

"Spelled M-A-R-S-U-R-O-U-N-D?"

"Yep. Let me know." A few minutes later he called back.

"Okay. Looks like a very up-market blanker company on Mars, as you would guess. Of course, they are also available on S.4 and just about anywhere else if you can afford the price. They cater for the jet-set just about anywhere and … erm … royalty."

"Royalty? You sure?"

"Yes sir. Unofficially of course." He laughed nervously. "Between you and me."

"Of course."

"I know it's late, Ochte. Can you do one more thing for me before you go off-shift. Find out if Marsuround has … or has ever had any dealerships on any of the moons of Jupiter?"

"Sure."

I went into my private quarters and sat back against my bed for a moment, cradling a double-vodka. Marcus was upright and leafy once more, under the bright UV light. *Much happier.*

I felt amusingly like Dusty the detective, now that I thought I was getting somewhere. I was considering what he might do next in my novel when Ochte's voice came over the intercom.

"Sir? I have some information, but it's not much."

"Go on."

"There was a small dealership … on Io, in Anderstown. Strictly a one-man operation on Aten St. It closed down years ago. Some scandal."

"Damn."

"But I have the name of the guy who owned it, and I happen to know where he works now."

"Good man."

"He is just an assistant now, in another blanker dealership on the same street. Place called 'To be's.' Name's Paul Danette."

"I just use Sensels myself."

"Most of us do. These are even cheaper though. Don't usually work properly. More mech than replicant if you know what I mean."

"Thanks. How did you find out all this stuff?"

"Let's just say I hang around there sometimes."

"We shouldn't be having this conversation. It's best I don't know why."

"Yeah. I think that's best."

"Thanks. No more calls … and you sleep well."

Before I slept, I looked this Paul Danette up on the military portal to Io's citizen database. Danette's real name was Paolo Giannetti. He was there, with his criminal-record and a photograph, a tall, blonde man in a sharp suit. The record said that he had been investigated during a case of 'inappropriate use of a blank replicant' but had been cleared.

Nine o'clock sharp the next morning I was standing outside 'To be's.'

What the hell am I doing here? Oh yeah. Hm. Just one more successful mission, become a success in Owen's eyes, and then I can go for the court-martial. Almost there.

It was a Saturday, and I thought they would have opened early to collect all the returns from Friday night's carousing, but I was wrong. I was dressed in civvies and ambled casually backwards and forwards for about three shop lengths either side of the store. At nine twenty-five, according to a clock in another shop, a scruffy, slightly paunchy and straw-headed guy in a cheap suit shambled up to 'To be's' and started to unlock the door. I had to look closely before realising it was Danette. I turned and looked at the long orange grotto ringing with the sound of water, running along the other side of the street and practiced what to say. "Excuse me. You don't remember me, but I remember you when you were with Marsuround." It sounded false, and I thought it would fail, but I couldn't think of anything better. I turned and walked up to him just as he was about to disappear inside the open door.

"Hi."

"Not open yet." His scowl convinced me to wait until he was ready. Five minutes later and probably one minute later than he was ready, he begrudgingly opened the door.

"What can I do for you? Most of the stock is out or being repaired."

"You don't remember me, but I remember you when you were with Marsuround."

His beady, brown eyes bored into me. "Nope. I don't remember you."

Shit.

I hesitated, but he carried on. "But then, what with drink and everything else, my memory is not that good. Maybe you were a customer. Is that it?" He smiled while he wiped the counter clean.

"Er. Yes."

"Marsuround was just the trading name. The name on the business cards and invitations was Courtesan Rouge. Only the very best, highly-trained replicants. I haven't talked to anyone about it in years."

"What happened to it?"

"Ha! What do you think? After the police had put their grubby fingers all over my client's accounts, I was poison to them. Marsuround wouldn't renew my franchise, and I was finished. I couldn't rent a domestic *robot* for two years."

"I understand … . I wanted to ask you a question though."

"You need to ask, or you want to ask?"

"Need, actually."

"Ah. You are Military aren't you? It's obvious. What is your name?"

"Nanden."

"There is a name to conjure with! Well, *Colonel* Nanden … . Am I right?"

"Yes, actually."

"Do you know what happens to old blankers?"

"Not really. I have heard rumours, but I try to ignore them. There are lots of hard-luck stories around. Who hasn't got one to tell?"

He laughed, a sharp high-pitched laugh.
"Well … anyway, they may be accurate; these rumours you've heard. Any minute now you will see someone

walk in that door behind you and through this door to my left. Don't stare, but take a look at him. If he is on time, and he usually is, it will be Tomas. Actually, not his real name, but he likes it that way. In the following half hour three more will come in, usually followed by the last, Melissa. They won't be hired today or tomorrow, probably not even next week or the next. But if they are lucky, on a festival night say, they will be the only blankers left, and they will earn enough money to see them through the next month."

"That makes me feel really bad. I use blankers myself, and that makes me a hypocrite. Of *all* people, I shouldn't … ."

The door behind me opened and a well-built guy in his fifties, with distinguished-looking grey hair and a slight smell of liquor, passed me, opened the door Danette had pointed to and went into the room beyond. I caught just a glimpse of a long sofa and a low table with plates and mugs on it.

"… do it," I finished.

"Ah. I see. Course, not all blankers are replicants."

"No? What do you mean?"

"Sorry, I mean full humans of the dirty-DNA kind. They do it sometimes. For money."

"Really?" I was genuinely astonished and curious.

"Nobody talks about it, and it's kept quiet by the authorities, but it happens. Guy, or girl, down on their luck, usually heavily in debt, decides to try it for a few years. That's the usual deal; no paperwork and it's very … whooo, under-the-counter. I mean, some people like to try different things, *if* you know what I mean, and some unscrupulous dealers will supply … them. Trouble is the drugs, not genetically tuned for it, the dirty-DNA-ers; they get kinda drunk. The effects don't wear off and poor buggers don't last long. I never heard of one actually surviving and getting out."

"So what happens to them?"

"On the streets or worse, dead. They are just recorded as drunks. This place had three go missing a year before my little incident, apparently. It was reported, but the police never found a trace."

"Sad."

"Yeah. Like you say, everyone has a sad story. Now … what is yours?"

"Ah. That would be a long one. I do need help though … er … I mean information."

"Oh, you do? Have you heard of Rudge's Robot Crimes?"

"No. I don't think I have."

"Well it's a good read if you have time. Anyway, the follow-up is called Rudge's Replicant Crimes. You will find out most of what you need to know in the third edition. Actually, some of the details were supplied personally by me. He, Rudge, interviewed me." He sighed deeply. "You will find it under 'Royal Court Murder' I think. *If* you really want to know."

"Okay. And you had nothing to do with it?"

"Well, ha! That is direct, anyway. Somebody did hire a replicant from me, and yes, he was used in an attempted murder plot, or that is what they say, anyway. Nobody was actually killed, except him and another replicant. But I knew nothing about what was going on until I saw it on the news."

"You didn't know the guy who rented it … I mean, him?"

"Never met him before, and anyway, he was found dead, outside a few days later."

"Outside?"

"Yeah. Outside; on the surface."

"Oh. I see."

"Never found his killer."

"Hm! Do you remember ever hiring to a Joachim Roanald?"

"Sure. I remember all my clients. Not always the name, but I remember him. Military type like you but a true romantic."

"Thanks!"

"No offense, but he truly was looking for something special, out of the ordinary. He was only looking for real high-nobility, something classy, but I don't think he found it. Hired twice I think."

"Why don't you think he found it?"

"Too coarse. Military type. Of course some of those ladies like a bit of rough … ."

"Okay. Thanks Mr Danetti."

"My pleasure."

After returning to S.4 and briefing Stone and Grinda about the mission I hoped to launch to Ganymede, I brought up the name Rudge on the terminal in my quarters. I chose Rudge's Replicant Crimes, picked the 'Royal Court Murder' and started reading. There was a long preamble, the author wishing to build up tension and make the most of the scandal element. During a visit by the Italian Royal family to Europa, no doubt to experience a Jupiter fly-by, they had stayed in the guest wing of the Governor's Palace and the personal aide to the Princess had been murdered by a lethal injection in his neck. His body had been hidden in a wardrobe and his place taken by the imposter-replicant, hired from Danetti's outlet for Courtesan Rouge. Curiously, the replicant himself, now made up and clothed as a butler, was found dead in the Princess's apartment two days later. Death had been by strangulation which would have been easy while the replicant was in a drugged state. The investigators traced the man who had hired the replicant to a Noam Eichter on Io, but as Danetti had said, he had been found dead on Io's surface outside Anderstown, shot with a round from an X.50. Since the round from an X.50 is untraceable, and there are as many X.50s as soldiers on Io, the investigators had to rely on other directions of enquiry after this but found no witnesses or evidence that pointed to anyone. The only other evidence they had, were the prints of size nine, army-issue Surface-Snake boots near the body.

Something Danetti hadn't mentioned to me was that the aide was himself a blanker, also hired from Courtesan Rouge, ID:Marsuround Blank Replicant Unit 43739, because the Italian Royal family were in fact in financial straits and trying to save money by cutting staff on the trip. It would have been easy therefore for the second blanker to inject the first. This was, however, the first known case of one blanker being used to kill another.

A planned visit by the King and Queen to a mine on Io, in which the King of Italy had an interest, had been postponed due to local volcanic activity that day, and the investigators concluded that the unexpected presence of the King's personal security guards in the Palace had led to the unauthorised entry of the blanker into the Princess Sofia's bedroom. They also concluded that whoever had organised the unauthorised entry, had killed the second blanker, ID 43822. The most likely motive had been murder but kidnap for ransom was also a possibility.

What interested me most was the name of the person in overall charge of security for the royal visit; Colonel J Roanald.

***

"Ah! Nanden," said Owens, sounding like a drunk snake. "Thanks for the weapons. Interesting. Have you tried firing one?"

"No sir. We are too worried about shooting holes in the skin of J.4. We just don't know how penetrating the beam is."

"Good. Well we have, and you are right, they are really powerful. Ten times more powerful than ours and fiendishly well-constructed. Too much so for IM I feel. I am even more interested in your little mission to Ganymede now. You still going?"

"If you have permission."

"Ah … . Permission. Yes, well I wouldn't exactly call it *official* permission. But you have my permission. Just keep it real low-key … and don't make a mess. And above all. Don't bother the scientists, okay?"

"Will do sir."

I called Stone, Danning, Grinda and Shaw to a briefing and told them we're going to Ganymede. There were open mouths at the name, but Grinda looked most eager to go. Stone had tried his magic on Grinda and Shaw but they seemed impervious.

"They are so close, they are like Tweedledum and Tweedledee, and they won't open up at all on Roanald." If Roanald had been at all involved in the Princess incident, I wondered if they would have been involved too. Again, I decided to take one of them with me and leave the other behind. Danning would be no good on the mission; he clearly didn't like to lead from the front, and I needed good combat men for a mission with so many unknowns. It made me sick with fear just thinking about it. An unknown environment, which we were entering illegally, with no support, in effect, and to look for something completely unknown too. I considered several times delaying the mission until we could get a reconnaissance probe sent there, but that would take months, and the IM, or whoever we were dealing with here, could have gone by then. I needed to impress Owens, and this seemed the best way to do it.

The briefing had ended with my instructions to Stone. "There are six of the new MCS Mark 7's in the bay Stone. We will be taking one of those. It's not ideal I know and will be slow to get to Ganymede but should suit our purposes once we are down. The main thing is that we all know the type and what we can do with them, and in a situation with so many unknowns that could be an advantage. Get one ready, and we will take it out later today to familiarise ourselves with this version. I read somewhere that there was a Ganymede kit available for this version, like there was for the Mark 6. Get hold of one if you can. I also want you to assemble thirty each of your best men and include DeTunne."

"Danny?"

"Yeah."

I ran my hands along the grey seribdenum surface of the Mark 7 in the vast flight-bay of S.4. There were two tired Mark 6s at the end of one line and the mangled remains of our old Mark 6 beyond. I couldn't bear to look at it.

It makes no sense to have salvaged it unless the army is so broke that it needs the money from its scrap sale.

The Mark 7 had the new anti-laser refracting armour which looked like so many polygonal scales on its skin. The pods were now grouped in pairs at the front and back, to provide protection in the event of high-speed impact, a move that many of us had called for, which gave it a bug-eyed look from the front. From the side, it looked like a truncated centipede, squatting on the deck. From the gantry, its top surface still looked a mass of pipes and vents but slightly less messy now with more armour plating covering it. My initial impressions of it on the testing flight had been good with the reservation that the cabins were all even smaller than the Mark 6 and that the extra armour plating had made it heavier and less manoeuvrable. The pods had shrunk to two-man crew size, and even with the bigger laser-guns this helped to compensate for the increased weight, as did the increased power of the new reactor. The MCS still felt a bit sluggish to me though.

Stone had called me a few hours after the briefing. "The Ganymede kit is available, in theory, but since nobody has ever requested one, they haven't yet built one. I've had the specifications sent, and it doesn't look too hard to implement most of it. Because there is nothing but ice on Ganymede, the vents and outlets on the side need to be ducted *inside* to the top and of course nobody knows if the teeth on the tracks will dig into the ice effectively. Probably not in my opinion. We have fitted smaller heaters to save some weight, because heating is not so much of a problem on Ganymede. There is one major downside though."

"What's that?"

"Well with the ice, the S-grav won't work."

"Back to the old grav-boots then."

"Yeah."

One now entered through a port between the two front pods, straight onto the flight-deck, and I followed Stone aboard. We launched minutes later and set a course for Ganymede, a journey that would take twenty-seven hours, even at full speed for the MCS, not designed for inter-moon space flight.

The journey to Ganymede passed almost peacefully. We had plenty to keep us occupied; we had to familiarise ourselves with the combat suits which we had been provided, similar to those used on the Moon, and we had brought two of those IM weapons with us to try out. But with everybody quickly slipping into well-rehearsed routines, a calm quickly settled on the crew. We were all gathered in the mess, wearing our grey army-issue boiler suits and Grinda hefted one of the weapons to get used to its weight. He swung it round his neck and aimed at Stone and I across his back.

"Careful!" I shouted.

"Don't worry. It has a little safety-catch right here," he said, leaning towards me and pointing conspiratorially to a small sensor on the stock.

"Okay. Okay. I believe you."

His long face creased into a grave-side version of a smile.

Stone busied himself reading the MCS Mark 7 manual. "Do you remember that argument about Diesel'o on that last mission together Cap?"

"Ha! Ha! Yes. That was you, wasn't it DeTunne?"

"Yeah! Wish Walsh was here now!"

"Says here the Mark 7 diesels have been tested in drive mode only once and were found to give a top speed of 4 mph. It is not, therefore, recommended that they are used for this purpose."

"Was it ever?" quipped Stone.

Twenty hours later, we put our combat suits on and strapped ourselves in as the MCS hurtled towards Ganymede's surface at 1000 mph, fast enough, we hoped, to be mistaken for a meteorite if anyone should pick us up on their radar.

***

I took the vid call from Katie while I had almost finished the report, glass of vodka in hand, in my quarters on S.4.

"Hi Jake! Oo. Drinking again on duty?"

"Nope. Off duty darling. Kids in bed?"

"Ha! Like you wish. You will *never* have kids with me baby."

"Is that a wish or a lament?"

"Hah! What u doin'?"

"Just finishing a report. I have to get it in in the next hour. I just need to read it back, and then I am done, probably."

"Oo. *Probably*," she aped. "So you got no time for your sexy pilot then. Even if I am naked?"

I swung round to look at the screen. She wasn't.

"Ah! Made you look. Mind if I hang around. We get so little time together. I was just gonna make a sandwich and tidy up, I can watch you while I work."

"Fine by me as long as you're quiet. Where you been anyway? I left a message nearly two weeks ago?"

"The fleet went on a little trip to Neptune. Top secret, so I can't tell you, but I really wanted to go."

"Oh. Okay." I returned to the report and read it back.

USAC Mission to Ganymede under Acting Lieutenant Colonel Nanden: 28 June 2101.

This mission: to investigate the source of a radar-return which we believed to be the receiver for a clandestine and unusual laser transmission system used by the Ionian Militia. MCS No. 177 was used as transport with 60 troops, Majors Stone and Grinda and Acting Lieutenant Colonel Nanden, as commander.

We landed Surface Ganymede 27th June at 04.00 approx. 5 miles from target and immediately proceeded to target. Sent PODs ahead from range of 0.5 miles, and they took up position around observed crater in which IM camp located. Approached east side of crater on foot. Approx. 150 feet deep, 1500 feet diameter. Observed target: Old Russian freighter: Pacific class, parked next to prefab units arranged as four sides around central open-square. Large radio dish observed in central square and smaller transmitter on top of one unit north east corner. No IM guards on perimeter. Disembarked 40 troops leaving 20 and Major Stone as backup on MCS with instructions to destroy camp in 1 hour if we could not extract. Apprehensive due to familiar and highly effective defensive arrangement of prefabs, requiring movement through entire ring while under fire to locate any target of importance. Also known to be favourite defensive arrangement of IM General Bogdanovic, a revered foe. Entered complex via single observed entrance in South East corner carrying 36 x X.77s, 2 x rocket launchers and 2 x IM new weapons which Major Grinda had already test-fired on Io surface previous to mission. Immediately under heavy fire from 2 guards in lobby using new weapons, taking out 4 of ours before eliminated. Moved north to first prefab and observed open-plan arrangement reducing cover to minimum. No opportune target observed and after losing further 10 troops moved to second prefab (4 per side of rectangle). Lost further twelve troops and now under attack from south entrance to prefab too. Left 10 as rearguard while 16, Grinda and I proceeded slowly towards north east corner, first viable exit into central square and location of transmitter. 4, Grinda and I reached fourth prefab. Unclear at this point if rearguard intact but casualties too heavy to continue. Surrendered to IM whereupon we were taken west, strip-searched, gagged, bound and contained within prefab with 2 guards inside room. Grinda and I mildly interrogated by General Bogdanovic, whom I thought dead according to battle reports in 2098. Gave him nothing. Returned to room with others. Joined by 2 survivors from rearguard. Spent first hour waiting nervously for Stone to make attack and then realised eventually it wasn't coming. Detained for 17 hours at subzero temperatures without food, water or clothes. Report as violation of Geneva Convention Amendment of 2051.

After that time Major Grinda overcame one of the guards.

My description of what Grinda had done didn't seem enough. I stopped reading, remembering what actually happened:

"Fuck it's cold," Grinda gasped. "They want us to just die of exposure, so they can claim it was an accident. No questions later. Whatever they're doing here must be *really* secret."

"I dunno Gr- … . John, isn't it?"

"Yeah. Nobody ever calls me that though."

"I dunno John," I continued. "Bogdanovic always was an asshole, and he hates my guts too. I was in a squad that wiped out his whole company years ago."

"Thanks. Why couldn't you have just left him alone? I am sure he is a ni-ice enough geezer." Grinda's voice shook from the intense cold. Five of us were close to hyperthermia, and the other three survivors were unconscious. We were too busy doing star-jumps and jogging on the spot to worry about them too much. Two of them were mortally wounded and had no chance anyway.

"If we don't do something soon, we're gonna die," Grinda said.

"Fuck yeah!" one of the grunts, a Joseph Lehmkuhl, said. "Let's just do *something*!"

"Okay" Grinda said. "You, you and you," he said pointing at the grunts still standing. "Go over every inch of this cell for anything you can find, cord, clips, anything they might have left behind. We are going to jump them." The room had only had a couple of chairs, some boxes and a cabinet in it when they brought us in. They dragged them out, and now it looked completely bare. The grunts crawled on the floor looking for anything at all they could use.

"A screw!" one said holding up a three-inch long screw after a few moments.

"Yeah! You can use it. I'll show you." Grinda took the screw and placed it between his first and second finger with the tip facing out and the head, resting inside his fist, against the back of the fingers. "Push against the head with your thumb. You will cut yourself and might break a finger, but you can penetrate the carotid or even the heart with practice."

The others stood up. They had found nothing else. "Right," Grinda said. "I'll use these," he said jabbing the air with stiffened fingers. "And you can help me Colonel. The rest of you will have to use fists. There'll be guards outside. There were two when they brought me back, and I am guessing there are still two. Maybe they're tired. We don't know, but we need to get their attention. I'll jump the first one into the room, and the rest of you take the second. At least one of you must make sure the second doesn't get away. You have to block his exit. Close the door if you have to. Nobody moves until I do. Okay?"

As an expert in urban survival myself, I could tell Grinda had done the courses and knew exactly what to do.

"If I'm right," he continued, "the one thing these guys won't be able to stand is silence. It will drive them nuts after a while." We had heard their voices occasionally, so we knew the door wasn't soundproof. "So from now on nobody makes a sound. This could take hours, but it's the only way. If you want to survive, keep totally silent."

There were a lot of nods, and nobody spoke after that. He was right. It did take, by my estimate, well over an hour before we heard a sharp rapping on the door. It made us jump, but nobody made a sound. We heard more rapping, and then a voice shouted:

"Eh! You in there! You all dead or what?"

A long conversation between the two guards ensued, and then the lock clicked open, followed by silence. Nothing and nobody moved. Grinda had taken up position to the right of the door, the side that would be open, and I crouched on the other side, along with Lehmkuhl. His would be the task of slamming the door shut while I pulled the second guard into the room and attempted to disable him. The grunt with the screw crouched to my left, ready to help me or move over the second guard as I pulled him down if there was a third guard. Our nerves were bow-tight and a metallic taste filled my mouth. This could be our only chance, and every man knew his life depended on him getting his part right.

Without warning, the door flew open and hit Lehmkuhl in the face. Everything happened at once, and yet I could see it all happening in slow motion. A laser barrel entered the room first. It dropped as the guard threw himself to his knees, expecting the worst. Grinda's first lunge missed, but he quickly swung, and threw his weight onto the guard, pushing him to the floor. At the same time, a white beam hit the far wall and scored a black line across it in a zigzag from top to bottom as the other guard fired, hoping for a target. He stayed out of the room; a problem for us. I reached for the barrel of the first guard's laser and, using the techniques taught to us, I grabbed it with both hands, throwing the weight of my hips over the stock, and at the same time twisted the barrel with all my strength to release it from the guard's grip. Fortunately for me, by this time not only was the guard more preoccupied with the fingers that Grinda had inserted so expertly into his eyes, but the other guard had paused to take careful aim at Grinda's head. The gun came away in my hands and completing my twisting fall I rolled over and aimed the laser at where I remembered the guard outside the door to be. I pressed the trigger, and his head exploded in a nova of white and red light.

Grinda had ripped off the first guard's helmet and begun strangling him, leaving the remains of the man's eyes on his fingers and splattered on the floor. The grunt with the screw offered the home-made knuckle-duster up to the guard's neck, but Grinda shook his head. I continued to use my weight to hold the guard down for Grinda. "*He's* dead," Grinda said finally, next to me and half under me.

"Sorry. I wasn't much help," added Lehmkuhl.

The two guards were smaller than both Grinda and I. "Put these on, both of you," whispered Grinda, grabbing a fist full of IM armoured uniform in his hand. "Keep your voices down." He looked at me. "What do you reckon?"

I read my report.

> After that, Major Grinda overcame one of the guards. While he did this, I grabbed the IM laser and killed the second guard, outside our cell. Grinda told two of the smaller grunts to put on the IM armoured suits, which were too small for him and I. I then took one of the lasers, went to the door of the North Eastern corner unit and opened the door. On the way, I found a cabinet, some crates and a pile of clothes but no target of opportunity. Seeing only two IM huddled over some electronic units, I burst in and killed them both with single charges. I memorised a radio frequency on a green display and ejected a disk before exiting the room, back towards exit point. I heard IM pursuing me, but the armoured door, which I closed, prevented their fire. Just before I reached the last exit before the lobby, shutting doors and shooting out lights as I went, I realised I had no way of reaching the MCS without a suit. I stopped in my tracks. I put my problem to the back of my mind when I heard the sound of laser-fire beyond the door.

I put the report down again, remembering what had really happened next:

Hearing the sound of IM boots behind me in the darkness, there seemed no way out, but I thought I would rather die trying to escape than be tortured by IM. I threw the lobby door open and saw a sight beyond, which I will never forget. Grinda was holding back a whole swath of IM troops, lined up on the south western exit of the lobby. They were lined up two deep at least, and a wall of laser-fire sought him out while he stood his ground. Two dead IM lay at his feet and, next to them, the last two of our men. But his demeanor astonished me most. He wore a pink shirt, half-buttoned up, a necklace, which swayed as he fired, jeans, and a cigarette hung limply between his lips. His eyes had the look of casual indifference while he fired single-handed in one continual burst along the lines of IM, causing them to jump and duck or jerk as they were hit. He seemed not to care if he lived or died and appeared to be enjoying it. He half turned and saw me from the corner of his eye. I could see one of our surviving grunts in the armoured airlock compartment waiting for the pressure on the surface and in the airlock to equalize, so he could exit.

"Only two suits here!" shouted Grinda from the corner of his mouth. "The rest of us have had it. I let Lehmkuhl and the kid go."

I nodded and joined in firing at IM from behind a desk near the door. Then it seemed like the world caved in. The outer wall next to the airlock exploded as the front cabin of the MCS crashed through it, and air started rushing out of the lobby into the near-vacuum of Ganymede's weak atmosphere. I grabbed the supports of the desk and dropped the laser, so that I could hold on to the disk which had been between my teeth. I saw IM guards flying across the lobby towards the ragged gaps around the MCS. I tried to gulp one last mouthful of air but swallowed almost nothing. I knew I only had moments before my blood boiled, and I passed out. Men were screaming, their faces contorting in pain, but I couldn't hear anything apart from a deafening roar. Grinda slammed against the wall, and blood burst from his head, but the seribdenum wall held, and he held on to his laser. After a few seconds, the rush of air stopped, replaced by an intense throbbing in my head and lungs while my vision turned red. I could see Stone through the MCS flight-deck window, gesturing for me to get to the vehicle but, totally winded, I felt on the very brink of blackout. I drunkenly stood and lurched towards the front hatch, now opening, while flashes of white light burst around me. I saw the other conscious grunt trying to drag the unconscious one to the hatch, and as I reached them, I grabbed hold of the other limp arm. With my vision almost gone and on the verge of passing outs from lack of oxygen, I forced my eyes open to look for Grinda and gestured for him to follow. One of his eyes had become a bloody pit while the other fixed in mad fury at the IM whom he blasted to pieces with the laser. Two of them had taken aim at us and had been about to fire before trying to exit through the doorway behind them, something that would probably be impossible without releasing all the air behind it as well. When I finally half dragged, half pushed the grunt into the MCS and the hatch closed behind all three of us, I could see nothing at all. My last sight of Grinda had been of him walking unsteadily through the open door in pursuit of the IM survivors. He disappeared into the black space behind the door, a place which offered no hope of salvation.

Again, I left the report as it was, shook my head and continued reading what I had actually written next.

Opening the door to the lobby I found Major Grinda defending the rest of our squad who were boarding the MCS. Major Stone had driven this into the complex, providing us with the only possible means of escape. The last time I saw Grinda, he was pursuing the remaining IM, after already killing perhaps fifteen of them, to give us a better chance of escape. I am recommending him for the Knights Cross of the Iron Cross for outstanding bravery and self-sacrifice in the face of overwhelming odds. While had I passed out, for perhaps ten minutes, one of the crew administered emergency first aid to me. During that time, Stone had reversed the vehicle and, when I came to, I could feel the MCS, climbing steeply and vibrating violently. I asked what was happening, because I couldn't see and demanded to be taken to Stone. He assured me the pods were covering us and that we would manage the forty-degree slope that the MCS now grinded up, bit by bit.

Actually, while Stone hunched over the controls of the vehicle, forcing it almost by will alone, inch by inch, up the slipping scree which rattled around the churning tracks, the rest of us were either praying or swearing at Ganymede's ice and our misfortune. We could do nothing to help. I must admit it, looked bad at this point, and I remembered what Stone had said about the diesels. If they were so underpowered, surely, we wouldn't make it.

"Fuck!" screamed Lehmkuhl. "To go through all that and die now. No! We gotta make it. Please God!"

"Oh God be merciful on all of us," muttered another man, Drozier, with his hands pressed together in abject supplication.

My vision in one eye partially returned, but everything became red and blurred. I stared in turn up at the ceiling and then at the tumbling scree through the window. The noise and vibration of the tracks on the slipping rock and incoming laser-fire tearing at hot metal were deafening; it felt like we were in a giant meat-grinder. I held on to the back of Stone's seat and willed the tired engines to keep going just a little longer.

Come on! Come on! You can do it.

Sweat poured off Stone's face as he shouted instructions to his co-pilot next to him and swung the wheel this way and that, searching for the tiniest bit of grip. All the while, laser-fire glanced off of the armour of the MCS with resounding clangs while missile strikes churned up the Sulphur either side. Then something at the rear of the MCS did explode.

Missile strike.

We occasionally caught glimpses of the PODs on our flank; they were trying to defend us, but they weren't doing too well either.

Finally, the tracks caught on something more solid. There came a moment of what seemed like profound silence while we danced on the edge of eternity, and then the MCS lurched forward and upwards. A few moments later, we drove over the lip of the crater and were safe. We all whooped and hollered.

"You fuckin,' crazy, talented bastard, Stone! Yes!" I slapped him on the shoulders. When we came to a halt at the extraction point, a few, small fires broke out inside, from the overheating water-cooled engines, which were on the point of seizing. They would probably never run again. We sat there, defenseless but for the two pods which had also made it.

I read the rest of the report.

> As I learned later, at the beginning of our
> interdict the MCS reactors had apparently
> been taken out by IM fire when they exited
> the complex via a hidden tunnel and bypassed
> the pods. They continued to harass the

stricken vehicle intermittently for the next
fourteen hours while Stone attempted to repair
it. Using diesel power alone, he finally
managed to make it to a vantage point directly
above the slope, where he halted to consider
his next move. After two hours, and shortly
before initiating an attack, he saw bursts of
white light from the lobby, followed by the
exit onto the surface of Corporal Lehmkuhl
followed by Corporal Drozier, some minutes
later. Corporal Lehmkuhl, seeing the MCS
and guessing he had been seen, gestured for
the MCS to approach, whereupon Stone drove
down the slope at 5 mph, the maximum speed
of the current MCS model plus some. With no
time to waste, Lehmkuhl indicated to Stone
that the MCS should impact the lobby, which
Stone accomplished, thus saving the lives of
the rest of the survivors. We then reversed,
turned and headed back up the slope, reaching
perhaps half-way up the slope, before the
loosened ice and grit caused the vehicle to
lose traction. I didn't believe we would make
it. It is only due to Stone's considerable
experience as an MCS driver, combined with
outstanding natural ability that we finally
reached the ridge and made it back to the
extraction point with the two surviving pods.
The MCS had sustained a lot of damage.
Finally, only the flight-deck remained
habitable. We had no chance of take-off, so
we sent out an emergency distress signal on
the USAC safe channel. USAC picked this
up, and a shuttle reached us in twelve hours,
just before the limited air in the cabin ran out.
The disk retrieved is probably high value,
because it contains what appears to be

> incomplete constructional drawings of some
> very large mechanical device with captions
> and instructions in an unknown, and so far,
> undecipherable, code. One Corporal,
> Lancotte, did not survive, although he still
> lived when we boarded the MCS.
> Conclusion of report. 12 July 2101

It sounded a bit 'Raymond Chandler' detective novel to me, like my own novel.

What the hell. I am only going to be in this game a little longer.

Apart from the details of Grinda's sacrifice, the fact that I had spent almost a week in hospital having my irises and corneas rebuilt and something Stone told me later, I had omitted nothing of significance. I made a couple of corrections and then pressed 'upload' on the keypad section of the plastic. The plastic connected to the terminal and the report appeared on screen. I called, "Email: General Owen. Subject: report," and it sent. I preferred writing on plastic, a skill few possessed these days, but I found that my thoughts flowed better. Only then did I notice the sound of Katie humming behind me. I went and sat on the bed where I could face the wall. "Project: wall. Fill wall." A holographic image of Katie in her cabin filled the space between the wall and I.

"Hey," Katie said.

"Hey."

"Finished?"

"Yeah."

"Let's have a jam!"

"What now? I'm tired."

"Oh, you're always saying that." She leaned over, picked up an old acoustic guitar and leaned against the wall. Perching the guitar on her crossed legs, she started to tune it.

"I don't have anything to play!" I protested

"Well, make something."

"Out of what?"

She seemed distracted by the guitar and mumbled, "Use your n-gen."

"Hey. I know it's not my old one; with that, it really would be impossible. But I don't think even this one can manage to make an instrument."

"Yeah it can. Just make a penny-whistle."

"Listen. This thing makes food and basic utensils and … good drinks but not musical instruments. We army grunts don't earn the money you guys get, and our stuff is the cheapest around."

She put down the guitar. "I thought of that. I will send you the program for a penny-whistle. I downloaded it just for you. Wait."

After a few moments, I heard her say, "Email: Jake. No subject. Check your email."

I downloaded the program to the n-gen, something I hadn't done in years, and waited for the few minutes it would take it to manufacture a penny-whistle. The n-gen 'dinged,' and I took out the whistle. I looked at it suspiciously. "I can't even play one!"

"Instructions in email," she said, continuing to focus her attention on the guitar. She started to pick up the rhythm and structure of her song.

"I need another drink or something stronger. Wait." I made another double-vodka and swigged about half of it while printing out the diagram of fingering for the whistle. I put my fingers dutifully in the right place and blew until I had become red in the face. "Nothing!" I gasped.

"Oh, you're useless. Come *on* Jake!"

I peered down the end of the whistle and saw that a thin membrane of white plastic blocked it the end. The n-gen had misread the plans or forgotten to hollow out the end. "Look! Ha! Ha!" I held up the blocked whistle to the screen, and Katie put her hand over her mouth:

"Oh my God! Ha! Ha! How useless is that! What sort of crap do they give *you*? You should throw that old machine out Jake."

"It's new! Ha! Ha!"

She replied with a bigger guffaw.

"Wait. I can fix it." I went to my uniform, took out the old-fashioned army-knife I kept in the pocket and proceeded to hollow out the end of the whistle. "Okay. Let's try." A beautiful clear note came out this time.

"Yeah!" she shouted, laughing and clapping her hands. "Okay. It's in G, so just play G, E and E in any combination, and you should be okay."

She started strumming the basic structure of the tune at quite a fast pace, moving from G Major to A Minor, D Major, back to A Minor and back to G Major again and so on. It would be quite a good rhythm to drive to and, with my random whistling, it sounded quite good. I wasn't that musical, but I could pick up a tune and keep reasonable time. Then she started to sing the verse; a couple of beats on high G and then high G, E and D.

Feeling old,
Feeling cold now.
Feeling sold,
Can't get hold now.

Of anything that matters … .
Of a time that matters … .
Everything is shattered … .
Everything is battered.

She shouted over the music, "I don't have a second verse yet, but we can work on it," and we kept playing what we had. Katie's music often seemed introspective, and sometimes the words sounded gloomy on their own, but with the music, I found it really uplifting. I really enjoying getting right into the music. I tried a few experimental notes which failed miserably and I looked sheepishly at the screen to see her gritting her teeth which just made me laugh.

Eventually, we had played enough and both wound down to some kind of a stop, laughing at each other and the fun we'd had playing together. I rolled back on the bed. "Katie. That was great! I haven't had so much fun in ages. It's a great song. It has to be a hit!"

"Ah! I'm exhausted! Any ideas for a second verse?"

"Nah! You know I'm no good at song lyrics. I want another drink."

"Oh, I have such good fun with you Jake. Why can't we be together, always?"

"We will be."

"Ah! I feel good. Now I think sleep might be quite good too. But not before a bed-time story."

"Bed-time story?" I said returning to the bed with another glass of vodka.

"Tell me about Earth Jake; that time you visited your grandma. I want to hear it again."

I called out, "Lights: low," and lay down on the bed. "Well, Barstow, where they lived, is really not that nice. It's right on the edge of the desert, and they had a kind of one-floor shack with a dusty yard and a black and white dog, which ran around a pole on a rope, barking at the flat-beds driving by. Hardly any trees or birds and just the odd coyote howling in the night. But the sky is big and blue. So big it just stretches almost like space with these tufty clouds drifting over, lonely as ghosts. Anyway, one day they took us for a drive up into the mountains. We went through Bakersfield, and that has more trees, you know, like fir trees, and the air is a little cooler. In Barstow it's really hot. I mean hot! Not like we ever experience on J stations or on ships. I mean you can't stop sweating even when you are sitting still."

"Yeah. So, Bakersfield and the mountains?"

"Yeah. So then we drove up into the mountain, and we drove all day until we came to the Sequoia National Park."

"What does Sequoia mean?"

"I don't know. I think it might be the Indian name for redwoods, which are the really tall trees."

"And they are like fir trees, yes? Like really big Christmas trees?"

"Much, much bigger! They can be over three-hundred feet high. It is so *green* there, you just can't believe it! It's like a really powerful drug-trip where green is redefined for you. It's just greener than green and more greens within each green if you know what I mean. It's nice and cool in the shade too and sometimes you see wolves, if you are really lucky. Not that we saw any, though."

"Did you see any eagles?" she asked sleepily.

"Well, I don't know … . We saw something *like* an eagle, soaring *way* above us, but it might just have been a buzzard. Anyway, then they took us to this tree, and I tell you, it would take about thirty people with their arms fully stretched to link arms around it. It has a name too, but I can't remember it now. Imagine that! A tree with a name. Like 'Old Smokey' or something. Ha! Ha! And you know these trees are like thousands of years old. Thousands! Not hundreds. They were there when the Romans were in Europe! How about that?" I glanced at Katie, but she seemed to be asleep. "It's really beautiful," I muttered. I felt tired myself and didn't feel like moving. I had that pleasantly warm glow from just the right amount of vodka.

I woke up, stiff from leaning against the wall behind my bed and slightly cold. I glanced at the clock. It was six in the morning, and Katie had broken the vid-link.

***

Chapter Five

I woke up in a sweat. I had been dreaming of a picnic with my mother on J5 when I had been sixteen. The images were so clear that it brought the emotions back as well. I had just joined the family and already suspected that I was a replicant, but after scoring my first ten runs in a game of cricket, I heard my mother call out something strange:

"Jake! You are such a talented cyborg!"

Even at my tender age, I knew a replicant wasn't the same thing as a cyborg, and I knew that she should know that, because her first husband had been a famous robot designer. Her words had always stuck in my head.

***

At the usual post-mission booze-up, Stone mentioned something to me which shed new light on the whole Roanald mystery. The party would be a short one, because there were so many dead spirits to drink to. Stone already rocked on his heels when I arrived at the bar.

"Here's to many dead souls," I said raising my beer to the departed.

"Bunny Grinda will be a *legend* soon, ya know that!" shouted Stone, before laughing idiotically, as drunks often do.

"Yeah!" rang out the chorus from the other survivors.

"A *real* legend! You know, Cap, there is something I been meaning to tell ya," Stone said conspiratorially. He leaned close to me, so that the others couldn't hear.

"Yeah? What's that Stone?"

"I heard something on the MCS, on the way to Ganymede that maybe you should know. At first, I thought it as a joke, but now I know, sorry, *knew* Grinda better, I think it may mean something."

"Okay. Tell."

"Well. Ya see one of the grunts, think it was DeTunne, dead now rest his soul, was saying Roanald was no good. He said that all he ever amounted to was a guy who had gone over to the IM. Course I am not saying I put DeTunne up to it, you understand what I am saying, but he may have got the wrong impression of Roanald from *me*! Ha! Ha! Anyway, I don't think Grinda knew I was listening, and he reeled off a list of stuff that ol' Roanald is supposed to have done, and one of them was mighty curious, if you ask me, um hm."

"Well?"

"He said that one time, Roanald was part of a negotiating team, negotiating for peace with the IM in some secret deal."

"Really? Go on."

"Well that's it!"

"Did he say when?"

"Nope!"

"Thanks Stone."

After the hangover had worn off the following evening, I settled at the terminal in my quarters to try to find out more about this peace negotiation. It must have been pretty secret, because I had never heard anything of it, and I could find nothing in Roanald's records about it.

I called Owens.

"Ah Nanden. Lucky again! Very interesting, that disk. We haven't worked it out yet, but we will do. Great job there. What's happened to the IM camp?"

"It's gone sir. We think they're still on Ganymede, somewhere, but perhaps underground. General Owens, I need to ask a favour."

"Well? Make it short Nanden."

"According to a source, Roanald was part of a peace negotiation with the IM. I can't find anything in, his records about it. As part of my investigation I really need to know everything you have on him."

"Hm. Give me five minutes Nanden. I'll call you."

He called back within three minutes. "Okay. Check his records now. You should have a new tab called 'special missions,' and under that you should find what you want. Gotta go. Out."

Sure enough, the new tab appeared after I had logged out and back in again. I found one mission listed there: Armistice Talks: IM 17-24 October 2098, a year before the blanker incident. I read the terse notes which told me little more, other than that the talks had taken place over Holo-link and that both USAC and IM ambassadors had been present, along with the Chairman of IM and the Director General of Io as well as Roanald and his opposite number in the IM, at the time, General Longe. Of course, the IM wasn't recognised legally by most countries, so the titles of Chairman and Ambassador were rather unofficial. The USAC were basically represented the United Nations on Io.

The brief report noted that the negotiations ended in stalemate, and no accord of any kind had been reached. After a further ceasefire of three weeks, which I remembered being one of the longer of many ceasefires over the last ten years, a violation by the IM restarted hostilities.

Well, well, well. I have never even heard of peace talks between the USAC and the IM. I wonder if there is a recording.

I checked Roanald's sessions for October 2098. I found none, perhaps, because the negotiators sat in a room and shared a vid-session. This would have used a 'black' link, an illegal and virtually untraceable link to the IM networks. I did see listed a personal link of Roanald's, a day after the negotiations ended, which had no IPZ number; the destination device address. This could be a black link, so I made a mental note to check it out later.

I found myself pouring another Vodka on the rocks and talking to Marcus. "What the hell is going on here? So many strands, and yet none of them connects! My head hurts." I put on some ambient music and rested my head on the edge of the bed, my tense neck muscles eased by the gentle pressure of the cool sheets. I closed my eyes and let the music wash over me.

10.00 pm had passed when I poured the drink, but I woke up at 4.13 am, the drink miraculously intact on the floor next to me. Shaking off the grogginess, I decided it wasn't worth trying to sleep before a meeting at six, so I paced the room, trying to get my brain working. I just needed a clue, any clue, as to what was going on here. I sat down at the terminal again and read the negotiation notes. Something, which hadn't interested me the first time, caught my attention again. On the second day, Roanald had been invited, along with the Director General of Io, to dinner with the IM Chairman, his wife and daughter. Unsure why, I looked for more information about the family. Chairman Ortega's wife was called Julia and his daughter, Andreya. I soon found photos of them. Andreya, about eighteen, I guessed, when the photo had been taken, was a beauty. She would have been twenty-one during the negotiations. Blonde, very tall, elegant, and with legs that went on forever, she would be impossible for Roanald to ignore at dinner. Moreover, his interest later in Courtesan Rouge might indicate an interest in classy, up-market women, I knew Chairman Ortega would be very rich and Andreya would have grown up pampered like a princess. Even though the IM were outlaws effectively, they had good trade contacts, particularly with Monrussia, both official and rebel sectors, and its close allies. In some ways the IM spearheaded the whole confederacy of outlaw countries and their black-market. As only-child of the premier family, Andreya would have had the best education and no lack of material wealth.

She might also be quite lonely.

I put in a not-too-hopeful request to Owens, via email, for access to the negotiation recording, if one had ever been made. Then I remembered the black link in Roanald's personal message log. I called the Comms Officer on duty and asked for the name of a tech who could tell me more about IPZ numbers. He gave me the name of Dickin but said he would be asleep for another thirty minutes. I considered calling Dickin anyway, but I didn't know what his duties would be that day. I went over the facts and clues I had so far, in my head, while I waited for the clock to tell me the right time.

"Dickin. It's Colonel Nanden here."

"Colonel! Yes sir!"

"It's okay. Relax. I just wanted to ask you a few technical questions."

"Sure. Fire away sir."

"IPZ numbers. What exactly is a black number, and how do I find one if it is missing from a log?"

"Well sir. What we call *black* numbers are numbers on the other side of router twenty-four. It's now sometimes called router X, but originally it was number twenty-four of twenty-eight. As you can probably appreciate, the network covered the whole of Io including what we now call IM territory. Of course, their network must be badly in need of replacing now, but it still works, for the most part."

"So how come they still have any connection at all to our network?"

"Well they don't, officially. All other connections between their part of the network, and ours were cut off years ago, but router twenty-four lay in an area that was heavily defended by them, and much of our own traffic went through it; probably why they fought so hard to keep it. Anyway, USAC put a lot of money into re-routing all the traffic so that, in theory, we didn't need it anymore, but for some reason they never cut it off completely. IM cannot send data-packets out, but we can send packets in, and as far as I know SCIA use it to infiltrate their network from time to time. That's what you hear anyway."

"Okay. And what about tracing a missing IPZ?"

"Well. I can't do that for you. I don't have access to that kind of information. You need to speak to a nerd at one of the civil data-centres. Probably one of the big ones in Anderstown would be your best bet."

"Thanks."

"No problem."

A shuttle-ride later, I was back in Anderstown, talking to the manager of one of the main data-centres. This time I kept my uniform on.

"We're always glad to help the military, Colonel Nanden. You need to meet Winston. Follow me." He led me down a long corridor and then through a door into a long room with a grated floor. Air cooling fans whirred deafeningly somewhere above and below us and a myriad of tiny red, yellow, green and, occasionally, orange lights winked at us in the semi-darkness. "Seen Winston, anybody?" the manager called to anybody that could hear him.

A voice came from behind a row of racks. "The Worm? Down the end, rack forty-seven boss!"

"Ha! Funny boys. They call him the worm. Don't take any notice of their jokes."

"Why 'The Worm'?"

"I dunno really, always been called that. I never asked. Ah! There he is. Winston! I'll leave you with him. Tell Winston to bring you out when you're finished."

"Thanks. Winston?"

"Yeah. That's me! Who wants to know?" a muffled voice said, from under the rack.

"My name's Colonel Nanden."

"Okay. With you in a minute. Just gotta get this new socket in."

"You still use sockets?"

"Sure. Modern stuff is all laser, laser-circuits, laser-optics and all the rest of it, but it's fragile. Everything in here belongs in a museum, some of it's on its last legs, and I have to buy it at trade-fairs, but it has one of the best up-times in the Solar System. Don't tell the boss, but we get mentions in 'RetroConnect' quite often. He wouldn't appreciate that sorta thing."

"Is that why they call you The Worm?" I asked when he straightened up, grinning and chewing gum. Bald as an egg, he looked about twenty-five had skin coloured a lucent white.

"S'cos I live down here. Never see the sunlight. Don't like it actually!"

"You're the man for me then, I reckon."

He laughed, slightly bronchially. "Why's that then? You don't seem like the normal military type. Haven't I seen your face somewhere?"

"Not down here. I need to know a lot about black numbers, and I need somebody who can get one, and tie it to a location."

"Oooh! That's difficult. Go on then. Try me!"

"Okay. I have the details of the connection time and I'm guessing this had been made to somewhere within the IM Director General's complex, but I don't have the IPZ number." I took out a piece of paper and read from it. "25 October 2098 21.47 from Colonel Roanald. IPZ number: 22323.63197,28964.99912."

"You realise what you are asking! *That* is like looking for a needle in a universe sized-haystack! I would have to check the log of every IPZ number, the black ones, mind you, in IM territory, which I might add, is highly illegal."

"Nothing is illegal if the USAC army authorizes it. That's the one good thing about being in the army."

"Hah! I bet it's not the only thing. Well I could write a program to trawl through; would take a long time, a *helluva* long time. Can't you, say, give me anything more local? A name? A room?"

"Hmm. Well, it's a guess, but try his daughter, Andreya. That help?"

"Well that makes it a big haystack. Still take a while, a few weeks at least."

"To write or run?"

"Both."

"Hmm. I can pay I guess. How much?"

"Well see it's like a hobby for me, it's not about the money. If you can get my boss off my back for as long as it takes, I will get it done. It will be fun. Unlimited time and resources, to do something nobody I know has done *before*! I'll get an article in 'Wire and Tap' for sure, and I will be set up for life!"

"Sorry. Has to be confidential, for now. Don't care what you do with the software after though."

"Ah! Deal then?"

"Sure. Let me speak to him. Can you lead me out of this dark maze?"

"Follow me."

"Thanks Winston," I said shaking his hand at the door.

"Call me Worm."

A few minutes later, the manager agreed to everything I had asked for.

I tried to turn my attention to other things for the first week of the wait. I finished off Lowell's 'Army Tutor to the Rank of Colonel' and read Hansegger's 'Dreams as the Road to Deeper Consciousness,' which I felt light and drew too much on Jung to really be called original. I had plenty of work to do, starting to reform K-Company and generally getting S.4 functioning the way I wanted it to. I also had a date with Diana Dalgleish.

Diana and I had dinner in a nice little restaurant on Ruwa Street in Anderstown and saw a movie after. She seemed to miss her family, who were on J1, especially her brothers. Too young for me to find anything much in myself that would interest her, I wondered if she might have been interested in me as a father-figure. But I didn't have time for that, so we consoled each other with a long night in a hotel, away from the prying eyes of J.4's crowd. She was beautiful, and I enjoyed our time together but found it empty and with the sad air of a lost time, as these things sometimes are. The whole thing could be summed up with one snatch of conversation in the restaurant:

"So what is she like?"

"Who?"

"Your girlfriend? You said you had one."

"Did I? Oh well it's a bit of a mess at the moment, and actually there are two, but my mind isn't focused on them right now." I lied but only partially.

"Oh? Well what is it focused on, or is that too impertinent for a grunt to ask of a Colonel?"

"Hah! No. It's complicated. Matters of lost identity and gropings in the dark."

"Really? I like the sound of the gropings, but really, I am too young to worry about identity yet. I am what you see."

***

After two weeks, I could resist it no longer, so I called Worm.

"Nope. Nothing yet. Maybe not far off though."

The waiting was killing me. Enormous stresses were building up in me; my stomach muscles constantly ached, and I couldn't sleep without a healthy dose of vodka inside me. I really wanted to apply for the Court-Martial of Enquine but knew I didn't yet have the kudos to carry it off. I tried composing my letter to Owens, but each time, I deleted it. I just couldn't find the words yet. At the same time, I couldn't seek support from the one person who had been like a rock for me over many years, Jena, because any conversation with her now came with strings attached. I felt increasingly angry, not with her, but that her demands had coincided with what I hoped would be the final stage of my army career. It just didn't seem fair that now, when I needed her the most, she was putting pressure on me to do something I couldn't yet do. And then another fear had emerged. One night, I had dared to wonder what I would do if I could leave the army. I couldn't think of anything, and that scared me. I had become defined, at least to myself, by my mission of justice. If I believed in myself at all, I did so, because I believed I could at least do this one thing.

Jena had once said to me, "Jake. You know people *believe* in you! I don't know why, but there is something about you. And yet the more I get to know you, the more I wonder why, and how, you don't believe in yourself."

It seemed that as long as I didn't stop too long to wonder what I *did* believe, kept swimming, I could keep going and give the impression to others that I knew what I was doing. Everything had come to a head, and I needed that information from Worm. Everything hung on that. On a day when I felt I could stand it no longer, he finally called.

"Good news boss!"

"At last! What have you got?"

"Yep. I can prove that the connection you gave me *was* to Andreya's terminal. Took a lot of doing. Do you want to see it?"

"See it?"

"Yeah. The holo-recording?"

"You mean it still exists?"

"Yep. Holo-casts date back to the days when we still kept backups of every file passed through the network for security reasons and holo-recordings were the last of these. They were streamed of course but so big that when the network was down, they would be buffered into large files and stored. I guess this was necessary 'cos they were so expensive."

"I definitely want to see it. Soon as possible. Can you send it to me somehow over the network?"

"Nope. Can't do that. It would never get through, modern connections just ain't up to it. Even if I compressed it into a file, it would be too big. Nothing can store that kind of size either. You'll have to come down here. I have hooked up an old holo-monitor to watch it. Should be fun."

I reached there within an hour.

"I guess you have already seen it?" I asked.

"Well yeah. Can't very well rebuild a file without that."

"No. Thought so. You may as well stay then. Not a word of what is on there to anybody though. Ever! You understand."

"Oh sure. I want to live a little bit longer. Not much on there to be honest."

We watched the two figures projected into the centre of the viewing room, the old projectors whirring noisily half way along each wall and the room getting hotter by the minute. I had forgotten the heat generated by holo-casts.

It was over in fifteen minutes. Roanald started off acting quite cautiously and politely, but their conversation became loaded with flirtation and ended with a bold kiss from Roanald. There could be no doubt that the two were embarking on a romantic liaison, which would have been extremely risky for both and had to have been kept as secret as such a thing possibly could. It had been all I had hoped for. I asked Worm to make me a vid-recording of the kiss and store the recording somewhere very safe.

"Thanks Worm. Hope you get your article in 'Wire and Tap.'"

My heart skipped beats like crazy on the shuttle back to S.4. Somehow, Roanald had managed to start up a romantic relationship with Andreya and had continued it with blankers. I could see no other way he could have done it. He could never have actually gone behind IM lines without being noticed, and Diana had said he was into blankers. With Holo-casts, one had no sense of tough, but with blankers one did. Maybe he *did* have something to do with those three blankers who went missing. I called

Paul Danette and asked if he could remember the date the three blankers went missing. He didn't know but called me back the next day. It was December, two months after the peace negotiations. It *had* to be Roanald.

***

As I thought about it more, I saw that there were several problems with my theory though. The IM had no blankers. Their ethical code, quite Protestant, forbade blankers, and they hadn't the resources anyway. On the other hand, it would have been impossible for Roanald to get one over there. I scratched my head, literally and metaphorically for days. I read again both volumes of Rudge, but they gave me no clues. The shortest gap between our lines and IM lines, three years before, had been about ninety miles at a point about twenty miles South of Anderstown. If you used some kind of transport, you would be picked up immediately on radar and taken in, either by police or USAC forces. To walk though, would be suicide. Even with a full tank of air and heavy protection against the radiation, you wouldn't get further than about twenty-five miles. Of course, Roanald could have made sure that the blanker wasn't picked up, but then that would put him at risk, and I didn't think he would do that. No, he must have worked through the guy that he had shot afterwards. I wondered if it would be possible with planted shelters and full tanks of air. But then the shelters would be picked up on radar. In the end I fell asleep that night with questions circulating restlessly in my head.

The next morning, as on every morning when we weren't involved in a mission, everybody who wasn't on the duty-roster did their two-hour workout in the gym which ended with two teams running in a relay. All the grunts feared letting their team down, because the punishment would be a day spent as a pariah. Girls competed equally with men and all competed fiercely when we reached the final few runners. My lap over, I noticed glances from Diana, which I tried to ignore, and then suddenly my eyes were fixed on the baton being passed to the last runner in her team. All morning I had not been able to stop puzzling-out the enigma of Roanald's blankers, but now, in a brightly-illuminated moment of clarity, I saw how it could be done.

As soon as I could, I studied a map of the Ionian terrain between the point 20 miles South of Anderstown and the IM lines. On a rough line from Anderstown to the nearest IM outpost, the ground rose gently to a ridge and then dipped into a large bowl feature, probably an extinct volcano crater. It then rose again to another ridge before descending to the IM outpost; walkable, and there would be cover from ground-radar while in the crater. It seemed a good spot to me. If Roanald had indeed done what I conjectured, it should definitely take its place in the Rudge book on replicant crimes, although technically, the replicants wouldn't have committed the crime.

Throughout the next few hours, I worked out the details, and I knew there could only be one way to prove it. I booked out a shuttle, filling in the purpose as 'Test,' and descended to Io's surface near the Anderstown edge of the crater, which lay about two-thirds of the way along the route the blankers would have had to take. During the descent, I went over the details in my head again.

Roanald hires some guy who then rents three blankers. Roanald supplies the guy with three suits and respirators with tanks for up to five hours air-time; the maximum available. The brilliant bit is this; the guy is paid to lie to the blankers telling each that there is shelter and air at the end of their twenty-five-mile trek and presumably a large cash donation. If the amount were big enough, they wouldn't ask questions about the exact purpose of the task but, for sure, each would be carrying a full air-pack himself and a large sealed container with a combination lock, the code of which would only be known to the guy organising it. In it, there would be another full tank of oxygen. The blankers would have to be wearing heavy duty, anti-radiation suits. These gave about another two to three hours protection over a normal combat-suit but were heavier. The first blanker would set out and run out of oxygen somewhere around the twenty-five-mile mark and then would be close to collapse. Normally, the correct drugs would allow the adrenalin of the host replicant to cut in when death becomes a threat, but the right kind of neural suppressant can stop this. If the will of the user drives the blanker on, it will keep going to the point of collapse. This whole process would have been repeated with the second blanker until he found the body, possibly tracked with SSGPS. The second blanker would also have a second, fresh tank in a container on his back, sealed with a code. The second, knowing the combination of the first lock, could replace the old oxygen tanks with the fresh ones and continue on, although he would be suffering from radiation exposure by this time. The second blanker would similarly expire with the container he carried, also containing a fresh tank of oxygen. Finally, the third blanker, traveling light with only one tank, would cover the whole fifty-miles in only five hours and would then shelter, possibly in a cave on the rim of the volcano. Finally, he would release the fresh tank from the second dead blanker and could continue on all the way to the IM lines, having not been exposed to radiation for more than five hours at a time.

If I was right, somewhere out there, near the ridge should be the body of a blanker.

I hadn't been able to tell anyone my destination. I didn't know if Shaw had been involved in the original crime or if perhaps he would still very loyal to Roanald for other reasons. Any other member of staff on S.4 could also have been involved. If any of them were, they would try and stop me. I didn't tell Stone, because everything I did from this point on would be for my own personal reasons. I might be ruining my own future in the army, but I didn't want to ruin his.

I stepped out of the airlock and onto Io's surface, wearing a red anti-radiation suit. Out of sight of Jupiter, my indicator patch showed 1800 REM. I smiled.

I guess that's why Roanald chose this spot.

With only the sound of my own breathing, I set off up the long slope towards the ridge, a few miles ahead of me. I looked for boot-prints. Io's rare atmosphere meant there was almost never anything you could call wind, although there were convection currents from heat variations. Any prints in the sulphurous crust lasted for many months, normally. I glanced up at the face of Ganymede, just disappearing over the ridge ahead of me. An intense loneliness settled over me, heightened by the fear that nobody would find me quickly if anything went wrong. My breath rasping in the tight, fabric-lined helmet, I struggled over boulders and up side-slopes to either side of the line I followed. I continued up a gully, looking for any prints in the Sulphur dust. Finally, I reached the top of the ridge and stared out over the vast crater before me. The southern slope on my right was shaded from the far Sun's light. If any cave for shelter existed, it would most likely be on this craggy rim. I cast around for a clue in the dust and the rock formations around me. Seeing nothing, I turned to my right and started off along the ridge. I checked my surface-time: almost two hours. After a fruitless search of half an hour, I turned back and repeated the search, this time to the north. Still I found nothing. I looked nervously down the slope, to the crater floor about two hundred yards below. Seeing a way down, I started cutting diagonally across the slope to the right and half way down, turned back and continued down in the opposite direction. Four hours surface-time had passed. I started to sweat profusely and feel nauseous. My vision blurred from time to time as I continued out into the disc of the crater floor.

"Damn! It must be here. There must be something!" my frustrated voice vibrated through my cheekbones. "Another five minutes."

Another five minutes became ten, and then I lost track of time. Jupiter's reflected light crept over the western rim of the crater, and its eerie light threw strange shadows across my face, distracting me. I heard myself laughing; I knew a combination of radiation and lack of clean oxygen as the re-breather struggled to cope, would affect me in this way. Suddenly, I remembered that I had forgotten something and thinking very hard, I remembered I had to check the time. Four hours and forty minutes! The upper limit for this suit would be five hours, and I wasn't using it in optimum conditions. I had to turn back. I turned and spotted a pattern in the dust at my feet. I laughed at myself.

It must be my own tracks.

But, looking closely I could see the tread pattern wasn't the same as my own. My heart leaped, and suddenly the heavy weariness and nausea left me. I looked back down the thread of tracks and saw that they had come from the slope of the crater only a few hundred yards north of the crag, which marked the spot where I had crossed the rim. I followed them using a gentle two-footed lope and continued up the slope. Everything had turned red, and I knew I would not stay conscious for much longer. At the top of the slope, gasping for air, I saw what I had been looking for. In a tumble of grey volcanic rock, a ragged hole marked the entrance to a shallow cave. Its base, hidden by a gentle slope, ran away from me but, as I approached the cave, I saw something red, half in and half out of the cave's shadow. My heart pounded as I reached down and pulled at the heel of the boot, dragging the body out of the cave. I turned it over and peered into the visor at the awful rictus of agony pasted on the dead man's face. My breathing stopped for a moment.

"Poor bastard!"

I peered up at Jupiter's awesome face in the surrounding blackness of space and smiled. A last glint of the Sun's rays hit the edge of my visor and pierced my eye, causing my brain to explode in a thousand painful thoughts of life and death. I gasped and then sighed. For a moment it looked as if, somehow, a pale sky really hung above Io, and I could have sworn I saw a face up there. I pressed the emergency transmit button. I had to try twice, clearing my throat and swallowing hard, before I could hear my voice clearly.

"Nanden to S.4 Nanden do S.4. Come in." An age of static passed before the reply came:

"S.4 here. Colonel? Are you okay?"

"Need assistance. Crater, twenty miles South of Anderstown. Two miles east of shuttle. On the rim. Ten minutes of air left."

"Roger. On our way."

***

Sitting up in bed didn't help the headache at all. In fact, it made it worse, but the doctor in Anderstown insisted I take some solids.

"I *did* it Stone! I found out and *proved* what Roanald was doing!"

"Yeah and nearly got yourself killed!"

"Did they recover the body?"

"Sure, but nobody seems to know what it's about. Shaw is quiet, but I don't think even he knows properly."

"Eat this please," a serious nurse said, holding a bowl of soup near my face. I tried to lift my arms but failed. I noted the tube hanging from a bandage around my left arm. The nurse tut-tutted.

"You army types are all the same," she scolded. "Get yourself into a mess and then expect others to pull you out."

Badly dehydrated and weakened from the radiation exposure, nevertheless, I could not stay in bed any longer than I had to and made sure Stone had me back in S.4's medical centre that night. In my mind, I was already composing my letter, indicting Enquine, to Owens.

***

Chapter Six

"Come on Jake. Let me dry you! Stop wriggling." I was wet from swimming, but I couldn't see my surroundings.

"Ha! Ha! Mum! Leave me alone," I said, laughing. She cuddled me close, and her arms felt as good as the wet towel felt against my freshly wet skin.

"I love you Jake."

"Me too mum."

She squeezed me even tighter.

But surely it was a false memory? I jerked awake and lay, watching the memory from a distance. It was the typical implanted memory of a replicant. I would have been about six; it had to be.

I stepped through the door into the hushed Court Room. A large room with an oak-paneled roof, it had been fitted out with soft blue chairs in neat rows, facing a dais. On it, judge and recorder sat with a chair for the witnesses. The USAC military emblem of the Eagle, arched over by two garlands of maple and backed by a giant maple leaf with both national coats of arms in front, had been hung from the wall behind the dais. All eyes swung to face me as I walked to the place indicated to me by my council.

Owens hadn't taken my request for General Court Martial too well.

"Nanden! This is outrageous! If not impertinent! If you weren't an even bigger hero now than you were a few days ago, I would have to turn you down. As it is you, put me in a difficult position." The paunchy General paced up and down in my office, looking all the more like an angry squirrel. "You haven't even worked with the man for seven years for chrissakes!" I kept quiet, hoping the storm would blow itself out. To my repeated silences, his final word was, "Okay. If that is what you want. I hope you know what you are doing." I saw a flicker of something in his eye, as if he knew something that he wasn't going to tell me.

The Roanald case had been closed before the Court Martial began. We had been able to prove, with more evidence from black links that Worm dug up later, that Roanald had continued his love-affair with Andreya right up until his death. In fact, he had been the one, through an intermediary, to hire the two blankers from Courtesan Rouge, thus implicating him in the Palace Murder attempt. So it seemed as if Roanald, whether through love for Andreya or blackmail, had become an agent for the IM.

After initial enquiries, the investigating officer for the Court Martial, Captain Reed, had asked for an Article 32 hearing which had led to a further twelve weeks of evidence gathering. I was extremely tense while I waited for the case to be dismissed, but it never was. I was most curious that Enquine had not asked to be tried by the judge alone. He had this right. Neither had he employed no civilian defense lawyer, also his right. In fact, as I glanced at him across the court, he looked almost serene, sitting with his arms crossed and occasionally glancing around the room as if with curiosity alone. His neat brown moustache made me despise him all the more. He wore it like a badge, proclaiming false valour or like a sticky-plaster, covering a gaping wound. His serenity astonished me all the more, because a verdict of 'Guilty' against the charge of 'Cowardice,' carried the maximum penalty of execution by firing squad.

I cranked my neck to look behind me, to where Roanald and Enquine's superior officer sat. They, like me, were there only as witnesses. Six military personal of mixed sex, rank and race would be the jury, and they fidgeted in two rows at the side of the witness plinth, chatting among themselves. General Court Martial had changed little in the past one hundred years apart from one aspect: with the trend of outsourcing more and more of USAC's armed forces functions to the private sector, psychological profiling included, the line had become blurred between civilian and military rights. Several Courts Martial had come about involving both military and civilian personnel. This had led to a revision of the court structure embodied in Amendment 19, October 20 2078, which allowed for inclusion of council for the key prosecution witness, who, in reality, often brought the Court Martial in the first place. This balanced up the court, rather like a civilian one, and helped the prosecution in cases where the civilian defense might be particularly skillful and experienced. My council, Captain Ning, sat next to me.

The judge, in full military regalia of a Major-General, lifting his hand, palm-out, turned to the presiding officer, and the voices hushed. "Have the jury all taken their oath?"

"Yes sir."

"Will the defendant please rise?" The Major-General had a sonorous tenor voice which belied his considerable girth, and he looked quite indulgently at Enquine.

This is not good.

"You are Colonel Gary Enquine, of 14th Regiment, currently stationed on Mars?"

"I am."

"Colonel, in a moment, the key witness statement, hm, or relevant part of it anyway as we don't all want to be here until Christmas, will be read to you, and then you will be questioned by the USAC Army prosecuting officer. At some point, your own defense attorney will be able to question the prosecution or even the key witness or any *other* witnesses, should he, or you, so desire. Is that all understood?"

"Yes sir. Very clear."

"You may sit down. Prosecution? You have the floor."

From my peripheral vision, I noticed movement above and glanced at the ceiling.

Mirrors!

Set into recessed panels within the natural-wood ceiling of the court, were four large mirrors. I couldn't imagine what logic had led somebody to put them there, but waves of vertigo passed over me. I stared hard at the floor and concentrated on the statement being read by the presiding officer.

"Colonel Enquine. The charge brought against you is one of cowardice, the maximum penalty for which is death. Specifically, on the occasion of 24 October, 2091, near Rikas Station on Io, while a Sergeant, you sent forward, then privates Nanden and Przeltski to reconnoitre an IM camp."

The next part of the indictment consisted a field-report which fitted exactly with events as I remembered them.

He went on, "Lieutenant Nanden further claims that Przeltski told him in sick-bay that night that he would seek a Court Martial for the then Sergeant Enquine. I am bound to point out that, although Private Przeltski's recovery had been hastened by early Cybo-technology in the form of artificial bones and muscle for his lower leg and Nanden's, similarly, by parts for his arm, this technology was in its infancy, and neither were fully recovered a week later when they were sent on another hazardous mission." The officer paused to take a sip of water, and I found myself swallowing hard, still trying to avoid looking up at the mirrors.

The statement continued with a mention that both Przeltski and I thought it to be a 'suicide' mission and a brief mention of what recourses we both thought each side had at the time.

He went on, "Both men were told to attack a laser position, which they had been briefed would be held by only five IM raw recruits, but, in fact, it had been manned by twenty-five of the best armed IM USAC forces had, to that point, encountered. Colonel Nanden escaped with his life, but Private Przeltski had been killed."

The presiding officer then questioned me first, simply to clarify my views on some points of the indictment. I also clarified that, in my opinion, Enquine was a coward. Nothing unusual occurred until the presiding officer pointed out to me that Enquine claimed that there were reported to be only five IM in the enemy position, and he had proof.

The presiding officer picked up a sheet of plastic and passed it to the first jury officer. They passed it among themselves and then passed it to me. I read the short extract from a radio log: "20:18, Incoming. Intel reports laser gun position at IM sector 8 only defended by five new recruits until 22:50." I felt a cold drop of something rolling down the back of my throat and swallowed. I didn't want to show it, but I felt confused.

I resisted the impulse to show my confusion and stated:

"It could be falsified or Enquine could have known it was inaccurate."

"Colonel Enquine," he corrected. I nodded. The presiding officer read the log out loud to the audience.

"That is all for now Lieutenant Colonel Nanden."

Damn. He made me look a fool.

My Council, Captain Ning gripped my arm. "Don't worry. It's not really that impressive."

I glanced over at Enquine. He still looked serene. For the first time since the begining of the Court Martial, I turned to look at Owen. He stared ahead stony-faced, as did the General next to him, Enquine's superior.

"The Prosecution has no further questions at this point. Would the witness council like to ask any?" asked the judge.

"Yes, sir." Ning stood up and followed Enquine to the chair. I couldn't help but feel a sense of victory, seeing him sitting there under the glare of a hundred eyes.

Ning started to question Enquine thoroughly but, at first, he made little headway against the calm man in front of him. They covered the fact that there existed no record of the radio traffic, because at the time it wasn't technically possible to record all radio messages in the field.

The sickening feeling of vertigo from the mirrors had been increasing, and my mind became filled with a tumult of thoughts and voices which mostly seemed disconnected and random. One voice pushing most strongly to the front; that of my mother speaking to me on that picnic so many years ago. "Jake! You are such a talented cyborg!" The words went round and round my head, like a backing soundtrack to the court case.

Ning tried the subject of Przeltski's intended indictment:

"Were you aware that Private Przeltski wanted to indict you?"

After a long pause, while he seemed to be weighing some odds, Enquine answered, "Yes."

"Did it bother you?"

"Of course. Yes." For the first time, Enquine sounded angry, irritated even.

"And yet, rather than address the issue, get both men, or even just Przeltski in for a talk, you decided to send them both on a suicide mission when neither man was fully recovered from their injuries?"

"Ye-es." He sounded uncertain of himself and Ning went in hard.

"How many fit men did you have available on that day, the second mission?"

"I don't know. Five, ten?"

"*Really?* Take a look at this." He handed the jury another piece of plastic which they read and then passed on to Enquine. He started to read it to himself. When he had finished, he lowered it to his knee and sat, impassive.

"May I?" Ning said, taking the sheet. He read it to the audience. "31 October. Sergeant Enquine's Section. Active roster: 17 men."

A hushed silence fell over the audience.

"So, including yourself, there were sixteen other men who were fitter than those two, who could have gone on the mission?"

"It seems so."

"And yet you chose those? Why?"

"They were the best I had." He sounded emphatic and confident.

"But only two? Against five? And two injured? One of them clearly shaken by his previous experience?" It was oh-so-clever of Ning to add that last sentence. It reminded the audience of Przeltski's accusation and at the same time pointed to Enquine's lack of experience at the time. It almost begged Enquine to plead incompetence. I could have clapped my hand at this point. "No further questions sir," Ning said, walking away from the plinth. Enquine sat, stunned for a minute, before getting up and returning to his bench. A continuous murmur came from the audience.

Suddenly, Enquine's council jumped up and called to the judge, "The Defense Council wishes to quote Article B, clause 17 and call for the case to be dismissed."

I glanced at Enquine, but he looked as confused as I was. I asked Ning what Article B, clause 17 was.

"Something about competence I think. I'll have to look it up."

"Court to take one hour's recess," called the judge. I followed Ning towards the door. Glancing back, I saw Enquine arguing with his council.

Out in the corridor, I queued at the n-gen machine, useful during sudden recesses like this. Ning had gone to study clause 17, and I heard Owens' voice behind me:

"Word with you in a moment Nanden?"

I looked at the selection of drinks when I reached the machine and chose orange-juice rather than coffee; I didn't feel that my head could take caffeine. I sipped from the cup while Owens talked.

"You look pale Nanden. Are you alright?" I nodded. "Well, listen you don't have a hope of winning this, I can tell you right now. For the sake of your career, why don't you just call the whole thing off?"

"I can't do that General Owens."

When we filed back into court, I couldn't see Ning. I sat down next to his empty seat and returned the judge's enquiring look with a stare. Just as he called for order, the door opened, and Ning came in. I leaned close to him to hear what he to say.

"It's not good. I have been trying to find a case that set some kind of precedent which we could use, but I couldn't find one."

The judge spoke. "The council for the defense has pointed out that Article B, clause 17 says, and I quote, that the 'key witness for the prosecution must be a human of proven competence, in particular with reference to the substance of the charges being brought.' The defense maintains that, because the witness in this case is, eh-hmm, a replicant, that he does not meet the criteria in the definition. They further cite Munser v. Davis in 2097, a case which dismissed with the same justification. Does the council for the witness have anything to add?"

Ning stood up. "Not at this point, General."

"Wait!" It was Enquine, looking very agitated, who cut through the rippling murmur. A silence that could be cut with a knife settled in the court. "I can't allow this. I have something to say." Suddenly the little voice inside my head grew louder, repeating my mother's words. But this time, an image accompanied it; I could see her face clearly. Like never before, I could remember exactly what had happened, and I could see an enigmatic smile on her face after she had spoken. It seemed as if she intended there to be a puzzle in her choice of words. I felt a great tide of emotion building up in me, and the seat underneath me seemed to fall away.

"I … I cannot use this defense," Enquine said. "My council has tried many times to use it, but I know something, which means I cannot use it. Lieutenant Colonel Nanden is *not* a replicant." I nearly fell from the bench, feeling the floor rushing up to meet me. A roar from the crowd added to my dizziness. "How do I know this? I grew up with Jake Nanden on J5. He won't remember, because his memory was wiped after a near-fatal accident. Since we both joined the Army, I have been watching out for Jake. That is all I am prepared to say at this point, but Major General Teigh can confirm this."

Through gritted teeth, I heard the judge say, "Court adjourned until tomorrow. I want General Teigh on vid-link in court at 10 am tomorrow. Somebody assist Colonel Nanden please."

I couldn't sleep. After a taxi took me back to my hotel, I ordered a bottle of vodka from room-service, drained half of it and lay on the bed, hoping that sleep would come. It didn't. I used the room pay-com unit to send a message to Jena.

"Record: message to Jena Ω. Hi Jena. Just been in Court Martial. Need to talk if you have time. Jake x."

As I sent it, Ning called:

"How are you?"

"Oh, you know; not too bad."

"Do you want me to come round?"

"No. It's okay. I really need time to get my head around what just happened. I'm not sure I understand why he basically withdrew his best defense."

"No. On the face of it, it doesn't seem to make much sense. See you in court tomorrow then Colonel Nanden?"

"Yes. Goodnight Ning. And thanks. You did a great job."

"No problem." He hung up. I lay on the bed for an hour and then sent a message to Katie, similar to the one to Jena. Finally, at 3 am Mars time, I sent one to my mother. I knew it must be mid-morning on J5, and although she would be paged, she wasn't one for gadgets like headbands, so if she was on the move, I wouldn't get a reply. I didn't.

When you really need someone to talk to, there's no-one there.

I finished the vodka and tried to focus on what Enquine had said, but it hurt my head to think about it. It felt less painful to watch the digital time pass, so I did, until dawn. Then I must have drifted off, because I woke at 7 am with my head pounding, not from the vodka but from lack of sleep, coupled with incoherent thoughts. I took a long shower and ordered breakfast in my room.

Entering the court at 9 am, all eyes watched me walk to the bench and sit down beside a red-eyed Ning.

"What's been happening?" I asked.

"I don't know exactly. I heard they have located the General, and he *is* going to testify. My guess is that you better seriously think if you want to continue. If they do have proof of what Enquine says … ."

"Court in session," the judge declared. A hush settled while we awaited his next announcement. "Open the link please," he asked the presiding officer. A large blue rectangle on the wall behind the judge suddenly turned white with the ashen face of a General near the age of retirement. With grey-hair and watery blue eyes, he peered down at us melancholically. He moved his lips, and a second later we heard his words:

"I can hear you and see you. Can you see me?"

"Yes, General Teigh," answered the judge.

The defense council stepped forward and addressed the slightly out-of-focus image on the wall. "Major General Teigh, am I correct in assuming that you have been familiarised with this Court Martial?"

"Yes. I already was actually."

"Oh? Why is that?"

"Because I have a particular interest in one of the participants, two in fact. *I* have followed Colonel Enquine's career *too*, with interest."

"And *who* is the other person you have been following?" The face on the screen didn't move a muscle; as if carved in stone, it stared passively ahead. Then the fleshy lips parted, and the words came forth:

"You are wanting to know what I know about Jake Nanden."

"Yes."

"I swore to his mother Mary that I would never utter a word about this unless it became strictly necessary, to save his life. But I find myself in the situation whereby I must do this to save somebody else's life; that of Colonel Enquine. I hope you will forgive me Mary. Roughly twelve years ago, Mary came to me and asked me for a favour. I had known her first husband, Douglas Nanden, personally and since his death, which, for the record, I still believe has not been investigated fully enough, I had taken an interest in her and her family. She told me that she needed a great favour from me and that it involved something very questionable, legally, and so she would only tell me what I *needed* to know. I agreed to help, and she told me that her son Jake had been involved in a near-fatal accident and lay in a coma. As some in your court may know, Mary was once Douglas Nanden's chief assistant, and there is not much she didn't know then about robotics and also cybernetics. She was also in at the beginning, developing android systems, and was one of those prosecuted for working on ways to transplant human brains into android, erm 'bodies' if you will." The limpid eyes widened slightly and great brows above them lifted in sudden animation when he mentioned the experiments. "Of course, Douglas Nanden was hounded for years after and, well, I am sure most people know what the general opinion is about his death. The experiments may have been unethical, but he *did* stop them, and is it right to hound a man to death for trying something he believes is for man's benefit? The replicant used would be the one-in-a-thousand which was either brain-dead or severely mentally damaged anyway. But I digress. Mary told me that Jake's body had been given significant replacement parts and that he no longer looked exactly like the little Jake I had once known. She asked if I could find a way to give Jake a place in the Army, in the replicant company, which in those days was just forming." The great head became still again for over a minute and the audience fidgeted. "That's all I can tell you. I did what she asked, and I have kept silent ever since. The only other thing I can add is that Gary Enquine *was* indeed a childhood friend of Jake's and volunteered in order to 'protect' Jake. I guess you could say I pulled a few strings to get Gary into the replicant company, but that is all. After that I played no part in his career. As far as I can tell, Gary has indeed kept an eye on Jake. And Jake?" He looked directly at me, smiling kindly. "You need to let what happened that day, go. That Polish private had his own battles to fight, but they are not yours. That is all I have to say."

The courtroom broke into uproar. People shouted across the room and Owens jumped to his feet and bellowed at the General next to him that he had known nothing. I stared at the face on the screen and tried to pierce those old, blue eyes. Could it be true? Could it really be true? Only one person could convince me. The judge rose to his feet, lowering his arms theatrically to quieten the court. Finally, I heard only an intensely restless silence, like a room of silent bees.

"Can this be proved General?" he said turning to the screen behind him.

"I have no doubt it could. You will find no record of a replicant sold to the Nanden family; in that year or any other year."

"That is not *proof*. One could have been bought on the black-market," replied the judge.

"DNA," somebody said. Everybody looked at me. I realised they were waiting for me to speak, so I cleared my throat. "DNA. You could test for it: if it matches my mother, then I am Jake Nanden and not a replicant, at least not a complete one." I smiled ruefully.

"So let's get this straight," the judge said. "You are saying, General Teigh, that Jake Nanden, the Jake Nanden in front of us, is a replicant's body with the brain of a human?"

"And face, I believe," added the General. "Brain and face. And possibly some other parts. I'm not sure."

The judge spluttered, "But that *is* highly illegal. It would make Jake Nanden the first of his kind. I thought it was impossible. The rejection?"

"Can be overcome," Teigh replied. "If the correct replicant is used; one which has been engineered *not* to reject human tissue."

"And how do you know this? I thought you said Mary Nanden hadn't told you about the procedure?"

"I was interested and researched it years later."

"You knew about this then. That makes you an accessory, were this ever to be investigated."

The General nodded slowly. "I know that."

"Very well then. Subject to the results of a DNA test on the relevant parts of your body Jake Nanden, and I mean the *real* Jake Nanden, do you still wish to pursue this Court Martial?"

"I don't know. I'm not sure." I looked at Gary Enquine, who smiled back. His council stood up.

"We have evidence to support my client's claim. May we submit it to the court?" He held up a photograph and passed it, first to the jury and then to the judge and finally to me. I looked at a photo of two boys on hoverbikes on J5. One looked like a young version of Gary Enquine, and the other looked a lot like me. We both looked about fifteen or sixteen. Both of our faces had wide grins spread across them as we stood with one foot on the ground and the other on the foot-board of the bikes.

"Is this genuine?" I said, facing Gary Enquine.

"Test it," he said.

"If it is genuine and the DNA proves what General Teigh is saying … ."

"You wish to suspend it?"

I glanced up at the mirror overhead and saw the other Jake, looking down, like a circus acrobat watching the ground, looking for somewhere to land.

"Yes."

"Very well. This Court Martial is suspended until we have results of both the analysis of the photograph for authenticity and the DNA results." The judge stood and left the room, which exploded into a chaotic cacophony of shocked voices.

"Come on. Let's get you out of here!" shouted Ning over the noise. I followed him out like a lost dog, and he called a taxi to take me to the hotel. We hadn't expected the crowd of news-reporters, which had gathered outside. A thousand photo-lasers hit my face, blinding me as Ning pulled me into the taxi.

"What's going on?" I mumbled.

"Don't you know? This is big news. It will be all over the papers tomorrow, from here to Earth."

He left me, after one drink in my room. No doubt he too had seen the flashing light on the com, indicating an incoming message. Even before the door had closed, I said, "Download," and the message appeared in front of my eyes. Contact: Mary "Jake. Sorry I was out. I am standing ready by my com. Mum x."

"Call Mary," I said and listened nervously to the bleeps before she picked up.

"Hi Jake," Her voice sounded thin and fragile.

"Hi Mum."

"It's all over the news Jake. I wish you had told me."

"So is it true?"

I could hear the sound of weeping at the other end of the line, and finally, in a little voice, she said, "Yes … . I am sorry Jake. It was all we could do to protect you. Will you forgive me?"

I stared out of the window to a point where the Sun's orb reflected off of the seribdenum dome above the city. While true that now, for the first time in my life, the life that I could remember, I could see a light at the end of a tunnel which I hadn't even fully acknowledged, with that hope came the fear of losing it. "I can forgive you, but I don't understand why you never told me, even years later."

"I wanted to, oh I wanted to, but it was too much of a risk. Even now there will be those that don't like it. You are in danger still Jake."

"Oh, come on. It was such a long time ago. I don't really think anything bad will happen to me now. Do you?"

"I don't know Jake. You should be careful. When am I going to see you? Will you come home soon?"

"Yes. Very soon."

"Then we can talk about all this. Will you be okay?"

"Yes Mum. I feel fine."

We talked for hours about lots of things, memories and ideas, beliefs and people, before finally I felt calm, and I sensed her fraught, nervy mood being replaced by weariness.

"Well I guess it's time to sleep … for now. Good bye mum." I had never said, "Love you," when parting with her before, but I felt like saying that now.

"Yes. Take care darling. Bye!" She sounded so lonely and fragile, almost childlike, that it made me feel guilty. I wanted to put my arms around her. I stood there for some time after disconnecting, before moving.

***

The Court briefly convened one week later. The results proved that the photograph had not been tampered with and that my DNA matched that of my mother. I confirmed, through my council, that I withdrew the charge and the judge made his concluding speech:

"Furthermore, it is the recommendation of this court that Lieutenant Colonel Nanden and Colonel Enquine serve in a duel-command on some challenging mission, to be decided by both their superior officers. This will allow them to reconcile their differences in battle."

***

Chapter Seven

Then the high voice said to the little voice:
"Can't you see the threat? It's coming."

I felt the sulphurous gravel crunch under my feet.

Somebody should invent a chum inhaler that works in these suits. I could do with one now! Maybe that's something I could use to build a business when I leave the army.

A small cloud of dust rose from Enquine's boots. The dust caught the faint sunlight at dusk, making it seem to glow.

"Careful," I said, pointing at the dust. He grinned through his visor.

"How the hell are we supposed to get in there?" Stone asked. "Are we supposed to *tunnel*?" He looked pissed off.

"No Frank. We are supposed to die!" I quipped, but Stone missed the old movie reference. "At least I think that is what *I* am supposed to do. Why did you come anyway? You stupidly volunteered for a suicide mission. Now I have to worry about you too. Why didn't you think of Martha for a change?"

The IM factory, if that's what it was, formed a black silhouette now on the plain below the ridge, but in daylight the tower had shone like a white sentinel, broad black slots near its wide top. Stone backed down the slope and stood up.

"We go in by truck," Enquine said. "Soon." He scanned the length of the track to our right, which disappeared behind the ridge and re-emerged to run straight up to the tower. Nothing moved.

***

Just before leaving my quarters, I had sent my resignation email to Owens.

I guessed that both Owens' and Enquine's Generals had both had their noses put out of join by the whole Court Martial episode, because the mission they chose was not just a challenge but very, very dangerous.

The briefing for the mission on Io had been tense:

As I entered the darkened briefing room, I saw Enquine sitting down in the right-hand of two seats facing the screen and Owens facing us. I took the chair to the left, scraping its legs noisily on the floor to draw it further away from Enquine's. We had a saying in the USAC Army: 'On the Field.' In other words, only what they did on the field of battle counted about a man, or woman. With the court-room behind us, I still saw Enquine as a coward, but now we would see.

Suddenly the screen lit up and, in the centre, I saw the 'clover-leaf' logo, like that on the IM lasers.

"According to our sources, the IM are building those clever little power-packs for the weapons *here*!" Owens snapped on a laser pointer and shone it at a cross in the middle of a desert region. "As you can see, it's about as deep inside IM territory as you can get and we cannot get anything near to photograph it. We do have this though. Next frame."

Up came a grainy photo of the tower, taken from a position similar to ours on the ridge now.

"We know trucks go in here several times each day, mostly with empty crates, and come out loaded with power-packs and other items. The power-packs are what we're interested in. I can tell you that they are bio-mechanical, some kind of biological matrix, so we will be sending specialists with you. That's all we have gentlemen. What we want you to do is; go in there, get some samples and any useful information you can get, and then blow the place. Sound simple enough?"

"Yeah… And suicidal," Enquine said. I smiled.

"Enquine, you will have overall command." Owens said before dismissing us. It stung, but I had to consider it one last test.

We had been dropped in five miles away and arrived on foot. It had been Enquine's idea to hitch a ride in to the tower on a truck. The only other way in would be through the vent system. Infra-red showed that the plant was kicking out huge plumes of heat and hydrogen wastes, so the vents had to be big and numerous.

***

Bright lights bobbed up and down on the track approaching the ridge behind us. "This is it," Enquine said. "Get the men, fifteen per side, down to the track now Major Stone!"

"Aye sir! Come on you lot!" ordered Stone.

While four grunts aimed at the antenna on the armoured truck, Stone tried to pass himself off as a guard and ordered the crew to let Enquine, he and myself on-board. To our amazement it worked.

Civilians.

The four IM guards in the tracked truck were no match for us, especially with the two IM lasers Enquine and I had, which were low on charge now. Stone questioned the driver at laser-point. One of Major Stone's less endearing qualities was his persuasiveness with IM grunts. After he'd obtained what he wanted, all three were tied and gagged and locked in a crate. Stone took the controls, and we headed towards the tower. The grunts were lying on top of the crates.

An IM guard, wearing an unfamiliar, heavily armoured white suit, stood in front of the truck when we stopped. Our intercom cracked into life. "Vehicle ID?" barked the speaker, synchronised with the IM guard's mouth.

Stone read from the papers he had taken off of the driver. "A-4290340."

"Codeword?"

"Crisis."

The guard's eyes closed, as if bored, and he indicated we should move forward with a sweep of his free arm. I watched his face as my window passed. Into the cavernous space between the walls of the tower, we passed. IM grunts lined platforms at cab height, either side, and the main doors ahead remained closed.

"Do we unload here?" asked Stone.

A second later, we knew the answer. "Back out! Now! Go Stone!" I had seen the barrel of an IM laser, raised to point at Stone by a nervous grunt. I had been half-expecting it, and my reaction had been instant. "Duck," I added. An IM round came crashing through the toughened window and shattered above our heads as the air started rushing out. Already, we were moving backwards at full speed, being bounced about it the cab like squash-balls. I struggled to get my visor closed and the air on.

"Off the track Stone," breathed Enquine into his helmet mike.

"Fuck!" Stone swore, bringing the truck to a shuddering halt in a cloud of dust right at the base of the tower.

"Out! Get out!" Enquine called to the grunts in the back as the main cargo door slid open. They poured out.

Shit. This is not good.

"Stone. No time to talk," Enquine continued. "We'll take six. Rest of you hold them off long as you can. Then get out. Wait at rendezvous." He nodded to me, and I tapped six grunts on the shoulders, as they emerged, including the biotechnologist, nanotechnogist and explosives expert. They followed Enquine and I as we set off bunny-hopping around the base of the tower.

"Here!" Two grunts blasted the grate locks at our feet until the grate released and swung down against the tower wall. "Down!" Enquine ordered me. Two grunts, and I jumped together. I heard a gurgling sound in my ears as I dropped. Spinning round on landing, I saw that one of the men who'd jumped with me had been neatly severed, right down the middle. His two halves lay like some medical exhibit complete with suit, the blood frozen within moments. I felt the gag reflex and turned away. "Don't look! We can't afford to puke! Somebody grab the … detonators!" Even while I spoke, the gag-reflex convulsed my throat.

Defense laser. There goes the explosives expert. Thank God I didn't know his name.

I frowned with disgust at my own thought. The others jumped down, and the grunts followed Enquine while I started crawling down the long metal-lined duct.

"I can't see a thing!" Hot gases were fogging my visor.

"We're trapped now!" shouted one of the grunts. "Flashes behind us!"

At a junction I turned left.

"You know where you're going Jake?" asked Enquine.

"Do you have to use my first name? Why not Nanden, like anybody else, and no, I don't know where I am going!"

"You will remember Jake."

I felt heavier as I crawled.

"S-grav," I said into the mike.

"IM don't have S-grav," Richardson, the biotechnologist, said.

"They do now!" replied Enquine.

The tunnel started bending to the right. I knew this, because I kept bumping into the left wall. Suddenly something hit me hard. The next thing I knew, Enquine was shaking me.

"Jake! Jake! You okay?"

"What the hell hit me?" I tasted something metallic taste in my mouth besides blood from my tongue.

"Shock barrier. You hit it. You're bloody lucky to be alive. Thousand volts, at least!"

Enquine took over and, after about another fifty feet, he stopped and announced:

"Blast of some sort of gas! On the right! This'll do! Get a grunt up here. Take it out soldier!" The locks burned away, and Enquine kicked in the grate. I backed into the room and dropped to the floor.

"Careful. It's a big drop!" I called out.

Store room.

There were rows of shelves with large boxes of something on top. One lay open, and I peered over the top. "Seeds!"

"Take the door out soldier," I ordered, tapping a grunt on the shoulder. I lifted my visor, keeping the air on, and took a gulp of air. "Okay to breath." I could hear a siren blaring behind the door somewhere. I glanced at Enquine, as he lifted his visor, and saw white foam on his moustache. "You okay?"

"I get a bit claustrophobic!"

Have to move fast now.

"Before they seal the doors!" I yelled.

Enquine pushed the grunt out of the way and aimed the IM laser at the door. In seconds he had cut half of it away, and we were out into the corridor.

"Air's normal here!" Enquine told us.

We all flipped up our helmet visors and switched off our air flow. Enquine turned to the right and broke into a run. The rest of us followed. I caught up with Enquine.

"Something's wrong!" he shouted.

"What? Apart from everything!"

"Too advanced! Never seen IM build anything like this!"

"I know."

We came to a corridor on our left. "This leads to the centre," I shouted. "Let's try it." Two IM guards fired at us, and Enquine took them out.

"Out of ammo!" he shouted.

At the end of the corridor, I saw a thick metal door with a transparent portion near the top. The door stood nearly eight feet tall, so I had to stand on my toes to see into the space beyond. "This is it!"

The door had no sign of a handle, or lock, but a panel on the wall had a small keypad.

"Now what?" Richardson asked.

I aimed my IM laser at the panel and blasted it out of its socket. I heard a 'clunk,' inside the door.

"That was stupid!" shouted Enquine above the sound of the siren.

"Maybe not!" I shouted. "Give me a hand." I pushed the barrel of the gun against the side of the transparent portion of the door and pushed towards the wall with the panel. Two grunts copied me and, slowly, the heavy door started to open. Enquine wedged his weapon into the gap and levered. Soon, he managed to get his whole body through the gap and push the door open.

The room we entered stretched as wide as a concert hall and about as high. It had white walls with galleries, higher up. Concentric rings of racking, about ten feet apart, filled the room and rose to near the roof, perhaps 100 feet above us. I saw ladders, up the side of the racks, and walkways, which extended out from the galleries. Bushy purple plants, about a hands-length in height, grew thickly in long trays on the racks. Surprising though this was, my attention became distracted by the sound of birds flying freely in the great hall. Then I saw something else:

"Butterflies! I haven't seen them for many years!"

"I ain't *never* seen a *bird*!" shouted one of the grunts. Half way through his sentence the siren stopped.

" … ollination," Richardson said quietly.

"They know where we are," I declared. "Three of you, you, you and you guard that door," As I swung back to look at the shelves, I saw a movement, high on one of the galleries. I stared, but I couldn't see anything. My skin crawled. I returned my attention to the plants. "What do you make of it Richardson?"

He scooped up some of the potting material with his glove and smelled it. "Looks like silicates. Combination of clay and sand with some other stuff thrown in. Some water." But then he took hold of a plant-stem and pulled it. "Wow! Really hard. Like stone. Flexible inside but covered with stone-like surface, like an insect shell."

"So? What is it?"

"No idea. Nothing I've ever seen. And where's the water? I mean there's water here but nowhere near enough." He pointed to a small drip-feed on the end of a tube that descended on the side of the shelving.

I reached out to touch the purple plants. "Their leaves are like clover leaves. Look Enquine!"

"Yeah! Like the logo on the lasers."

"Wait a minute!" the nanotechnologist, Schluter, said. "These tubes are coming *from* the pots, not going *to* them! The water is coming out and being taken away in these pipes! The plants are *making* water."

"It's possible," added Richardson. "Some silicates have oxygen and hydrogen in them. Have you noticed too that there's no ultra-violet light in here. Just plain lighting. I guess they need the birds and insects for pollination-..."

I cut him short:

"We haven't got time to talk about it now. Richardson; grab some kind of container and put some of this purple stuff in it; keep it alive for a few hours. The rest of you, stuff your pouches with some of this," I ordered, holding a clump of the purple plants.

"We still need to know how the batteries are made," Enquine added.

"Yes. Up there, I bet. The tower stood at least twenty storeys outside. This room is half that."

"Factory floor!" added Richardson.

"Argh!" One of the grunts by the door screamed. He had been hit and flew into the room, knocked back by the force of a shot. Thin threads of red spurted from his white suit.

"Ladders!" I screamed. Shouldering the heavy laser, I started to climb. The clumsy suit made it a struggle. The racking shuddered as a short slammed into something below. I almost lost my fragile grip with the bulky gloves. I stared ahead grimly and climbed.

Must have been one of ours. Dead!

Something hit my sleeve below my left shoulder, and I smelled burning k-plex, the suit material. Gasping for breath, I finally gained the refuge of the first gallery and found Enquine and Schluter standing beside me. Richardson struggled up moments later, the front of his suit unlocked and nestling a box of the green plant. Laser-fire came directly up at us now. I looked at my sleeve and saw the tear, which meant death if we ever escaped into the vacuum outside the tower. I put the thought to the back of my mind.

"The others!" shouted Richardson as we looked for a way out.

"Through here!" shouted Enquine, holding a door open.

"Come on man!" I yanked Richardson's sleeve as he leaned over a railing and hauled him through the door. A bird followed us.

Always one clever one.

Outside, to our left, I saw first a set of descending stairs and, just past them, a flight of ascending stairs. Enquine took the ascending ones. Three floors above, we found ourselves in a curving corridor, similar to that leading from the gallery. Enquine followed it. At a corridor on the left, he stopped me with his glove held up and, moments later, darted across the gap. I peered into the corridor and saw two guards in lightweight suits, saluting each other about twenty-five feet away. One held

up his gloved hand with the little finger and third finger
apart, like children do when imitating a dog's ears in
shadow-puppetry. The other repeated the salute. The
gesture reminded me of something else, but I didn't have
time to think. The guards had thin tubes emerging from
the suit, which stopped just short of their noses and
mouths. One of the guards turned around, and the other
followed him out of sight. I crossed the gap and beckoned
Richardson and Schluter forward.

A little further on, we saw a door on the right with a
label that read, 'Production Bay 1: Clean Suits Only;
Breathers Required.' Below, there were some hieroglyphs.

I stared at the door, not quite believing what I saw
seeing, and then pointed. "See that! That symbol. I have
seen it before!" The symbol looked like the simplified
silhouette of the head of a jackal with long ears.

"Where?" asked Enquine, sounding impatient.

Numis.

"At a fair on the Moon. On … On a token."

"Anubis," added Schluter.

"*Come on!*" Enquine said. "We don't have time for
history!"

"But … !"

Enquine shot off the lock, and we piled through. We
entered a room with black walls and no windows, roughly
the same shape as the one below but covering only a
single floor.

"Santa's Grotto!" Enquine said.

"Yes," Richardson said, walking in and picking up
something purple from a bench.

Rows of benches ran across the round room, with
aisles between groups of four benches. At intervals on the
benches, sat transparent machines, like n-gens. Between
these were trays of the purple plants. Inside two of the
machines, on the group of benches closest to us, a
flickering light highlighted a plant. I stooped to the trays
of purple plants and brushed my gloved finger through

the leaves. Separating a stem, I smiled to myself. It looked just like a clover. I picked up something green from a tray next to the nearest machine.

"Compound resistor!" I said out loud. "Or that's what it looks like!"

Schluter held up something from a tray on the second bench. "Super-capacitor. Maybe!"

"Semi-conductors. Very nice," Richardson said, from the third bench.

Enquine held something close to his eyes at the fourth bench. "Here it is! This is what we came for. A power-pack! Grab a handful each and anything else you can get in your pockets. Let's set the charge and get out of here!" He tossed something to me. "Jake. Reload!"

I flipped open the power-bay on the laser, as the tech team had taught us, and pressed the catch which released the old pack. I pressed home the new one and saw the power indicator light up white, indicating a full charge.

I walked along the row of benches with the power packs and saw a pile of plastics. I picked one up, looking for any kind of label. The plastic felt much lighter than the normally-light plastics I used. I grabbed four of them; about six inches by ten, unfastened the front of my suit and stuffed them inside.

From the machine nearest me, a cable for power extended. It terminated, not in a power socket, but in a tray of the completed green power-packs, which sat on a bed of more silicates.

What the hell ... ?

"Look at this!" I cried. "This is amazing!"

"No time Jake. Grab what you can and let's get out of here. Who has the detonators?"

"I got 'em!" shouted Schluter. "Does anybody know how to set them?"

Finishing stuffing my pouches, I grabbed one of the four detonators from Schluter. "It won't be fancy, but

Enquine and I were shown the basics. Hold the laser! How long?"

"Ten minutes! Come on Jake!" shouted Enquine. He held the door open and Schluter and Richardson ran through it.

Crouching down, I released the sandwich-box sized pack from my belt onto the floor and found the detonator hole. I stuck the detonator all the way in and moved the slider to 'Ten.' I pushed in the red end, hard, and ran for the door. Just before I reached the door I saw a movement from the far right of the hall. I saw something big, moving fast, but when I looked again, I saw nothing there.

I followed the others back to the stairs and down.

"Does anybody else feel dizzy?" panted Richardson at our first halt for breath, three flights down.

"Too much nitrogen in that room," Schluter said. "I feel sick."

I bent over, ready to vomit too. My head pounded. The corridor spun every time I looked at it. "That was … what … those tubes were for!"

"What tubes?" asked Enquine, gulping for air.

"Saw two guards with tubes to their noses and mouths," I gasped.

"We've got to go!" Enquine said.

Schluter ran ahead, as we moved anti-clockwise around the curving corridor, and then he stopped, his hand going to his head briefly before falling to his side. Enquine caught him as he fell to the floor. "Back!" he shouted and ducked as incoming laser-fire hit the wall above him. We turned and the three of us ran back past the stairs and on. We ran on and on, trying several side corridors, but each time found our path blocked by IM.

"We're running out of time!" Enquine shouted.

"Here! This one. Maybe it's a store room."

I tapped the door on our left, and Enquine stopped. "Try it!" I shot off the lock and pushed the door open. I saw another door on the far side of the room, and I shot the lock off of that too while running at it full speed. Yanking the door open, I entered a corridor, empty of IM.

Thank God.

I led the way to the right and a corridor, wider than the rest and sloping down, opened on our left. A huge explosion rocked me off my feet and, a moment later, the boom echoed along the corridor. "Too late!"

With the corridor still shaking violently, I stumbled down the slope and arrived at a large double-door. Like all the doors we had come across, it looked air-tight, having huge flexible black seals around the edges. For once, it wasn't locked. I barged it open and pressed on. The sirens again started clanging. Another set of double-doors stood in front of me, just like the first. Again, I barged through and then stopped, stunned.

The siren had masked the sound of activity behind the doors, and I found myself standing in a vast loading bay, filled with crates, IM guards and technicians, coming from side corridors, ran towards a pair of huge gates, opposite us. About fifty feet high, they were ribbed like the insides of an old ship and made of iron, judging by what looked like rusty patches. On either side were steps up to airlocks, at about the same height as the platforms we had seen outside the entrance. Between us and the doors, were an old fork-loader, piles of crates, some open and some closed, and a large open floor. I took all this in in an instant.

Shit!

Richardson slammed into the back of me, and we both struggled to keep our feet. I elbowed him backwards. "Back out!" I said, trying to keep my voice low, and he must have heard, even above the din of the sirens, because he backed away, too late. A guard had spotted us. Laser-fire burned through the crates ahead of us. I dived to the right, but Richardson moved too late. He caught the laser-fire full in the chest, and the slit of light went right through him.

He should have been dead, but as he fell to the floor, in the white-hot, horizontal rain, next to me, I could hear him still moaning. Bits of burned crate were hitting me in the face and all over my body. As I covered my face with one hand, I felt something slice into my leg. I felt no pain, so I ignored the sensation. I reached out, grabbed Richardson's arm and pulled his limp body out of the main path of fire.

No crates left soon. Fork-loader.

I dragged Richardson forward and further to the right, until we were leaning against the sheltered side of the fork-loader. As we reached the vehicle, my second finger on my left hand felt suddenly cold. I looked at it, but it had gone, torn off by a laser.

"Ouch," I said. But really, I felt nothing.

Jena will kill me.

I leaned against the solid weight of the fork-loader and looked back, toward where I hoped Enquine would be. His mouth moved as he shouted but, against the sound of firing, I couldn't hear him. He beckoned us, but we were stuck. Then, he too had to dive for cover behind a crate. I looked at my leg and saw a deep wound above the knee. It looked as if a laser had severed the bone, and it bled copiously. Richardson tried to tell me something, so I leaned close to him.

"I'm incredibly hungry," he muttered, putting his hand to the hole in his chest. I pulled his hand away. The hole went right through where his spine should be; I could see only splinters of his jagged bone inside.

Why isn't he dead?

"Do you have anything to eat?" he asked, meekly.

"Here!" I fumbled for my Snookie bar, emergency rations, and unwrapped it for him. He held it weakly and took a bite.

The laser-fire continued, I could hear its hissing, screaming sound, but I couldn't see any slits of light near us.

Richardson's innards moved when he swallowed, and the sight made me want to retch.

"At least they missed the two important bits; our little purple plants and my wedding tackle," he said. "Not sure if I want to get married. You been married?"

"No. Painful for the man during, woman after. So they say. Why do you need a piece of paper or a metal ring if you love each other?"

He didn't reply.

Dead.

"Jake!" I could just hear Enquine's voice over the angry hiss of lasers. "Jake! You gotta get here now! They're burning … ." But I couldn't hear the rest of his sentence. Then I knew what he said. A shaft of hot, angry white light burst through a hole, dribbling molten metal, in my side of the fork-loader, and just missed my face. I remembered the purple plants at the last moment. I grabbed the pot from Richardson and crammed it inside the front of my suit, feeling like a kangaroo. Metal bubbled all over the surface of the fork-loader, and its yellow paint ran in gobbets onto the floor.

In slow motion, I struggled to my feet and dived for Enquine, sliding to a halt well-short.

Still too far to go!

I started crawling and Enquine's own laser-fire passed inches above my head. I felt the hair on my head starting to sizzle. I slid my own laser over to Enquine and he started firing with that too.

"Come on! Come on Jake! Argh!"

It's taking too long to crawl. We'll both die like this.

I turned on to my back for a second and saw the fork-loader had become just a pile of steaming metal parts. Many of the IM guards were advancing towards us, using crates as cover.

I turned to face Enquine. He now backing through the doors which he had propped open. I tucked my knees under me and stood on my one good leg, the other hanging uselessly at an odd angle. I hopped once and then dived again. This time, I reached him. I could see he had been hit in the hand, but it didn't look too bad.

He turned me over and stuck the laser in my good hand. "Cover me!" I pressed the trigger and fired at random; I didn't care what I hit.

I could see Enquine's laser-fire pointing to the roof and glancing up, I saw what he aimed to do. A gantry-crane, under the roof, equipped with a cab, ran on wheels along a track. He aimed at the base of the jib, burning through the metal frame with his laser. If he could get through, it would fall between us and the IM, giving us some cover while we escaped. But I knew, even as I thought this, that I wouldn't be escaping, not from this building. My suit had been riddled with holes.

"Come on Enquine!" I kept firing and watching the jib. Suddenly it tilted, hesitated for a moment, and then my heart leaped as it came crashing down, bouncing me into the air for a moment. A cloud of dust and packing material rose up between us and the IM. "Whooa! Nice one!"

"Jake!" I twisted around to face him. "There's not much time!" He had a look in his eyes of great sadness and compassion. Suddenly, I didn't hate him anymore. "I have to go. We both know you aren't going anywhere like that."

"Yeah."

"Listen! Gonna find a way out and come back for you! Okay?"

"Yeah. Okay. Here! You better take this." I started to remove the pot of purple plants from my suit-front, but he grabbed a small handful of the little plants and grinned.

"This is enough. Set the charge for ten minutes." He tapped me once on the head and turned for the door, just as the IM started up again. This time they were even more determined. I wanted to release the doors from the slivers of wood which Enquine had used to wedge them open, but I had no time. I turned around for a moment but Enquine had gone, so firing with one hand, I clumsily set the charge with the other.

Plenty of charge in the laser. Get to the door.

I couldn't back up without stopping firing, because the weight of the suit meant I had to prop myself up on my elbows, and the lethal white rain wouldn't even slow down if I didn't keep firing. I swung the barrel from left to right in wide arcs, aiming for every head I saw. Several of them were out wide enough to see around the jib, so they had me pinned down.

Enquine won't be back. Coward after all. I'm a dead man.

During a half-second respite, I looked around me. I saw no protection at all and another six feet to go before I could get through the door. It might as well be miles.

Only one thing to do. Forward.

I turned onto my belly, at the same time twisting to face them and crawled behind the protection of the jib, which had been distorted by the intense heat of the lasers, theirs and mine. For a beautiful moment, their firing ceased. What was left of Richardson's body still lay a few feet in front of the jib. His feet were almost under it.

Protection. The armour.

It wasn't much, but it might be enough. Where my finger had been, I felt only a throbbing pain, but my leg hurt more. As soon as I stopped firing, it became almost unbearable. I took out two ano-morphine capsules, unscrewed the lids and jabbed one into each wound.

The soldier's friend.

I had felt its embrace before and, at times like this, you couldn't do without it.

I calmly took hold of Richardson's boots and dragged his body under the jib, towards me, incurring a little light IM fire in the process. His body wasn't a pretty sight.

"Sorry Richardson. One last job for you."

I dragged him back to the maximum distance I could reach behind the jib without being fired upon and then a bit further.

Nothing!

I turned over, into a sitting position, with his body propped in front of me, and inched away from the jib.

Then it started. The IM who most outflanked me, took deadly aim, and a charge drilled straight through my helmet, grazing my forehead and burning my hair.

Jesus! This is it.

I had to keep going. Richardson's body disintegrated in my hands until I had very little left to hold, but now there were only about four needles of light coming at me.

Most of them must be gone!

I made it thought the door and dropped Richardson's remains. The remaining IM were climbing over the jib, but I hit one of them. He slumped over the melting metal, and steam engulfed his suited body. This made the others angry, and they came on faster.

I swung the laser barrel wildly, hoping for hits, and then saw something which almost made me release the trigger. Something like a man but, I would guess, nearly ten feet tall, sprung in one leap from the loading-bay floor to the top of the stairs, eight feet above. Black, with very long arms and hands the size of spades, its head looked like that of a jackal with very long ears, and it screamed something at the men around it before moving towards the airlock doors. It seemed to be constantly moving, as if struggling to hold its position in the thick air, which made it seem even more like an apparition. Men fell back before it, either out of fear or awe. Then it had gone. For seconds, I felt stunned and just kept firing. Then I refocused.

Lintel

I aimed at the top of the door and turned the laser up to full power. Bits of concrete flew in all directions, exposing the metal work, and I aimed to separate a large chunk of the frame from the rest. Several needles of light converged on my chest, and I screamed reflexively, but to my astonishment, they moved off of me. Just as one of the IM grunts peered around the doorway, the lintel came loose and crashed down on his head. The others stopped firing when dust from the debris concealed me. Exhausted, I lay back, gasping. Then I saw a burst of white light.

I had imagined what it would be like when the tower blew. I knew that the S-grav would finally destabilize, and then there would be a small nuclear explosion of a few megatons. A fireball would engulf what the tower remains in a fraction of a second, and it would become a vaporized part of a wave of enormous power, that would spread out, first in a rushing horizontal wave of biblical destruction and then upwards. Less than it would have been on Earth because of Io's weak atmosphere, still it would reach to the heavens in rings of cloudy, ungodly delight. Some IM who were perhaps a mile away or more, might survive, but this was the end for me. I gave in to it and waited.

Darkness again.

I thought I heard a distant boom but not as loud as I had expected. Cautiously, after a few heartbeats, I opened my eyes. The debris around me had settled, and I could see I still lay in the corridor of the tower. I hadn't expected Heaven, but this was disappointing.

Why am I still alive? Maybe there was no explosion.

I seemed alone, and it seemed quite peaceful, apart from the siren, wailing pointlessly.

Then I remembered my wounds and saw that I lay in several coalescing pools of blood.

The IM must have all gone. Including that monster. Did I actually see it? Need to get out.

I rolled on my stomach and dragged myself back to the jib. I crawled under it and out on to the loading bay floor; empty now of enemies. Among the debris, my elbow rested on something sharp, and I saw a roll of old copper cable.

Must have come out of a crate.

I cut off two lengths of it. I wound one around the top of my leg and the other around my arm to make two crude tourniquets. I crawled on, to the bottom of the steps and then dragged myself up onto the platform. I could only reach the control panel, still blinking, by standing, so I levered myself up onto my feet and pressed the default emergency escape code, which worked on most airlocks; '1, 2, 3, 4.' I waited for the reassuring hiss, but it didn't come. I tried again and still nothing.

They've locked it! The bastards! The sick bastards!

I fell back to the ground and laughed at the hopelessness of it all before a great feeling of sadness came over me.

All the things I'll never get to do. I'm just too tired to do any more.

I closed my eyes.

Then, again, I saw a burst of white light. I smiled to myself.

Not so easily fooled.

"Jake! Come on Jake!"

The voice sounded familiar, but I refused to open my eyes or respond. I wanted to say, "Go away!"

"Jake!" The loud voice had to be right next to my helmet. Something lifted me up. I opened my eyes, reluctantly. I saw, upside down, at the back of somebody in a suit just like mine, descending the stairs.

"Hold *on* Jake! We have to get out!"

The huge doors of the gate were open slightly. We passed through them as I bobbed up and down sickeningly.

"Enquine?" I asked.

"Yes. It's me Jake. I said I'd be back. I don't know why you're still alive. There's something about you Jake! You set the charge? How long?"

I tried to look at the panel on my suit, but everything was bounced around, blurring my vision. I thought I would soon pass out from blood-loss.

"I can't read it. Stop!"

"No time!"

I tried one last time, opening my eyes wide and then screwed them up to focus on the bouncing read-out. For just a fraction of a second, I thought I could read it. "Ninety seconds!" I shouted.

"Jeez! Jake, close your helmet. I don't know if your leg and arm are sealed enough. I am making for the truck. You might make it!"

He doesn't know about the finger.

Every suit had wrist and ankle seals. Combat suits had three settings, 'release,' 'seal,' and 'tourniquet,' the third being self-explanatory. I selected it. I gritted my teeth as the band bit into my wrist.

Painkillers wearing off.

"IM bastards sealed the airlocks. Only way I could get in was through the big doors! Fortunately, they have a giant airlock too. Way beyond anything I seen for IM before. You seen these panels?"

I didn't reply. I felt sick. I just hung there limply while Enquine operated the outer airlock side-doors which still operated.

"You came back for me … Gary?"

"Yeah! I said I would."

"Did you see the alien?"

"I saw something. Or I thought I did, getting in the back of an IM truck."

"Like a jackal." I laughed, but he didn't hear me.

"Almost sealed. Close your helmet!"

I did and heard my own, gasping breathing. Then we were outside, and I lifted my head to look back. Inside the open, outer gates, I could see a large transparent wall, like a giant plastic green-house. As Gary had said, it seemed beyond normal IM technology to have a curved transparent surface like that which could seal a space inside. He turned left and jogged towards where I remembered the truck to be. I found myself subconsciously counting-down.

"Sixty seconds!" I guessed. I could hear Gary grunting and gasping for air to fill his lungs. Then, "Jake. You still holding that … laser?"

"Yeah," I answered, my voice sounding strange as I bobbed up and down.

"Drop it! You don't need it anymore."

Fifteen seconds later he slowed, and I could see the truck wheels through his pounding legs.

"Found it intact! Surprised?"

"Yeah," I rasped, weakly. "Thirty seconds!"

He moved to the loading door and I recognised the upside-down Stone, leaning against the truck, by his over-sized dagger.

"Stone! Get in the truck! St-…" I yelled.

"He's dead!" cut in Gary.

I felt a pain in my stomach, knowing that my friend had gone.

Gary slung me on the floor of the truck and pressed the panel to seal the door before leaping into the driver's seat.

"Go!" he shouted at the old truck as he gunned the engine. It roared into life, and we bounced across the Sulphur. He spun the truck around and headed away from the tower. I counted down to zero and then closed my eyes. Even through my eyelids, the intense light hurt. It felt like jabbing your fingers into your eyes hard. Reflexively, I looked away and opened them, but I couldn't see anything. Gary was still driving flat-out even though I doubted he could see anything either. Then there came the blast.

"Here it co- … ." We rattled around like hard-boiled peas in a tin. For a moment, I heard near silence, just the revving of the engine, as the truck tried to continue on, slipping, with sulphurous gravel pounding it from behind. As some vision returned, I saw Gary struggle into the seat again, and then I felt the almightiest trembling.

"We're being sucked back!" he screamed.

The truck laboured at a crazy angle, as if crawling out of a near vertical hole. The tracks fought for purchase, the engine revs erratically rising and falling. I glanced, for one terrible moment, behind us and saw that the tower had disappeared and had been replaced by a pit of boiling ground which was collapsing in on itself as the singularity of the tower's S-grav ran out of control.

I had no time for thought, only for trying to keep my balance in the thunder of collapsing ground and the truck's desperate struggle to escape the pull of the vortex. The struggle went on and on, and then suddenly we were motionless although I could still hear the engines roaring.

"Stop!" I shouted weakly.

"What's happened?" I couldn't answer but just lay there.

We had come to rest with most of the truck under a sea of solidified glass, which a few moments before had been molten. The sides of the truck were bent and twisted by the crushing force, but somehow, we were still air-tight. Only the cab windows in front of Gary were now above ground.

"We're saved!" shouted Gary. "Whoa!"

Not quite.

A few moments passed before he remembered how badly hurt I was.

"Now let's take a look at you. The IM are long gone. We'll be picked up soon I am sure. We just need to wait here."

I smiled weakly.

He inspected my wounds quickly and pulled the remains of the plants and the plastics out of the front of my suit. Most of the plants had dropped out when I had been upside down, but a few remained. The plastics were shattered into pieces.

He whistled and showed me the burn marks on some of the plastics. "You were lucky! Whatever this stuff is, it deflected the laser-fire. Strong stuff! The front of your suit is burned away! Okay, we need to get a caut-o-lase on this."

Severed limbs and deep cuts were the normal injuries for modern warfare and most medi-packs had at least one cauterizing tool called a caut-o-lase, but they were often out of power. Gary found the medi-pack in the truck but, as usual, the caut-o-lase's indicator showed no power.

"Don't worry. We'll soon fix this!" Gary said. "I just need one of those power packs … Let's see now …" He took one of the little green power-packs, which we had taken from the tower. He untwisted two 'shoots,' which extended and wrapped around the packs like old-style positive and negative wires.

"I just need to unscrew the back of the caut-o-lase thus, take out the batteries – useless old IM batteries – and touch this wire to here and this other wire to here … ," he explained. I heard the high-pitched buzz of the caut-o-lase coming to life and smiled. But then I grimaced, as I prepared myself for the pain.

He touched the contact to the wound on my leg, the worst wound, and an intense pain raked my body, making me convulse and hit my hands against the side of the cabin.

"Hold still! Just need to do the arm …"

"Agh!"

"And finally, the finger ..."

"Agh!"

"There! All done. Now you can rest for a while. I'll just unwind these wires, so the blood can flow again."

I must have fallen into a deep sleep, because when I next saw his face, it was lit by the gentle blue neon glow of the cab's night-lights.

"How long have I been asleep?"

"Since yesterday afternoon."

"So it's morning."

"No. Evening."

"That long? IM?"

"Long gone, or dead."

"Dead?"

"Our own fighters would have wiped them out once they were beyond air cover, unless their forces were coordinated, which I don't think it was. We're all alone now. I guess our own forces think we're dead."

"A *whole* day, we've been here? Air?"

"Yeah! It's a problem. Not much left mate. I did try to get off a few messages in code using the radio, but I don't think it has much range, and the battery's almost out now. Probably too much traffic. I'll try again later. We need what's left for the recycler. I'm going to turn the lights off now."

"Okay."

"Best to try and rest now. Use as little air as possible."

The day slowly dawned, and as the sun rose, Jupiter's familiar arc filled the sky.

***

I was finding it difficult to breath.

"We've had it!" answered Gary.

"Try the radio one last time. We won't need any light or recycling tonight, we'll be out of air."

Gary sent a brief message for help, giving our grid-reference just before the juice ran out on the radio and then turned it to 'Receive.' "Nothing!"

From the ether, suddenly, came first a crackle, louder than the rest, and then, weakly, a voice. "Reading you Foxtrot Alpha. Have assistance on the way. ETA thirty Earth minutes."

***

While we waited for rescue, we talked:

"I never thought you would come back for me."

"You still don't remember me, Jake, do you? But you will."

"Were we really that close?" I tried to remember anything in my childhood that might have had Gary Enquine in it.

"Yeah. We were."

"Tell me about the accident that nearly killed me."

"You don't remember? You don't remember at all? Don't you remember the Sunbreakers?"

"No."

"We had hired Daiwa Sunbreakers, micro-light wings which you could strap on and fly with. Do you remember the craze? Of course, it's a professional sport now, but it was still a novelty then, and the only place you could do it was on Space Stations like J5, in the spoke-tubes that ran down to the Central Terminal. Gravity was 1/6th normal there. It was a bright sunny day and college was out for the summer. We were happy, and you wanted to try and go higher and further than ever before. Sometimes, we would fly close to the panels that opened to let the sunlight in. It was bloody dangerous to fly near them, because the material of the wings was only a few microns thick and would melt if it became hot. You were a mad kid though, and you wouldn't listen to any warnings. You wanted to go closer to the panels than any of us had ever gone. You talked me into going up there with you. I watched as you flew closer and closer to the panels, each time swerving away and then trying again, lifted on the thermals that rose from below and thrown about by the turbulence of warm air coming in through the panels. It was too dangerous, and I shouted and shouted for you to stop. But you had this mad grin on your face, and you couldn't stop yourself. 'I've done it! I've done it!' you screamed, just before the material melted, and you started to fall. I tried to catch you, managed to get my wing under your broken one for a moment, but then you fell away, screaming all the way down, spiraling like a broken butterfly as you tried to slow your speed. But in the end, you couldn't stop yourself, and you fell to the ground."

"Yes! Yes! I think I remember!" My mind's vision suddenly filled with a memory that had been lost, half-guessed, perhaps for many years. I remembered the Daiwa manufacturers stamp on the black alufibre tubes as I assembled my Sunbreaker, and I remembered flying so close to the Sun, so close that my eyes were nearly seared, and I was filled with the bright glowing light … .

***

You can buy NOW the complete Kindle or paperback version of Iron II: Unknown Place, Unknown Universe on Amazon: http://bit.ly/amziron2

Appendix

Ionian Militia

The Ionian Militia (IM) was formed by miners on Io, moon of Jupiter on June 1 2089. Their living conditions were already touch but falling iron prices led to smaller pay-rises and longer hours. They went on strike and in the long summer of 2080 Earth News bulletins were full of items about iron shortages and skirmishes between USAC troops and miners on Io. Led by Richard Ortega, the miners demanded some concessions, most prominent being that their families could live with them. This was granted but shortly after their families arrived, the miners were subjected to further pay-cuts and reductions in supply of essential equipment. From the Ionian Iron Miners Union was formed the Ionian Miner's Union, led by Ortega. This powerful union then began receiving equipment and other supplies directly from the Rebel Alliance on Earth, a move that was seen as highly provocative by the USAC forces, then in administrative control on Io and then attempted to block these supplies and suppress resistance using overpowering force. From the Ionian Miner's Union Ortega then formed the Ionian Militia, a small but highly trained and well-equipped force which operated using guerrilla tactics against USAC. The force gradually grew in size and strength until, ten years later, they are a significant force on Io, controlling one half of its surface. Only a few mines remained loyal to USAC, raising Solar System prices of iron and putting an end to the building of the great J stations.

Mobile Command Station (MCS) – Mark 6

The MCS officer's cabins were at the rear with the flight-deck sandwiched between the two shuttle bays. Behind the flight-deck and also between the shuttle bays

was the reactor and behind this the mess where the private
soldiers spent all day, sleeping in hammocks. The mess
was to the left of the MCS with windows along one edge
next to a row of benches, raised to cover one of the four
backup diesels. On the other side of the mess was the
wash-room for the grunts and a door to a short corridor to
the commander's cabin. This was in the right rear corner
of the vehicle and the other officers had, or shared,
smaller cabins next to this along the rear edge of the
MCS. The beds in the smallest cabins covered a second
backup diesel; the third and fourth being underneath the
flight-deck.

Mobile Command Station (MCS) – Mark 7

Very similar to the Mark 6 but entrance was through a
hatch in the centre of the front which led straight onto the
flight-desk. The Mark 7 had the new anti-laser refracting
armour which looked like so many polygonal scales on its
skin. The pods were now grouped in pairs at the front and
back, to provide protection in the event of high-speed
impact, a move that many of us had called for, which
gave it a bug-eyed look from the front, and from the side
it looked like a truncated centipede, squatted on the deck.
From the gantry, its top surface was still a mass of pipes
and vents but slightly less messy now with more armour
plating covering it. My initial impressions of it on the
testing flight had been good with the reservation that the
cabins were all even smaller than the Mark 6, and that the
extra armour plating had made it heavier and less
manoeuvrable.

SU 401

As with most modern space-fighters they were pencil-
shaped, with engines in four pods, separated from the
main hull by wing-lets. The pods allowed the engines to
be used for propulsion in any direction, and the main
difference between the SUs and the FAs was the wing-

lets. These were bigger on the SUs for some direction stability in the thicker atmosphere on Mars.

IM Clover Leaf Laser Rifle

It looked a lot like an X.50 but was much more compact, and clearly its charge was much more powerful at greater ranges. It was light; extremely light for its size. I couldn't see a maker's name anywhere on the black stock or trigger assembly. The only thing I could see was an embossed sign like a four-leafed clover on the side of the trigger mechanism. The laser rounds from it were white rather than the usual green.

***

Biography of Lazlo Ferran

Lazlo Ferran: Exploring the Landscapes of Truth.

Educated near Oxford, during English author Lazlo Ferran's extraordinary life, he has been an aeronautical engineering student, dispatch rider, graphic designer, full-time busker, guitarist and singer, recording two albums. Having grown up in rural Buckinghamshire Lazlo says:

"The beautiful Chiltern Hills offered the ideal playground for a child's mind, in contrast to the ultra-strict education system of Bucks."

Brought up as a Buddhist, he has travelled widely, surviving a student uprising in Athens and living for a while in Cairo, just after Sadat's assassination. Later, he spent some time in Central Asia and was only a few blocks away from gunfire during an attempt to storm the government buildings of Bishkek in 2006. He has a keen interest in theologies and philosophies of the Far East, Middle East, Asia and Eastern Europe.

After a long and successful career within the science industry, Lazlo Ferran left to concentrate on writing, to continue exploring the landscapes of truth.

From the author:

Thank you for reading my story and I hope you liked it. I value very much feedback from people and need this if each book is to be better than the last, so if you could take the time to either post a comment on my blog or simply email me, I would appreciate it.

Where to find Lazlo Ferran
Amazon: http://amzn.to/144HYR4
Email: lazloferran@gmail.com

www.ingramcontent.com/pod-product-compliance
Lightning Source LLC
Chambersburg PA
CBHW070451120726
47910CB00003B/1010